I0672675

The Emmon Fields

Nelhelm

Jeremy Stroop

Dedication

For my wife, Tracey.

CONTENTS

About the Author

Jeremy Stroop is a long time IT guy and even longer connoisseur of religious and mythological texts. He and his wife, along with their three four legged children, call the Appalachian mountains of Virginia home. You can visit him online at

https://www.jeremystroopbooks.com/

Page Blank Intentionally

1

Glenwood

Jace Alexander stood at the edge of the Glenwood Forest, his tall frame casting a long shadow in the early morning light. His dark hair, tousled by the wind, framed a face that bore the map of the mountains in its contours—sharp cheekbones, a square jawline, and piercing steel blue eyes that scanned the horizon with an intensity born of his survivalist upbringing. He was dressed in a simple flannel shirt and jeans, the attire of a man who knew the value of practicality over fashion.

"Always thought you'd get hitched in a camo tux," teased a voice from behind him

"Never pegged you for a comedian, Emma," Jace replied without turning around, his voice carrying the timbre of rolling thunder—a sound as much a part of him as the soil beneath his feet.

Emma Williams stepped beside him, her gentle brown eyes reflecting a myriad of emotions. Her blonde hair caught the sun's rays, creating a halo effect that, to Jace, symbolized the light she brought into his life since they met those years ago in middle school after her family relocated to Glenwood.

"Remember our first hike up here?" Emma asked, wrapping her arms around herself against the chill.

"Like it was yesterday," Jace said, turning to her with a smile that softened his rugged features. "You were so out of your element, city girl."

"Hey, I've come a long way since then," she countered, a playful spark in her gaze. "I even know how to bait a hook now."

"Your parents still think they're nuts for settling down here."

Jace's eyes turned thoughtful as he glanced toward the Williams' estate, perched on the outskirts of town. Liz Williams, with her literature-filled past, and Nicholas, who steered his shipping business from the chaos of Philadelphia to the tranquility of the mountains—both of them refined, wealthy, and yes, secretive—never seemed to mesh with the rustic tapestry of Glenwood, holding onto their cosmopolitan air-like armor against the unknown.

Emma nodded, her expression turning somber.

"They wanted a different life for me, one filled with... more." She searched for the word "predictability."

"Yet here you are," Jace said, reaching for her hand. "Choosing this unpredictable life with me."

"Here I am," she echoed, though her voice held a tremor that didn't escape Jace's notice. For a moment, he wondered if there were depths to Emma he hadn't yet explored, secrets nestled within her heart. But the thought dissolved as quickly as it formed, overshadowed by his resolve to be the pillar she needed.

"Two weeks until 'I do," he whispered, pulling her close. "Are you ready to be Emma Alexander?"

"Ready as I'll ever be," she murmured, her words muffled against his chest.

Yet, something lingered unsaid—an elusive whisper that danced just out of reach.

Jace let out a breath he didn't know he'd been holding. The wedding marked not just the union of two high school sweethearts but a convergence of past and future—a promise of constancy in a world full of variables. He felt the weight of that promise, the expectation of steadfastness, and clung to it like a lifeline.

"Whatever happens," he vowed silently, "I'll keep us anchored. For better or worse."

"Jace?" Emma's voice jolted him from his reverie.

"Yeah?"

"Promise me we'll always find our way back here," she said, gesturing to the woods, the mountains—the very essence of their bond.

"Always," he affirmed, his determination echoing through the trees, strong and unwavering as the mountains themselves.

The mountains of Glenwood rose like ancient sentinels around the small town nestled in their embrace. Here, the Appalachian wilderness was a living tapestry of hickory and hemlock trees, with secrets whispered by the wind that danced through their leaves. In this cradle of nature, the townspeople of Glenwood lived lives deeply entwined—each birth, wedding, and passing woven into the communal quilt with threads of shared joy and sorrow.

"Ma, I'm heading out!" Jace called, his voice echoing off the walls of the family home, a modest two-story affair that had weathered storms and seasons much like the Alexanders themselves.

"Wait up, Jace!" Sarah's voice carried from the kitchen.

The scent of apple pie, a hallmark of her culinary affection, trailed behind her as she emerged, wiping flour-coated hands on her apron.

"I packed some of your dad's jerky for you. I know you like to have it when you go up there."

"Thanks, Ma." Jace took the offered package, a familiar warmth spreading through him at the mention of his father's recipe. "It always tastes better when I'm out in the woods."

Sarah studied her son, her eyes the same shade of blue as his—a mirror reflecting back his image and the lineage of resilience they both carried.

"Just like your father," she said softly, pride apparent even as a shadow of loss crossed her face.

Jace's father, Dale, stood tall with broad shoulders and a strong, weathered frame due to his years working in the woods. His hair was peppered with salt and framed sharp, focused eyes that seemed to have a direct line to the truth. Unfortunately, a logging accident took him away just seven years ago.

Jace reached out, his hand finding her shoulder with an assurance borne of years of being each other's rock.

"He loved these mountains as much as we do," he murmured, the unspoken 'and we love them together' hanging between them.

"Be careful, Jace," Sarah added, her tone blending concern and trust. "The trails can be treacherous this time of year."

"Always am," Jace replied, though his mind was already tracing the path to the waterfall, where his heart was unburdened and complete.

His fingers curled around the leather strap of his hiking bag, feeling the weight of its contents—supplies meticulously chosen for utility and comfort, another testament to his resourceful nature.

As he stepped outside, the bustle of Glenwood greeted him. Neighbors waved from porches adorned with swings and flower pots overflowing with marigolds and petunias.

Mr. Jenkins, the local mechanic, called out from beneath the hood of a car, "Good luck with the hike, Jace! Say hello to the mountain gods for me!"

"Will do, Mr. Jenkins!" Jace shouted back, his stride steady as he passed the row of shops that marked the town's main street.

Each storefront bore the mark of personal touch: hand-painted signs, displays of local crafts, and the ever-present hum of conversation that spoke to the shared history of every soul within.

He could sense the pull of the forest, the allure of solitude that promised a reprieve from the whirlwind of wedding plans and expectations. Yet, as he left the town behind, a flicker of unease stirred within him—a premonition, perhaps, or simply the nervous energy of a groom-to-be venturing into the wild to find clarity before the vows that would anchor him to another soul for a lifetime.

"Remember who you are, Jace Alexander," he whispered to himself, the leaves rustling overhead as if in response. "Son of the mountains betrothed to Emma, beloved of Glenwood."

The words were a talisman, grounding him in the identity that had been shaped by the town and its people—an identity as enduring as the peaks that now beckoned him onward.

Jace's boots crunched against the gravel path leading away from the heart of Glenwood, a sound that echoed the rhythm of his racing thoughts. The town, with its woven tapestry of lives and shared memories, seemed to fade into a watercolor blur as he approached the outskirts, where Allen's modest home stood nestled among the pines.

"Jace!"

Allen called from his porch, his sandy blonde hair catching the sunlight in a way that seemed to crown him with a halo. Allen's average build was deceptive, for beneath his unassuming exterior lay a strength honed by years of learning alongside Jace's father, Dale, learning the ways of the woods.

"Hey, Al," Jace greeted, his steel blue eyes reflecting a camaraderie that had weathered countless adventures and trials. "Just wanted to drop by before heading up to clear my head."

As Jace and Allen stood on the porch, a mischievous squirrel scurried by, pausing briefly to steal a wedding favor left behind on Sarah's porch. It darted away with a cheeky grin on its furry face as if mocking the upcoming nuptials.

Jace chuckled, shaking his head.

"Wedding jitters and thieving squirrels... I never thought those two would be connected."

Allen laughed, his eyes twinkling.

"Well, they say marriage is all about compromise. Maybe this little thief is just reminding you to share your cherished possessions with Emma."

"Ah, so this is my lesson in marital harmony," Jace mused, watching the squirrel disappear into the distance. "Note to self: hide the nuts and bolts from now on."

Their laughter filled the air as they shared this humorous moment, reminding Jace that even in the face of wedding jitters, there's always room for a good laugh and a playful reminder that love and laughter go hand in hand.

Allen nodded, understanding the need for solitude that often gripped Jace.

"You always did find peace in those mountains. Remember when we camped out near the summit? You could practically read the stars without a telescope."

"I could never forget," Jace replied, the memory bringing forth a warmth that offset the chill mountain air. "But this time, it's a waterfall calling my name—a place to pause and... reflect."

"Emma's okay with it, then?" Allen's tone held a note of concern.

"Actually, I'm about to ask her."

Jace exhaled, his breath misting in the cool air as he started back toward town with purposeful strides. He knew Emma would understand his need for this; the mountains were his sanctuary, a place to commune with the spirits of nature and his own soul.

"Be safe, brother," Allen called after him. "And come back ready to be the best damn husband Glenwood's ever seen."

"Count on it," Jace threw over his shoulder, a grin breaking across his face.

The day was waning as Jace entered the house. He and Emma had been painstakingly decorating for their life together. The scent of pine from the furniture mingled with the aroma of fresh flowers—Emma's doing, no doubt.

"Emma?" Jace called softly, finding her in the kitchen, her golden hair aglow in the evening light streaming through the window.

"Back so soon?" she said, turning from the oven with a questioning look in her warm brown eyes. Her gaze lingered on him, searching, perhaps sensing the undercurrent of his restlessness.

"Listen, Em, I need to ask you something." Jace leaned against the doorframe, watching the play of emotions across her face. "I want to take a hike tomorrow morning, up to the waterfall overlooking Glenwood, just to have a moment alone before everything changes."

"Tomorrow?" There was hesitation in her voice, a flicker of something unreadable in her eyes before she masked it with a soft smile. "Of course, you should go. Clear your mind. When will you leave?"

"Sunrise," he responded, noting the brief shadow that passed across her face—a secret held close to her chest. "I'll be back before you know it, and then nothing but you and me and 'I dos'."

"Sunrise," she repeated, her voice steady even as her hands betrayed a slight tremor. "I'll wait for you, Jace. Always."

"Thanks, Emma. It means the world."

And with that, Jace felt the weight on his shoulders lighten just enough to breathe easier. He stepped closer, wrapping his arms around her in a silent promise of return, his resolve fortified by the love that had grown since those middle school days.

As they parted, Jace's gaze lingered on Emma's form, the curve of her spine as she returned to her baking, and he wondered if the mountains might also hold answers to the quiet mysteries hidden within the heart of the woman he was about to marry.

The morning sun spilled its golden light over the peaks of the Appalachian Mountains, casting a warm glow on the dew-speckled ferns and mossy boulders that dotted the landscape. Jace Alexander stood at the edge of a narrow fire road that would lead him up to the waterfall—a winding ribbon of dirt and gravel cut through the dense canopy of trees like an afterthought. The ancient mountains rose up around him, silent sentinels swathed in a cloak of emerald green, their jagged profiles softened by a haze that clung to their edges.

"Nature's cathedral," Jace muttered under his breath, his steel-blue eyes reflecting the splendor of the woodlands.

His gaze followed the path upward, where the elusive call of a distant bird mingled with the rustle of leaves. He took a deep breath, tasting the crisp air that promised solitude and revelation.

"Got everything you need?" a voice called from behind, jolting Jace from his reverie.

"Almost," he replied, turning to see his mother, Sarah, emerging from the house with a small bundle wrapped in cloth. "Thought I'd double-check."

"Can't be too careful," she agreed, handing him the package. "Fresh biscuits and some of that apple jam you like. A little bit of home for when you reach the top."

"Thanks, Mom."

He smiled, accepting the bundle. Jace opened his backpack, already loaded with essentials—a map, a compass, a water bottle, and a first-aid kit. His fingers brushed over the pocketknife his father had given him years ago, its handle worn smooth by countless adventures. He packed the food next to a lightweight jacket and gloves.

"It should hold you over until you get back to Emma's cooking," Sarah said, her tone light but her eyes betraying a touch of concern. "You'll watch your step?"

"Always do," Jace assured her, zipping up the backpack. His mother's support was as unwavering as the mountains themselves, her faith in him a stronghold against doubt.

"Good boy."

She reached out to ruffle his dark hair, a gesture he'd long outgrown but never resisted.

"It's not just the trail that's got me worried. It's what waits at the end of it."

"Emma?"

"Emma," Sarah confirmed, her voice softening. "She's a good girl, but there's more to her than what meets the eye. You know that."

Jace nodded, recalling the tremor in Emma's hands the night before.

"I suppose we all have our hidden depths."

"Suppose so." She pulled him into a tight embrace. "Just remember, whatever you find up there or in here," she tapped his chest, right over his heart, "You're not alone."

"I won't forget."

He hugged her back, feeling her strength bolstering his own.

"Sunrise isn't going to wait for you, my boy."

Sarah stepped back, her voice thick with emotion that she tried to mask with practicality.

"Nor will I tarry for it," Jace replied, a grin breaking across his face as he shouldered his pack.

He checked the fit of his hiking boots, ensuring they were snug against his feet—their well-worn leather familiar and reliable.

"Take care, Jace," his mother called as he started down the fire road, the gravel crunching beneath his steps.

"Will do," he shouted back, not daring to look behind lest the pull of what he was leaving become too much. Instead, he focused on the path ahead, on the intertwining branches that formed archways, beckoning him forward.

As he walked, his mind wandered to Emma—her laughter, her warmth, her mysteries—and to the life that lay ahead. But for now, it was just him and the mountain and the promise of clarity that awaited him at the summit. The forest swallowed him whole, its whispers merging with his steady breaths and the rhythmic beat of his heart.

Jace's shadow stretched long and thin across the fire road as he made his way past the last of the sleepy houses of Glenwood. The sun, a fiery eye on the horizon, watched him with a silent promise of the day to come. His boots crunched over gravel and fallen leaves, a steady drumbeat marking the time until he would stand face-to-face with the grandeur of the Appalachian wilderness.

"Nature's cathedral awaits, old friend," Jace muttered to himself, the anticipation bubbling in his chest.

The mountains loomed ahead, a formidable wall of green and stone that had witnessed countless dawns. He adjusted the straps of his backpack, which contained all he'd need for the journey – water, food, a map, and the compass that had been his father's.

The fire road began to ascend. The air was crisp, redolent with the scent of pine and the musky tang of earth. Here, away from the town,

Jace felt the first stirrings of solitude, an old companion that welcomed him like a whisper among the trees.

"Solitude's a fine thing," he said aloud, though there was no one to hear him. "But Emma's voice is finer."

He smiled at the thought, his heart carrying the weight of her absence even as he embraced the freedom of the trail. The path narrowed, and he found his rhythm, each step a further entanglement in the wild's embrace.

The forest closed around him, a verdant tunnel where only slivers of light pierced the canopy. Birds stirred their calls, a tapestry of sound that stitched sky to earth. Squirrels chattered, darting from tree to tree, their presence a reminder of life's persistent bustle even in the quietude of nature.

"Easy does it, Jace," he coached himself when the incline steepened.

Beads of sweat gathered at his brow, his breaths becoming labored.

"It's just a little farther."

At last, the dense foliage gave way to a clearing, and the waterfall revealed itself in a cascade of silver threads. It poured down from the clifftop, a sheer drop that turned the water into mist before it reached the pool below. Sunlight danced through the spray, casting rainbows that arced across the grotto.

"Would you look at that," Jace whispered, awestruck.

He dropped his pack and approached the water's edge, the roar of the falls filling his ears. Droplets kissed his skin, cool and refreshing after the climb. He let out a long breath, feeling the tension in his muscles ease.

"Emma would've loved this," he mused, tracing the arc of a rainbow with his eyes. "She's the missing color in all this beauty."

His hand lingered over the small velvet box in his pocket—inside, a ring that was a testament to promises made and soon to be kept. For now, though, he put aside thoughts of future vows and allowed himself to be present in the raw majesty of the moment.

"Two Saturdays, I'm hers," he declared to the falls, to the trees, to the very mountain itself. "But today, I am my own man, free as this water, strong as these rocks."

He sat beside the pool, legs crossed, the mist enveloping him like a cloak. In the ceaseless rush of water, he found a peace that ran deeper than thought, a silent understanding that flowed between him and the ancient world around him. This was a place of power, of renewal—a fitting altar for the last moments of his bachelorhood.

Jace's fingers played absently with the edges of a maple leaf, its crimson hue a stark contrast to the greens and browns that made up the forest palette. The sun was playing hide and seek among the leaves, dappling the earth with shifting patterns of light and shadow. He followed the trail, his boots finding purchase on the uneven ground with an ease that spoke of countless such ventures.

"Who would've thought," he said aloud, a grin tugging at the corners of his mouth, "That Jace Alexander, the boy who once got lost in his own backyard, would find solace in these woods?"

He chuckled at the memory, the sound mingling with the distant call of a jay. Once, as a child, he'd ventured no further than the garden's edge, afraid of what lay beyond. How far he had come since then.

"Life's funny that way," he mused, stepping over a fallen log, his hand brushing against the rough bark. "You grow, you change... I guess that's what I'm doing now, isn't it? Growing. Changing."

As the trail wound upwards, the air grew crisper, the scent of pine sharper in his nostrils. A bead of sweat trickled down his temple, a testament to the exertion of the climb. Yet there was something exhilarating about the burn in his thighs, the steady rhythm of his heart.

"I never thought I'd be the marrying type." His voice seemed small amidst the grandeur of nature. "Dad always said life's a journey, not a destination. I hope you're right, old man."

The wind whispered through the trees, offering no answers, only the rustle of leaves like a thousand hushed voices. Jace could almost imagine his father's laughter carried on the breeze, a sound from long ago that still managed to warm him.

"Emma, though..."

His thoughts drifted to her smile, the way her eyes lit up when she laughed.

"She's my compass—always pointing me true north."

A sudden gust shook loose a shower of golden leaves, and Jace watched them dance their way to the ground. Life was much like those leaves, he pondered—fleeting, fragile, beautiful. Today, he stood at the precipice of a new chapter, each step toward the waterfall a step closer to a shared future.

"Tomorrows for promises," Jace declared, his words swallowed by the cascade ahead. "Promises that I'll keep till my last breath."

The hike had stripped away the veneer of ceremony and expectation, leaving him raw and open. Here, in this natural sanctuary, he faced himself—not Jace Alexander, the fiancé, the son, the friend—but simply Jace—the man who found wisdom in the silence of the mountains, the man who sought clarity in the solitude of the wilds.

"Life is an adventure, Emma loves to say," he whispered, looking up at the towering pines that stood sentinel around him. "Well, here's to our greatest one yet."

The waterfall roared in agreement, a symphony of water on stone that drowned out all other sounds. Approaching the edge, he peered into the churning pool below, seeing his reflection merge with the froth and foam.

"Here's to love, to life, and to the unknown," Jace said to his watery twin. "May we navigate it with courage and grace... together."

With that, he took a deep breath, filling his lungs with mountain air, and turned his face to the sky, where the late afternoon sun began its descent, painting the world in hues of amber and rose. At this moment, he felt a profound sense of belonging—a thread woven into the vast tapestry of existence, ready to embrace whatever tomorrow might bring.

2

Target

Jace Alexander stood at the edge of the waterfall, the cool spray kissing his face as he gazed down at the churning waters below. Lush green foliage surrounded him, and the scent of damp earth filled his nostrils. The mountains offered a cathedral of solitude and tranquility, their jagged peaks clawing at the sky like ancient guardians. He felt alive.

"Emma would've loved this," he whispered to the wind, imagining her laughter as she splashed in the shallow pool beneath the falls.

He could see her dark curls, damp with droplets, cascading down her back as she smiled up at him. Above average height and athletically built, Jace was no stranger to the call of the wild, and it was moments like these that he treasured the most.

Taking a deep breath, he reluctantly tore himself away from the mesmerizing sight and began descending, following the path carved out by countless years of rainfall and erosion. Ancient roots snaked across the ground, providing handholds for his strong fingers as he navigated the steep terrain. His steel blue eyes scanned the landscape, appreciating the delicate balance of nature, untouched by the blight of civilization.

"Such beauty," he mused, recalling passages from ancient texts he had studied with his father. "A testament to the divine."

As he continued his hike, the sun played hide-and-seek among the trees, casting dappled shadows on the forest floor. Birds sang sweet melodies from their hidden perches high above while insects buzzed and hummed, creating an orchestral symphony that soothed Jace's soul.

"Hello?" he called out, his voice barely audible above the cacophony of life around him. "Is someone there?"

He paused, straining his ears for any sound that might betray the presence of an observer. But the woods remained silent, save for the chattering of the wildlife.

The rustling grew louder, and Jace's instincts kicked into overdrive. He crouched down, his body coiled like a spring, ready to react at a moment's notice. His heart pounded in his chest, the blood roaring in his ears as he focused on the source of the noise.

"Show yourself," he demanded, his voice steely and unwavering despite the adrenaline coursing through his veins.

Without warning, the undergrowth parted, and a group of men emerged from the shadows. Their faces were covered in ski masks, and their eyes were cold as they leveled their guns at Jace. There was no mistaking their intent.

"Who are you?" Jace demanded, his voice steady even as fear clawed at the edges of his consciousness.

"Doesn't matter," one of the men sneered, his finger tightening on the trigger. "We have a job to do."

Time seemed to slow as Jace braced himself for the inevitable. His mind raced, desperately searching for a way out of this dire situation. He could see the glint of malicious intent in the masked men's eyes, and his heart sank.

"Easy now," Jace said, raising his hands in a gesture of surrender.

But his mind raced, searching for an escape route, an opportunity to turn the tables on his attackers. He knew that these men would not hesitate to kill him if he gave them the chance.

As if in response to his desperate thoughts, a flicker of movement caught his eye. A small stone rolled down the hillside, dislodged by the shifting earth beneath it. Jace's gaze followed its path, and as he did so, he saw the solution he needed.

"Such a shame," he mused aloud, his tone casual despite the sweat beading on his brow. "I was just admiring this beautiful landscape. It truly is a wonder of creation."

"Shut up!" another man barked, but Jace continued, his voice filling with passion.

"Have you ever considered the divine artistry that went into crafting these mountains? The intricate balance of nature, the delicate interplay of light and shadow…"

His words served their purpose, drawing the men's attention ever so slightly away from him and toward the scenery he described. In that split second, Jace sprang into action.

He lunged to his left, and the loud crack of the gunshot echoed through the forest, followed by the high-pitched whistle of the bullet as it sliced through the air with terrifying speed. He scrambled up the steep incline with practiced agility, using the uneven terrain to his advantage. Rocks and roots provided handholds as he ascended, his breath coming in ragged gasps.

"Get him!" one of the men shouted, their footsteps pounding on the earth behind him.

Jace's heart hammered in his chest, and his muscles screamed in protest, but he forced himself onward. He knew that to stop was to die. And so he climbed, higher and higher, driven by an unyielding will to survive.

Having scaled the rugged mountainside, Jace paused for a moment to catch his breath. The forest ahead seemed dense and impenetrable, yet he knew it was the only way out. Drawing on the strength of his resolve, he threw himself forward, sprinting headlong between the trees.

"Stop him!" a voice bellowed from behind, echoing through the forest.

The underbrush clawed at Jace's legs, but he refused to be slowed. Twigs snapped underfoot as he dodged fallen branches and leaped over gnarled roots in his path. His heart pounded in rhythm with his thundering footsteps, echoing the primal drumbeat of his ancestors' hunts.

"Emma," he thought urgently, "I'll find my way back to you."

Jace's breath came in ragged gasps as he burst through the undergrowth, emerging into a small clearing. The old stone chimney stood tall and proud, the only remaining structure of the once grand Alexander homestead. The crumbling gray bricks were covered in moss and vines, a testimony of time's relentless grip. He had always loved this spot, coming here often to reflect and reconnect with his roots.

But now was not the time for nostalgia; Jace quickly scanned his surroundings, searching for any signs of pursuit. Seeing none, he cautiously made his way to the chimney, taking cover behind it.

Just as the voices of his pursuers began to fade, Jace stumbled upon a hidden path that he had never seen before. It was narrow and overgrown, barely visible beneath the tangled foliage. He hesitated, torn between continuing his current trajectory or taking this mysterious route. In the end, desperation won out, and he veered onto the path.

"Curse these forsaken woods," he muttered to himself, casting a wary glance back over his shoulder.

As Jace pushed further along the path, an eerie silence fell over the forest. Gone were the cries of birds and the rustle of leaves. Even the wind seemed to hold its breath. A shiver shot down his spine, and his instincts screamed at him that something was amiss.

But Jace pressed onward, driven by the knowledge that the men with guns were still pursuing him.

The ground beneath Jace's feet grew softer as he ventured deeper into the woods. The trees grew thicker and taller, blocking out most of the sunlight and casting the forest in a deep, eerie gloom. He could barely make out the path ahead, relying on his instincts to guide him forward.

The energy in the air was palpable, and Jace felt like he was being torn apart and then reassembled again. His vision was filled with unknown colors as the world seemed to collapse around him. Amidst the chaos, a symbol appeared before Jace, glowing and suspended in midair. It resembled pitchforks arranged in a wheel, with ancient writing between the tines that Jace couldn't make out in the brief moment it was there. As quickly as it started, the experience ended, leaving Jace breathless and disoriented.

"Where...?" he choked out, his voice barely audible against the backdrop of unfamiliar sounds.

Jace struggled to regain his bearings, his mind reeling from the impossible reality before him. Though a forest still surrounded him, it was clear that he was no longer in the same one he had been only moments ago. The air was thick with the scent of decay and damp earth. There was also a strange, musky smell that reminded Jace of a mix between wet fur and burnt wood.

With his heart racing and his body sore, Jace presses on with determination to reunite with the life and love he left behind. Little did he know the challenges that awaited him or the unfamiliar world waiting in the depths of this mysterious forest.

As he notices the world around him fading away, he realizes it's his physical form, succumbing to the journey into this new realm.

Jace's vision swam as he struggled to regain consciousness, his body sprawled on cold stone. The air was damp and heavy with the scent of ancient scrolls, and the faint glow of torchlight flickered on the walls of the small castle chamber in which he found himself. With a groan, he forced himself to sit up, cradling his pounding head in his hands.

"By all that is holy," he muttered, steel blue eyes widening at the sight of peculiar artifacts scattered around the room. "Where am I?"

His gaze lingered on a tapestry depicting monstrous creatures locked in battle before darting to a shelf lined with bizarre objects – twisted metal sculptures, glass orbs filled with swirling storms, and scrolls bound with delicate golden chains.

"None of this makes sense," Jace thought, his heart racing with confusion and fear, yet a strange sense of wonder.

The chamber's high-vaulted ceiling and arched windows spoke of an architectural style he had only ever seen in ancient buildings, but there was something undeniably otherworldly about the place.

"Think," he urged himself, trying to calm the torrent of thoughts threatening to overwhelm him. "How did I get here? And more importantly, how do I leave?"

"Hello?" he called out hesitantly, his voice echoing through the chamber.

There was no response save for the distant water drip and the wind murmur outside the window.

"Alright then," he said, taking a deep breath. "Let's figure this out."

With cautious steps, Jace began exploring the castle, searching for clues that might help him understand his situation. He marveled at the intricate stonework of the spiral staircase as he descended into the depths of the fortress, his footsteps echoing softly in the darkness.

"Nothing about this seems familiar," he mused, feeling the rough texture of the walls beneath his fingertips. "If only there were some kind of sign or inscription..."

As he continued to examine the strange artifacts that seemed to fill every corner, Jace couldn't help but feel a growing sense of awe and dread. It was as if he had been entirely transported to another world filled with wonders beyond his wildest dreams and dangers too terrible to contemplate.

"Stay focused," he told himself firmly, pushing aside the wild fantasies that threatened to distract him from his goal. "Remember Emma and the life you left behind."

And so, his determination renewed, Jace pressed onward through the castle's twisting corridors and shadowed halls, certain that somewhere within its ancient walls lay the key to his salvation.

Despite the eerie atmosphere of the ancient castle, Jace refused to succumb to despair. He knew that somewhere within these walls must lie an escape, a door, or a passage back to his old life – and he was determined to find it.

"Think, Jace," he muttered under his breath as he paced the candlelit halls, fingers tapping at his chin in thought. "There has to be something... some sign or symbol..."

It was then that he noticed a heavy oak door partially hidden behind a moth-eaten tapestry. His heart pounding with anticipation, he pushed it open to reveal a small courtyard bathed in the fading light of day.

"Fresh air, finally," Jace whispered, inhaling deeply.

He stepped outside, eyes scanning the distant horizon for any signs of familiarity. Instead, he found himself gazing out upon a vast expanse of rolling plains dotted here and there with patches of thick forest. The landscape was unlike anything he had ever seen, yet it held a haunting beauty that stirred something within him. The sprawling land is filled with rolling green plains and pockets of dense forests. In the distance, Jace can see towering mountains, their peaks shrouded in clouds. The sky above is a vibrant shade of blue, with fluffy white clouds scattered across it. The sun casts a warm golden glow over everything.

"Where am I?" he wondered aloud, his voice barely more than a murmur on the wind.

But there was no answer, save for the rustling of leaves and the distant call of a bird.

"Alright then," he said, steeling himself for what lay ahead. "Time to get to work."

Jace's resourcefulness and keen instincts served him well in this strange new world. He quickly discovered a nearby stream where he could refill his canteen and a cluster of fruit-bearing trees that provided sustenance. He even fashioned a makeshift spear from a sturdy branch, just in case he encountered any unwelcome surprises.

Jace stood at the edge of the forest, taking in the unfamiliar scenery before him. His breath formed clouds in the cool air as he surveyed the forest, alive with the sounds of rustling leaves, chirping birds, and scurrying animals. The occasional creak of tree branches.

"Where am I?" he murmured to himself, squinting into the sunlight as if it might reveal some hidden truth.

He had found food and water nearby, but this new world was far from comforting.

"Emma," he whispered, her name coming to him unbidden like a prayer. "If only you were here."

"Talking to yourself now, Jace?" he chided himself, feeling the weight of isolation settle upon his shoulders.

The castle, its stone walls stretching high into the sky. The grey bricks were cold and foreboding, as if they held secrets within their ancient walls. The windows were narrow and barred, and the only visible entrance was a grand wooden door Jace had used.

"Maybe I'm losing my mind," he mused, running a hand through his dark hair. "But if I'm going mad, then so be it. Anything is better than giving up."

He knelt by the stream he'd discovered earlier, cupping clear, icy water in his hands and letting it spill over his face, cleansing the grime and sweat from his skin. As the water cascaded around him, he couldn't help but think of Emma – of the life they'd planned together, a life that now seemed so impossibly distant.

"Remember, Jace," he told himself, steeling his resolve as the last drops of water slipped through his fingers. "You're doing this for her. You'll find a way back home, and nothing will stand in your way."

"Emma," he whispered again, his voice carried away on the wind as if she could hear him across time and space. "Wait for me."

With renewed determination, Jace set off into the unknown, traversing the strange, alien landscape with a will that could not be broken. He trekked through the tall grass, his heart heavy with longing and memories of a life left behind.

As he walked, Jace couldn't stop the memories from flooding his mind—memories of Emma's laughter, her kind heart, and her unwavering support; memories of their first kiss, their shared dreams, and all the moments they had planned to spend together.

But amidst the bittersweet nostalgia, Jace felt a growing sense of unease. The forest seemed to be getting denser and more ominous with each passing mile. The trees loomed over him like shadowy giants, their branches reaching out as if trying to snatch him away.

But even in this desolation, Jace refused to give up.

The sun dipped below the horizon, casting long shadows across the strange world Jace now found himself in. The colors of the sky melted together like a painter's palette, streaks of red and gold giving way to the encroaching darkness. As he wandered back toward the castle, his eyes were drawn to the small patches of forest, their twisted branches reaching out like desperate fingers.

"Seems like I'm not the only one longing for something familiar," Jace murmured under his breath, a wry smile tugging at the corners of his mouth.

The castle stood tall and imposing, its massive stone walls jutting up toward the darkening sky. Turrets and towers loomed overhead, casting ominous shadows across the surrounding land. The castle's architecture was a mix of Gothic and medieval influences, giving it a foreboding appearance.

Weary from his initial search and the emotional toll of his isolation, he trudged up the castle steps, each footfall echoing through the desolate halls. It was as if the very stones beneath his feet were urging him forward, whispering secrets of this place that he could not yet grasp.

"Sleep," he thought, the word resonating in his mind like a distant drumbeat. "I need rest before I can make sense of any of this."

And so, Jace began to explore the upper levels of the castle, seeking out a place where he might find some measure of comfort. He passed through ancient chambers adorned with tapestries depicting battles long forgotten and feasts that had gone cold centuries ago. The air was thick with dust and history, pressing down on him like an unseen weight.

"Empty rooms all around, yet it feels as if these walls are closing in on me," Jace mused, feeling a sudden chill run down his spine.

He shook off the unease and pressed onward, finally stumbling upon a small room hidden behind a partially open door. Curiosity piqued, he opened the door, revealing a simple cot nestled in the corner. Its frame was made of sturdy oak, and its mattress was worn but inviting.

"Better than nothing," Jace said aloud, his voice breaking the silence that had enveloped him.

Jace reclined on the cot, exhausted but unable to fall into a peaceful sleep. His mind raced with thoughts of his home and loved ones, wondering how long he would be trapped in this strange world.

As he lay there, staring up at the ceiling, Jace realized that he had yet to see another living being in this place. It was as if he was truly alone, with only his own thoughts for company.

He spoke quietly into the dark, "I can't quit; I have to keep going."

His resolve hardened, Jace closed his eyes and allowed sleep to claim him. As he drifted off, images of Emma danced through his mind, their laughter mingling with the distant howls of the wind outside, a bittersweet lullaby for a man caught between worlds.

3

Nelhelm

The howling winds tore through Jace's dreams, wrenching him from the warmth of a fading memory of Emma's embrace. He found himself sitting up in bed, surrounded by darkness and the relentless sound of the storm raging outside. His heart pounded in his chest as if it were trying to match the fury of the tempest.

"Easy," he whispered to himself, rubbing his eyes and peering into the pitch-black room.

It seemed as though the darkness had seeped into every crevice, consuming even the faintest glimmer of moonlight. Jace swung his legs over the edge of the bed, feeling the chill of the stone floor beneath his feet as he rose. He moved cautiously towards the window, his hunter's instincts guiding him through the inky void.

As he leaned against the cold windowsill, he could see nothing but swirling darkness outside. The wind roared like an angry beast, shaking the very foundations of the castle. Jace squinted, trying to make out something, anything, in the impenetrable blackness.

Suddenly, a demonic face appeared in the darkness, its twisted visage contorted in malevolent glee. Jace stumbled back, his heart leaping into his throat. The terrifying image vanished as quickly as it had appeared, leaving him questioning whether it had been real or just a trick of his imagination.

"Get a grip, Jace," he muttered to himself, his breath visible in the frigid air. "You're letting this place get to you."

He stood there for a moment longer, listening to the wind's mournful cries before finally retreating back to the cot. As he lay down, he couldn't shake the feeling that there was more to the storm than met the eye. Something about it felt...alive. The darkness seemed to slither around him, whispering secrets he couldn't quite decipher.

"Maybe this is all just a test," Jace thought, his father's teachings echoing in his mind. "A trial to prove my worth."

With that thought, he forced himself to close his eyes and will away the fear that gnawed at the edges of his consciousness. Sleep eventually reclaimed him, wrapping him in its cold embrace as the storm raged on outside. And though he didn't know it yet, the howling winds carried with them whispers of an ancient power, one deeply entwined with both the mysteries of the castle and his own destiny.

The first rays of morning light fought their way through the storm-battered windows, casting a warm glow on Jace's face as he stirred from his restless slumber. He blinked away the remnants of sleep and sat up on the cot, rubbing the stiffness from his neck.

"Alright, Jace," he murmured, steeling himself for the day ahead. "Time to find out what this place is all about."

He swung his legs over the side of the cot and stood up, stretching his arms above his head before stepping out into the dimly lit hallway. The air was heavy with the scent of ancient stone and wood, the quiet stillness only broken by the distant echoes of his footsteps.

As Jace ventured deeper into the castle, its grandeur revealed itself in magnificent arches and vaulted ceilings that seemed to reach for the heavens. Intricate carvings adorned every surface, forming a visual tapestry of stories long forgotten and worn tapestries draped across the walls, depicting scenes of heroism and valor.

"Who were these people?" Jace wondered, his curiosity piqued by the detailed artwork.

A feeling of reverence filled him as he continued exploring the castle, each new discovery further cementing his fascination.

His gaze fell upon a row of statues, larger-than-life figures carved from solid marble. Their faces were etched with determination and strength, yet there was something haunting in their eyes – a sense of loss and longing.

"Were they kings? Warriors?" he asked himself, studying their features with growing admiration.

As he moved down the corridor, his attention was drawn to the stained-glass windows that lined the upper reaches of the walls. Each one was a masterpiece, the vibrant colors and intricate designs blending seamlessly together to form breathtaking images. They depicted mighty storms, raging seas, and fierce battles between otherworldly beings.

"Could this be a manifestation of the storm from last night?" Jace mused, recalling the demonic face he had seen in the darkness. "Or perhaps it's a representation of something more...something greater than I can comprehend."

He paused, deep in thought, as he contemplated the windows and their potential significance. The enigma of the castle had captivated his mind, tempting him to explore its hidden secrets.

"Okay, Jace," he whispered to himself with resolve. "You've made it this far. May as well continue."

And so, with each cautious footstep, Jace descended further into the maze-like core of the castle, fueled by a relentless curiosity and an intense need to unravel its enigmas.

As Jace delved deeper into the castle, he couldn't help but notice that the sculptures grew more complex and intricate. The large humanlike figures were now accompanied by dark shadow creatures, their forms blending seamlessly into one another. And despite the eerie atmosphere these images created, Jace felt a strange sense of familiarity.

"Father," Jace whispered, recalling the countless evenings spent poring over ancient religious books with his dad. "You would have loved this place."

He could almost hear his father's low chuckle in response, the sound warming his heart even amidst the cold stone surroundings.

Jace examined one sculpture in particular that depicted a fierce battle between a towering Titan wielding a massive sword and a horde of sinister shadow creatures. The scene was breathtakingly detailed – each muscle on the Titan's body straining against the weight of the sword and the monstrous expressions on the shadow creatures' faces frozen in time.

"Could the storm from last night be related to these beings?" he wondered, his mind racing with possibilities. "Were they trying to warn me or test me?"

He continued to study the sculptures and windows with a renewed fervor, his thoughts swirling like a tempest within him. The more he explored, the more he became convinced that there was a deeper connection between this ancient world and the one he had known all his life.

"Perhaps," he thought, "The key to understanding this place lies not just in its art but in the stories my father and I loved so dearly. In the tales of gods, Titans, and the eternal battle between light and darkness."

Lost in his musings, Jace scarcely noticed how far he had wandered from his starting point. The castle's winding corridors and grand halls seemed to stretch on for miles, each turn revealing yet another beautiful piece of artwork that begged for his attention.

"Something brought me here," he concluded, feeling a newfound sense of purpose settle within him. "And I cannot leave until I uncover the truth hidden within these walls."

With that thought echoing in his mind, Jace pressed onward, his eyes shining with the fire of curiosity as he continued his exploration of the ancient halls and their secrets.

The sun began to set, casting the castle in an ethereal glow. Shafts of golden light filtered through the stained-glass windows, illuminating the grand hall with a kaleidoscope of colors. Jace stood transfixed, his eyes roaming over the intricate details of the glasswork as the shifting hues danced across the floor and walls like a living tapestry.

He marveled at the lifelike quality of the figures depicted in the windows – the mighty humanlike beings holding aloft lightning bolts, their faces etched with both determination and serenity. The dark shadow creatures recoiled from the divine presence, their writhing forms seeming almost alive as they twisted away from the onslaught of light. It was as if some unseen force had breathed life into the very glass itself, creating a story that unfolded before Jace's awestruck gaze.

"Beautiful, isn't it?" said a voice, startling Jace out of his reverie.

He turned to find a tall, slender man with fiery red hair standing beside him. The stranger's vivid green eyes regarded Jace with an intelligent curiosity, and something about the way he carried himself suggested a coiled, predatory grace. His presence seemed entirely at home amid the grandeur of the castle and the legends immortalized in the artwork.

"Who are you?" Jace asked, his mind still racing with the implications of what he had discovered so far.

"My name is Reynard," the man replied, a faint smile playing on his lips. "I am a scout for the El, and I've been watching you ever since you arrived in this realm."

"Realm? What do you mean?"

"Welcome to Nelhelm," Reynard said, gesturing around them with a sweep of his arm. "You have crossed into a world unlike any you have known before."

"Are these...your people?" Jace asked, gesturing toward the towering figures in the stained glass. "Are they your people?"

"Indeed," Reynard said, nodding. "Our ancestors were beings of great power who walked the line between god and mortal. They fought the shadow creatures that sought to consume all that was good and pure in the world. The lightning bolts you see were their weapons, symbols of their mastery over the elements."

"Were you the one who brought me here to the castle?" Jace asked, his voice laced with suspicion.

Reynard nodded calmly. "I had to get you somewhere secure," he said. "The shadow creatures are after you."

Jace's heart skipped a beat when he heard about what he had witnessed the night before. He had not completely forgotten about it, but his fascination with this unfamiliar world had pushed the storm to the back of his thoughts.

"How did you know they were after me?" Jace asked, fear creeping into his voice.

"I am a tracker," Reynard replied simply. "I could sense their presence on your trail as soon as you crossed into our world."

"Why am I here?" Jace asked, his mind racing with questions about this mysterious new world and his place within it.

"That, my friend, remains to be seen," Reynard replied cryptically, the smile never leaving his face as he studied Jace intently. "But for now, know that you are not alone. I will be your guide in this strange land, helping you to understand its secrets and navigate the path that lies before you."

Jace felt a mix of relief and trepidation at Reynard's words. He knew he had much to learn about this strange new land and its denizens, but he couldn't ignore the gnawing feeling that there was more to this place – and to his own presence here – than met the eye.

"Thank you, Reynard," Jace said sincerely, extending his hand in friendship. "I'm Jace Alexander. Nice to meet you."

Reynard passed a warm smile as he clasped Jace's hand, reassuring him.

"Don't worry about it," he said. "We have a lot to uncover together, Jace Alexander. It seems like fate has played a part in bringing us together."

As the sun dipped below the horizon, plunging the castle into darkness, Jace felt a new sensation, the weight of destiny resting on his shoulders.

Reynard's sharp eyes narrowed as they scanned Jace from head to toe, taking in his dark hair and steel blue eyes. He appeared skeptical, perhaps even cautious, but something about the young man intrigued him nonetheless.

"Before we begin," Reynard said, his voice tinged with wariness, "You must know that my people, the El, have been wary of outsiders for good reason. Trust is not freely given here in Nelhelm, especially to one who seems... out of place."

As they walked through the grand castle, the setting sun cast eerie shadows across the ancient sculptures and stained glass windows. The air was thick with a sense of mystery and wonder, leaving Jace feeling both overwhelmed and oddly at home.

"Understandable," Jace replied, trying to hide the uneasiness in his voice. "But I didn't choose to come here. I'm just trying to find my way back to where I belong."

"Ah, yes, your world," Reynard mused, studying a particularly intricate carving of a lightning bolt. "We shall see what can be done. But first, you must learn the ways of this land if you are to survive."

Jace nodded, grateful for any guidance he could get. They continued onward, their footsteps echoing through the dimly lit corridors. As they walked, Reynard began to share his knowledge of Nelhelm – its history, its customs, and its many inhabitants.

"Nelhelm is a land of balance, where light and dark are in a constant state of war," Reynard explained, gesturing towards the striking stained-glass windows that depicted the various gods and creatures of the realm.

As they explored the castle's many chambers and hidden alcoves, Jace marveled at the intricate craftsmanship that had gone into creating such a breathtaking place. The knowledge that he was experiencing something most humans could only dream of filled him with awe and reverence – emotions that were not lost on Reynard.

"What is this place?" Jace asked, staring in awe at the massive castle that towered above them.

"This is a garrison castle for the El," Reynard responded

Jace gazed up at the towering walls with awe and fascination. He had never seen anything like it before – massive stones stacked perfectly atop one another, forming a formidable barrier against the darkness beyond.

"Amazing," Jace breathed, unable to tear his eyes away from the intricate carvings and runes etched into the stone.

"It is not just for show," Reynard said, leading Jace towards a section of the wall where smaller, more delicate symbols glowed faintly in the fading light. "These are ancient wards created by our ancestors to protect this castle from shadow creatures."

Reynard reached out and traced one of the symbols with his fingertips, causing it to glow brighter for a moment before fading back to its previous state.

Jace's mind raced with questions. A world of magic was something he had only ever read about in books or seen in movies. The fact that he was now standing in such a place left him speechless.

"But why do you need protection from shadow creatures?" Jace finally managed to ask.

Reynard's expression turned grave as he turned and led Jace through a hidden passageway in the wall. As they walked, Reynard explained that while Nelhelm was a land of balance between light and dark forces, there were those who sought to tip that balance in their favor – beings who were drawn to darkness and sought to spread its influence throughout the land.

As he stepped into the corridor, Jace's eyes widened as he took in the sight of warriors, both human and otherworldly, training and preparing for battle. He couldn't help but feel out of place amongst all the magic and strength surrounding him.

"Your eagerness to learn is admirable," Reynard observed, a hint of approval in his voice. "Perhaps there is more to you than meets the eye."

"Thank you," Jace said, trying to suppress the pride swelling in his chest. "I've always believed that knowledge is a powerful tool."

"Indeed, it is," Reynard agreed, his initial skepticism towards Jace slowly giving way to respect. "And with it, you may yet find your way home."

Jace couldn't help but feel a sense of hope and determination rising within him. With Reynard as his mentor, he would face whatever challenges Nelhelm had in store for him and, perhaps, unlock the secrets of this fantastical world.

Jace's gaze was drawn to a particular sculpture, an El warrior standing tall and proud, a shadow creature crouched at his feet. The details were so vivid that, for a moment, he forgot they were made of stone.

"Reynard," he said, "What is the connection between the El and these mythological creatures? How did I end up in this world?"

Reynard scratched his chin thoughtfully, studying the statue alongside Jace.

"The El has long been intertwined with the creatures of myth, but as for how you came to be here..." He shook his head. "I'm afraid I do not know. Perhaps your arrival is tied to the very fabric of our world."

"Perhaps," Jace mused, turning his attention to the stained-glass windows that allowed shafts of colored light to dance across the castle's floor.

The scenes depicted there mirrored the sculptures: the El and the mythical beings locked in battle or standing side by side, united against some unseen foe. What struck Jace immediately, though, were the lightning bolts – they seemed to connect the two worlds, binding them together.

"Reynard, the lightning bolts... They must mean something more, right?" Jace asked, eyes widening as he began to piece together the puzzle.

"Indeed," Reynard replied, his voice taking on a somber tone. "The lightning bolts symbolize the bond between the El and the storm's power. Our people harness the power of nature to protect our world and maintain the balance between light and darkness."

Jace gazed back at the warrior sculpture, taking in every minute detail – from the determined set of its jaw to the delicate etchings on its armor. He now understood that the El were more than just skilled warriors; they were also protectors of a fragile balance, guardians tasked with preserving Nelhelm from the chaos born of untamed power.

Together, they continued their exploration of the castle, each step bringing Jace closer to unraveling the secrets of his new home and revealing the true nature of the El's sacred connection to the storms that defined their world. And though many questions still lingered in his mind, Jace took comfort in the knowledge that he was not alone in his quest for answers – he had a mentor in Reynard, a newfound friend in an unfamiliar land.

The sun had long dipped behind the horizon, casting a warm orange glow gradually fading into twilight. Jace and Reynard stood in front of the castle's grand entrance, their shadows stretching out before them like dark fingers reaching for the night.

"Reynard," Jace began, steel blue eyes sincere as they searched the El scout's face. "I just want to say... thank you. I don't know what would have happened to me if you hadn't found me or if I'd be able to make sense of this place without your guidance."

"Jace," Reynard replied, his red hair catching the last embers of sunlight. "It is my honor to help you. As I said before, our paths are intertwined by fate. Besides, I find your company quite refreshing. You're a quick learner, and your curiosity about our world is infectious."

A smile tugged at the corners of Jace's mouth, but it wavered as the weight of uncertainty settled upon him. He couldn't shake the feeling that his presence here had some deeper meaning, something tied to the essence of Nelhelm and its storms. But for now, he pushed those thoughts aside, focusing on the immediate future.

"Where do we go from here?" he asked, voice tinged with determination. "If there's anything more you can teach me about the El and Nelhelm, I'm eager to learn."

"Patience, Jace," Reynard chided gently. "There is still much for you to discover. Tomorrow, we'll journey to an El camp where you can meet others of my kind and continue your education. There, you will not only gain knowledge about our people but also hone your own skills – both physical and mental. The road ahead is long and arduous, but I have faith in you."

"Thank you, Reynard," Jace said, his heart swelling with gratitude. "I promise I won't let you down."

"Very well," Reynard nodded, his eyes glinting with a mixture of pride and anticipation. "We leave at first light. Rest now, Jace Alexander, for the next chapter of your journey is about to begin."

As they retreated into the castle's embrace, the night descended upon them like a heavy cloak, shrouding the mysteries that still lay hidden within the walls. In the darkness, the lightning bolts etched in the sculptures seemed to pulse with an unseen energy, whispering secrets yet to be unveiled.

As Jace drifted off to sleep on his cot, he found himself reflecting on his family and the worry they must be feeling.

4

Missing Man

Glenwood, a quaint and serene town nestled at the foot of the majestic Appalachian Mountains, was the kind of place where time seemed to stand still. The townspeople lived simple lives, tending to their farms and small businesses and attending church on Sundays. Stone cottages with sloping thatched roofs lined the cobblestone streets while a babbling brook meandered through the heart of the village. It was a close-knit community where everyone knew each other's names, and secrets were few and far between.

"Alright, folks, listen up!" Sheriff Tom Callahan bellowed as he stood before the assembled crowd of Glenwood's residents. His tall, broad-shouldered frame lent him an air of authority, which was only further accentuated by the steely glint in his eyes. "We're here to find Jace Alexander, who has been missing for two days and last seen hiking to the waterfall. And I'll be damned if we don't bring him back home safe!"

"Damn right!" Allen chimed in, clapping a reassuring hand on the sheriff's shoulder. His sandy blonde hair fluttered in the breeze, framing a face etched with determination. As Jace's childhood best friend and deputy, it was no surprise that Allen was at the forefront of the search efforts. He had known Jace since they were boys, learning side by side from Dale Alexander's survivalist teachings. Though Jace had always been the more adept student, Allen's loyalty and steadfastness were beyond question.

"Let's divide into groups," Allen continued, addressing the crowd. "Sheriff Callahan will lead the first group up the northern ridge while I'll take the second group up to the waterfall at the top of the mountain."

The waterfall in question was a sight to behold—a cascade of crystal-clear water that tumbled down the mountainside and pooled into a tranquil basin surrounded by lush green foliage. It was a place of respite and contemplation, where locals often ventured to escape the monotony of their daily lives. But today, it would serve as the starting point for a desperate search that would span the treacherous expanse of the Appalachian Mountains.

"Remember," Sheriff Callahan added, his voice tight with resolve, "we leave no stone unturned. Check every cave, every crevice, and call out Jace's name as you go. He could be injured and unable to respond, so keep your eyes peeled for any sign of him. Godspeed, everyone."

As the townspeople murmured their assent and prepared to set off on their respective missions, Allen couldn't help but feel a growing knot of worry in the pit of his stomach. The thought of Jace lost and alone in the unforgiving wilderness was almost too much to bear. But he knew that now was not the time for fear—now was the time for action.

"Let's move out," he said firmly, leading his group towards the waterfall. As they began their ascent, Allen offered up a silent prayer, beseeching whatever higher power there might be to watch over his friend and guide them to his side. For in this vast, untamed landscape, only hope and determination could light their way through the darkness that lay ahead,

Despite the worry gnawing at their hearts, Emma and Sarah held onto an unwavering hope for Jace's return.

Emma's hands clenched in prayer, her gaze fixed on the jagged outline of the Appalachian Mountains. A fierce determination radiated from her eyes, a beacon that even the creeping presence of doubt couldn't extinguish.

"Jace is a survivor," Sarah murmured, placing a hand on Emma's shoulder as if to ground them both. "He knows these mountains like his own heartbeat. He will survive."

Emma nodded; it was a headstrong affirmation rather than an agreement. They had to find him. "We'll locate him, Mrs. Alexander."

Sarah managed a brave smile, "Call me Sarah. We have to believe we can."

While search parties bustled around them, finalizing procedures, Emma's parents approached Allen and Sheriff Callahan. Their expressions were taut masks of worry —their usual joviality replaced by furrowed brows and restless glances.

As the search parties dispersed and began their arduous trek into the mountains, Emma's parents stayed behind with Allen and Sheriff Callahan, eager to help in any way they could. The four of them huddled together, mapping out a plan of action.

"We will do everything in our power to find Jace," Sheriff Callahan assured them, his voice heavy with determination. "But we must prepare for the worst as well. These mountains are unpredictable and treacherous, especially during this time of year."

Emma's parents nodded solemnly, understanding the gravity of the situation. They were well aware of the dangers that lurked in these mountains—the rugged terrain, brutal weather conditions, and wild animals that called it home.

"We stand with you," Emma's father said firmly, placing a reassuring hand on Allen's shoulder. "Please let us know how we can assist—arranging supplies, equipment or money."

Emma's mother chimed in, her voice trembling slightly with emotion. "We want to do everything we can to help bring Jace home safely."

Sheriff Callahan acknowledged this unity of purpose with gratitude glistening in his eyes, "Your solidarity goes beyond words. We'll keep you updated on every bit of progress."

"And we expect nothing less," replied Emma's father—his belief echoing the sentinels of hope surrounding them all.

Underneath the looming presence of the Gray Mountains, the townspeople of Glenwood assembled in a bustling wave of determination. They had congregated at the foot of the mountain trail, their breaths steaming in the crisp morning air as they exchanged murmurs and nods of encouragement. The sun had barely crested the horizon, yet the urgency that gripped the community could not be quelled by mere darkness.

Sheriff Callahan's gravelly voice boomed above the crowd. All eyes turned to him and Allen Walker on their makeshift platform. Allen's sandy blonde hair danced in the wind as he scanned the crowd intently.

"Today, we're going to find Jace Alexander," he declared, his voice steady and resolute. "All of you have been divided into groups, each responsible for a specific area of the mountains."

"Group A -" The sheriff continued, pointing towards the left, "-you'll be starting at the waterfall. Remember to look for any signs of disturbance or tracks leading away from the site."

"Group B will comb through the forested area to the South of the waterfall," Allen interjected, his gaze catching Emma's for a brief moment. Her heart clenched, but she steeled herself, knowing her own inner turmoil paled in comparison to the task at hand.

"Groups C and D will cover the west side of the mountains and the valley below," the sheriff finished, his eyes glinting with determination. "We've provided maps and supplies for each group. Radios are available for emergency contact only. And remember," he paused, allowing the weight of his words to settle, "We're searching for one of our own – Jace is family."

As the townspeople dispersed into their designated groups, Emma found herself standing beside Sarah and Allen in Group A. Her parents, clad in clothing ill-suited for the mountain terrain, had insisted on joining as well, their worry etched upon their faces like a stormy sky.

"Alright, team," Allen murmured as he glanced at each of them. "We're going to find him. We have to believe that."

Emma nodded, her pulse quickening with renewed determination. She could feel the cool mist of the waterfall beckoning them, stirring something deep within her – an ironclad resolve to bring Jace home.

"Let's do this," she whispered, her voice barely audible above the roar of the cascading water. And with a collective breath, the search party stepped forward, embarking on a journey that would test the very limits of their courage and perseverance.

The waterfall's mist clung to Emma's skin as she, Allen, and Sarah ventured deeper into the mountainous terrain. A refreshing mist rose, carrying the scent of untouched nature - clean, crisp, and invigorating. The earthy fragrance of wet moss and ferns added a soothing touch to the air. The search party moved in harmony, like a living organism, following the river upstream.

"Sarah, you check behind those rocks," Allen called out, his voice carrying over the rush of water. "Emma, let's look around this bend."

"Understood," said Emma, her breath hitching as she contemplated the rugged path ahead. The air was heavy with the scent of damp earth and moss, and the soil seemed to cling to her boots, weighing her down. She felt Jace's presence in every rustle of leaves, every bird that broke the silence – but he remained elusive, a memory just beyond her reach.

As they pressed on, the landscape shifted beneath their feet. What had begun as a gentle slope grew steeper, crumbling away into loose rocks and treacherous ravines. They were forced to move with caution, eyes trained on the ground for any signs of Jace's passage.

"Careful, Emma," Allen warned, reaching out to steady her as she stumbled on a slippery stone. His grip was firm, grounding her amidst the chaos that threatened to sweep her away.

"Thanks," she whispered, her heart pounding as she stared at the chasm yawning before them. "How are we supposed to cross ?"

Only one way," Allen replied, determination flashing in his eyes. He crouched low, then leaped across the gap with surprising agility, landing safely on the other side. "Just keep your momentum up, and you'll be fine."

"Right," Emma murmured, steadying herself.

With a deep breath, she launched herself forward, her thoughts filled with images of Jace – his laughter, his kindness, the way he'd looked at her since they were children. As she soared through the air, she knew that nothing, not even the treacherous terrain or her own fears, could keep her from finding him.

"Are you alright?" Sarah's voice called out, concern lacing her words as she approached the chasm. Her gaze was fixed on Emma, assessing her for any sign of injury.

"Fine," Emma replied, smiling through her exhaustion. "You can do it, Sarah. Just jump."

"Alright," with a nod, Sarah gathered herself and leaped across the gap, landing safely beside Emma and Allen. She straightened up, brushing dirt from her hands. "This is where the trail splits. We should divide our efforts – I'll take the left path while you two carry on to the right."

"Good idea," Allen agreed, his eyes scanning the horizon for any indication of Jace's whereabouts. "We'll keep in touch via radio. Stay safe."

"Of course," Sarah replied, her voice steady despite the tremor that ran through her body. "And remember, we're doing this for Jace. He'd never give up on us, so we can't give up on him."

With those parting words, the search party split, each member carrying with them the weight of their mission – to find Jace and bring him home, whatever the cost. And as the mountains loomed above them, casting shadows over the landscape like ominous sentinels, they knew that their journey had only just begun.

The sun dipped toward the horizon, casting long shadows that stretched across the craggy terrain like spindly fingers. Allen, Emma, and the rest of their search party pressed on, undeterred by the waning light or the treacherous landscape. They had been searching for hours, and every step they took seemed to echo with the fervent hope that they would find Jace unharmed.

"Jace!" Allen called out, his voice hoarse from hours of shouting. "Can you hear us?"

"Jace!" echoed Emma, her own voice strained but determined. She refused to give in to the creeping sense of despair that threatened to overwhelm her. If she lost hope, then they might as well abandon the search altogether – and that was something she simply could not do.

"Look over there," said one of the townspeople, pointing to a cluster of rocks that stood sentinel-like amidst the rugged terrain.

"Let's check it out," Allen replied, his eyes never leaving the path before him as he led the group onward.

As they approached the rocks, they found Emma's parents, Mr. and Mrs. Williams, huddled together against the biting wind. The older couple was ill-prepared for the harsh conditions, dressed in regular clothes that provided little protection against the cold. But despite their discomfort, there was a fierce determination etched upon their faces – a testament to the deep love they held for their future son-in-law.

"Any sign of him?" Mr. Williams asked, his eyes full of worry as he scanned the rocky outcrop.

"Nothing yet," Allen admitted, frustration seeping into his voice. "But we're not giving up. We'll find him."

"Of course," Mrs. Williams agreed, her voice a mixture of hope and fear. "He's like a son to us. We won't rest until he's safely home."

"Jace!" Emma called out again, her voice reaching across the desolate landscape like a lifeline.

She could feel the weight of worry pressing down on her chest, but she refused to succumb to it. Jace had always been there for her – strong, steadfast, and unyielding in his love. Now, it was her turn to be his rock.

"Jace!" her parents echoed, their voices joining hers in an anguished chorus that seemed to reverberate off the mountains themselves.

The search party pressed on, their footsteps crunching through the rocky terrain as they continued their desperate quest. They were not just searching for Jace; they were searching for hope, for reassurance, for the promise of a brighter tomorrow. And though the shadows grew longer and the wind whipped mercilessly around them, they held onto those precious dreams with every ounce of strength they possessed.

"Jace!" Allen called out once more, his voice echoing through the twilight. "Jace, where are you?"

"Jace!" Emma cried, her heart aching with unspoken prayers as she imagined him somewhere out there, alone and afraid.

"Jace!" Mr. and Mrs. Williams shouted, their love for their future son-in-law shining through the gathering darkness like a beacon.

And although the night closed in around them, the search party remained undaunted, fueled by their unwavering belief that they would find Jace – and bring him home once more.

The sun dipped lower in the sky, casting long shadows across the rugged mountain landscape. The search party's breaths came out in ragged puffs, visible in the crisp air, as they continued their relentless pursuit of any trace of Jace. With each passing hour, the crimson hues of the sunset painted a more somber picture, and a sense of urgency settled like a shroud upon the group.

"Emma," Allen said, his voice strained and weary. "We should call the others back. It's time to regroup."

Emma nodded, her eyes scanning the landscape one last time before she let out a piercing whistle. "I hope someone found something," she murmured, more to herself than to Allen.

"Perhaps we'll hear some good news when we gather," Sarah offered, her voice holding steady despite the fatigue that creased her face. She had been a pillar of strength throughout the day, bolstering the spirits of the townspeople with her unwavering faith.

As the members of the search party trudged back towards the meeting point, small groups began to coalesce, sharing their findings – or lack thereof – with one another. Despite their exhaustion, there was a palpable sense of camaraderie among them, as if the shared experience of searching for Jace had bound them together in an unbreakable chain of unity and hope.

"Any luck?" Mr. Williams asked, his clothes torn and dirty from scrambling over rocks and through thickets, yet his determination remained undimmed.

"Nothing yet," admitted Allen, disappointment lacing his words. He looked around at the assembled townspeople, noting the worry etched on their faces. "But we can't lose hope. We must press on."

"Agreed," said the sheriff, stepping forward to address the crowd. "We've covered a lot of ground today, but the mountains still hold many secrets. We'll rest tonight and resume our search at first light."

"Jace is out there, somewhere," Emma said, her voice resolute as she searched the faces of her friends and neighbors. "We can't give up on him. He wouldn't give up on us."

A murmur of agreement rippled through the gathering, and as the sun vanished behind the mountains, the flickering glow of a campfire illuminated their shared determination.

"Tomorrow, we keep searching," Allen affirmed, clapping his hand on Emma's shoulder. "Together, we will find Jace."

The search parties had dispersed once more, their voices echoing through the valley as they called out Jace's name. Emma, Sarah, and Allen climbed higher up the mountain path, their breaths coming in ragged gasps as they pushed themselves onward. The air was thinner here, biting at their lungs with each inhale.

"Jace!" Emma screamed, her voice raw and desperate, hoping against hope to hear a response.

"Jace, where are you?" Allen joined in, his heart pounding in his chest.

The wind howled around them, carrying their calls away into the vast, unforgiving wilderness. Sarah shivered, pulling her coat tighter around herself as she peered into the shadows cast by the towering pines.

"Emma," she whispered, grabbing Emma's arm. "Look down there."

She pointed to a small group of hikers who had emerged from the tree line, their faces etched with concern. They had overheard the cries for Jace and now hurried towards the trio.

"Did you find him?" one of the hikers asked breathlessly, his eyes searching theirs for any glimmer of hope.

"No," Emma choked out, tears streaming down her cheeks. "But we won't stop until we do."

"Wait," another hiker interjected, his face pale. "We were camping up here last night, and we heard gunshots. We didn't think much of it at the time, but maybe...maybe it has something to do with your friend?"

The words hung heavy in the air like a dark cloud threatening to engulf them all. Gunshots? What could that mean for Jace?

"Where did you hear the shots?" Allen demanded, his mind racing with grim possibilities.

"Near the old Alexander homestead," the hiker said, gesturing further down the mountains.

The search party gathered around the hiker, their expressions grim as they processed the news. Gunshots near the old homestead could only mean trouble.

"We have to check it out," Mr. Williams said, his voice low but firm.

"Agreed," said the sheriff, his hand resting on the handle of his gun. "But we must be cautious. It could be dangerous."

Together, they set off towards the Old Chimney, following a narrow path that wound its way through dense foliage and over rocky terrain.

Allen led the way, pausing occasionally to point out landmarks or warn of steep drops.

As they approached the old homestead, an eerie silence settled over the group. The chirping of birds and rustling of leaves gave way to an oppressive stillness that seemed to vibrate in the air.

Allen noticed Emma's unease, but his false assurances fell on deaf ears this time.

"Emma," he had said in a hushed voice, offering empty platitudes. She responded with a tight expression, her gaze unconsciously drawn back onto the path ahead.

5

The Camp

As Jace and Reynard traveled across the vast plains of Nelhelm, it was difficult not to be awed by the untamed beauty that stretched out before them. The land seemed to go on forever, a patchwork of rolling fields and dense forests whose trees reached for the sky like ancient, gnarled fingers. The sun cast golden hues on the grass, making it shimmer with an otherworldly light. It was so different from the familiar landscape of Glenwood, and yet there was something eerily comforting about it. In the distance, majestic mountains loomed against the sky, adding to the breathtaking scenery.

Jace directed his gaze towards the towering mountains in the distance. "What do you call those mountains?" he asked Reynard.

The latter responded, "Those are the Mountains of the Stars. They stretch across the northern region of Nelhelm."

"Nelhelm is just one of the three realms within the Emmon fields," Reynard elaborated.

Jace couldn't help but be fascinated by the mention of different realms. "What are the other two realms?" he inquired.

"In due time, Jace," Reynard replied with a mysterious smile. "For now, we should focus on our journey."

Jace couldn't help but wonder what Reynard was keeping from him, but he decided to trust his companion and let go of his curiosity for the time being.

"How much farther until we reach the El camp?" Jace inquired, his steel blue eyes scanning the horizon for any sign of their destination.

"Nearly there," Reynard replied a spark of excitement in his voice. "You'll see it soon enough."

Jace's thoughts drifted back to Glenwood, and he couldn't help but wonder what his family was going through. They had no idea he'd been whisked away to another world, leaving everything he had ever known behind. And Emma... his heart ached at the thought of her. He could only imagine the pain and confusion she must be feeling, believing him to be gone without a trace. The guilt weighed heavily upon him, but he knew that he needed to find a way back to her – to make things right again.

"Stay focused, Jace," Reynard cautioned as they navigated the terrain. "I know your mind wanders, but we must remain vigilant. There are dangers in Nelhelm that would prey upon any moment of weakness."

"I understand," Jace said, forcing himself to push aside his concerns and concentrate on the task. "I'm ready for whatever lies ahead."

As they climbed a ridge, the El camp came into view, stretching out like a live thing in the middle of the forest.

Jace felt a mixture of excitement and apprehension course through him, sending shivers down his spine. He was eager to learn more about the El and their world, but he couldn't shake the feeling that his life would never be the same again.

"Here we are," Reynard announced, his red hair catching the light like a flame as they descended toward the camp. "The heart of my people."

Jace took a deep breath, steeling himself for whatever challenges awaited him within the El camp. He had come this far, and there was no turning back now. With each step, he hoped he was one step closer to finding his way home – to the ones he loved and the life he'd left behind.

Upon entering the El camp, Jace's senses were immediately assaulted by the sights, sounds, and smells of a bustling military settlement. Everywhere he looked, there was activity – from sharpening weapons to tending to wounded soldiers. The atmosphere hummed with anticipation and tension, as though those within the camp were preparing for an imminent clash.

"Jace Alexander," boomed a deep, resonant voice, cutting through the din of the camp. A tall figure emerged from the crowd, his commanding presence demanding respect even in the chaotic surroundings. Forset, the captain of the El army, stood like a titan among men; his piercing gaze seemed to bore right into Jace's soul. "So, you are the human who has found himself in Nelhelm."

"Please forgive my straightforwardness," Forset added with a slight nod. "I am Forset, a captain in the El army."

Jace found himself nodding in response, feeling suddenly tongue-tied in the presence of such an influential figure.

"Y-yes, sir," Jace stammered, unnerved by the intensity of Forset's scrutiny.

"Few humans ever make it to Nelhelm. And even fewer survive long enough to tell their tale," Forset continued, his voice heavy with unspoken knowledge. "You must know that your existence here is nothing short of a miracle."

"Reynard has been helping me," Jace replied, gesturing to his red-haired companion. "I wouldn't have made it this far without him."

"Indeed," Forset said, nodding at Reynard, whose expression remained impassive. "But our world holds dangers, unlike anything you have ever known, human. Creatures that would rip you apart without hesitation. You have much to learn if you wish to stay alive."

"Speaking of which," Reynard interjected, "we should inform him of the ongoing war with the Cambions."

"Ah, yes," Forset agreed, his brow furrowing with concern. "The Cambions are a scourge upon our land, demons. Their dark powers are formidable, and they serve their lord Belloch with unyielding loyalty."

"Who is this Belloch?" Jace asked, his curiosity piqued by the mention of such a fearsome adversary.

Forset's eyes seemed to darken as he spoke of the enigmatic figure. "Belloch, an embodiment of malice and darkness. He is cunning and ruthless and seeks to expand his power over Nelhelm and your world."

"Will I be fighting against these Cambions?" Jace questioned, feeling the weight of responsibility settling on his shoulders.

"Perhaps," Forset answered cryptically. "But you have much to learn before you can face them in battle. We will teach you what we can, and in time, you will understand the true nature of our struggle."

"Do you know why Belloch wants to conquer Nelhelm?" Jace persisted.

"Patience, human," Forset replied sternly. "You will learn more when the time is right. But for now, focus on mastering the skills necessary to keep yourself alive."

Jace nodded, swallowing the questions that burned within him. He knew better than to push the captain further. Instead, he resolved to absorb every lesson he offered, determined to become a warrior capable of standing beside the El in their fight against the Cambions – and ultimately finding his way back to the life and people he'd left behind.

As the sun slowly descended, Jace found himself making his way into the tent provided by Reynard. Even now, he couldn't quite fathom that he was in a completely different world, and it all felt like a dream. Exhaustion overtook him as he waited to wake up, and he drifted off to sleep.

The following day, Jace was already wandering around the El camp. The air is filled with the aroma of wood smoke emanating from the cookfires and forges scattered throughout the camp. Fresh pine needles and earth mix with the delicious scent of cooking meat and herbs.

After having breakfast, Jace stood among the El soldiers, their ethereal presence both awe-inspiring and unnerving. The male El, with fierce expressions on their faces, spoke of untold battles fought. Their bodies were adorned with intricate armor, every curve and edge blending harmoniously with their powerful forms. The female El were breathtakingly captivating, the spark in their eyes fiercer than any other force. Their beauty was lethal as it was bewitching.

"Your education begins now," Forset declared, his voice echoing across the expanse of the camp. "You will train alongside our finest warriors, learning the skills necessary to survive in Nelhelm."

"Thank you, Captain," Jace replied, his voice steady despite the uncertainty gnawed at him. He couldn't help but feel like a child among giants, these otherworldly beings with their ancient knowledge and unfathomable power. But he would do whatever it took to find his way back to Emma and the life they had built together.

"Remember, Jace," Forset said, his tone softening slightly. "The Cambions are a formidable enemy, their dark powers born from an unholy union. If you wish to stand against them, you must learn all you can."

Jace nodded, not fully comprehending Forset's words, but he knew it didn't matter. He could not – would not – fail. As Forest strode away, leaving Jace to join his new comrades, Jace's heartbeat quickened. The battle for survival had begun, and that was one thing he knew how to do.

In the days that followed, Jace threw himself into his training with a single-minded focus, the images of the monstrous Cambions he saw that one night in the castle never far from his thoughts. The El soldiers were patient but relentless in their instruction, pushing Jace to his limits and beyond.

"Stay focused," one of the male El warriors advised as Jace struggled to maintain his grip on his sword. "Your mind is your greatest weapon."

Jace continued to observe and study, slowly making his way towards swordplay and archery training, but only when the El deemed him ready.

"Captain Forset," Jace said one evening after an especially grueling session, sweat dripping from his brow. "I am grateful for all that you have taught me. But I cannot forget why I am here – to find a way back to my world, to the people I love."

Forset acknowledged Jace's determination with admiration, their eyes meeting with an intensity that sent shivers down Jace's spine. "You don't have to do this alone," Forset reassured him. "We will work together to find a way to bring you home."

With one final nod, Jace turned away, steeling himself for the challenges ahead. He would face them head-on, knowing that the power of the El was behind him, and he would not stop until he had reclaimed everything he had

Jace stared in awe at the area transformed into a bustling battleground. Fierce, armored warriors with the heads of snarling wolves and intricate tattoos on their arms moved through the crowd of El while the females glided gracefully across the field. Their twisted bodies seemed almost immune to the lethal power they held, as their swords appeared to be an extension of themselves in their deadly dance. The sun shone off their long, silken hair, highlighting the beauty behind their martial artistry.

"Watch your footing, Aydis!" one of the males, El, barked as he deflected a blow aimed at his female counterpart.

"Remember, Ahat," the female warrior called out, her voice melodic yet firm, "precision over force."

As Jace continued to observe the El soldiers sparring, he found himself drawn particularly to two individuals - Aydis and Ahat. Aydis possessed an ethereal beauty that belied her deadly skill. Her eyes, the color of moonlit silver, sparkled with intelligence and determination, and there seemed to be an aura of otherworldly power surrounding her.

"Jace, you should join us," Aydis suggested, a playful smile touching her lips. "It's time for you to learn our ways."

Ahat, on the other hand, was a stoic male warrior. His face was a tapestry of scars and tattoos, each telling a story of battles fought and victories. Despite his harsh exterior, Ahat's eyes held a surprising warmth that spoke of loyalty and camaraderie.

"Indeed," Ahat agreed, sheathing his sword and extending a hand to Jace.

"Alright," Jace said, hesitating momentarily before taking Ahat's offered hand. "I'm ready to learn."

Throughout the training sessions, Jace formed a friendship with Aydis and Ahat. They pushed him to his limits, encouraged him when he faltered, and celebrated his successes as if they were theirs. In their company, Jace felt a sense of belonging that had eluded him since arriving in Nelhelm - a place where he could make a difference and protect those he cared for most.

"Remember, Jace," Aydis whispered one evening as they practiced archery, her eyes never leaving the target, "trust in yourself and your instincts. They will guide you true."

Jace hung on every word of his newfound comrades, feeling a fire within him begin to grow. It was as if a power that he'd had all along was slowly awakening from its slumber.

The sword in Jace's hand gleamed in the golden light of the setting sun. The blade was sharp and polished, the hilt adorned with intricate designs and symbols, his grip firm yet uncertain. His eyes darted between the male and female El warriors – their lithe forms and fluid movements mesmerizing. It was like watching a dance of death, each step calculated and flawless.

"Focus, Jace," Ahat's voice cut through his thoughts. "You must become one with your weapon."

Nodding, Jace turned his attention to the wooden target before him. He took a deep breath and swung, but the sword felt clumsy and unwieldy in his hands. Frustration crept into his chest as he watched the other soldiers spar easily.

"Perhaps you'd do better with a bow," Aydis suggested, her voice soft and melodic. She had been a constant presence in Jace's training, her ethereal beauty captivating him even amidst the chaos of battle. Her golden hair shimmered in the fading sunlight, framing her delicate features like a halo.

"Give it a try," Ahat grunted, handing Jace a beautifully crafted bow. The bow was a work of art, its smooth curves and polished wood glinting in the warm sunlight. Golden accents adorned its tip and grip, giving it an elegant yet fierce appearance. The strong EL warrior, his stern gaze never faltering.

Drawing back the bowstring, Jace found a natural rhythm, breathing steady as he aimed at the target. He released, and the arrow flew straight and true. A sense of pride was inside him – perhaps this was his weapon.

"Good!" Aydis exclaimed. "Now, let's see how fast you can fire."

Jace focused on the target, feeling a strange energy stir within him. With each arrow loosed, the sensation grew more assertive. Jace glowed with an ethereal light as his arrows struck the target, landing with an unnatural heaviness. Faster and faster, Jace fired until the target could take no more and flung backward in defeat.

"Remarkable," Reynard murmured, his eyes gleaming with a knowing smile.

The warmth of the flames danced across all the El's skin, their eyes filled with amazement and admiration. They were awestruck by Jace's remarkable display of power.

Forset approached, his towering figure casting an imposing shadow over the training grounds. "I have heard of humans like you before, Jace. They are called 'Gaians' – warriors who come to the El to aid in our fight against the Cambions. But I have never seen one until now."

Jace swallowed nervously as he felt all eyes turn towards him. "Me? A Gaian?" Jace's mind raced, grappling with the revelation. He thought of the power he had just unleashed. Was this his destiny? To stand among these legendary warriors and defend a world not his own?

Forset's words echoed in Jace's mind as he stood before the towering El leader. The weight of his new identity as a "Gaian" settled heavily on his shoulders. He had always known he was different, but now it seemed he had a purpose – a destiny.

"Do you accept this fate, Jace?" Forset's voice cut through his thoughts.

Jace looked around at the expectant faces of the El warriors, their eyes filled with hope and trust. He thought of his world, torn apart by war and chaos. Perhaps this was his chance to make a difference, to fight for something greater than himself.

"I accept," he said, his voice steady despite the turmoil.

A smile tugged at the corners of Forset's mouth. "Good. Then let us begin your training in earnest."

"Your strength, Jace, lies not in untapped potential but realized capabilities," Forset stated, his tone firm. "We stand at the threshold of a long and strenuous journey. The lurking shadows of Nelhelm will challenge us; yet, be mindful, salvation lies within you."

As the sun dipped below the horizon, Jace stood tall among the El soldiers, the weight of his newfound purpose settling upon his shoulders. With each arrow fired, he would grow stronger, embracing his role as a Gaian warrior. And with each battle won, he would move closer to reuniting with those he left behind.

The cool evening breeze whispered through the trees, carrying the faint scent of woodsmoke. Jace leaned against a sturdy oak, his fingers unconsciously tracing the lines and grooves of its bark as he gazed into the distance. The plains of Nelhelm stretched out in undulating waves of green and gold.

"Hard to believe you've come so far, right?" Reynard's voice broke Jace from his reverie, the older El's eyes soft with understanding.

Understanding Jace's concerns, Reynard placed a comforting hand on his shoulder. "Your loved ones occupy your thoughts—you're in a position here, Jace, with an opportunity that can potentially lead you back to them."

As the last light of day faded, painting the sky in hues of purple and orange, Jace took a deep breath, steeling himself for the battles ahead. He thought of the power he had unleashed earlier, the raw energy courting through him like a raging river. This was his path now, and he would walk it tirelessly, seeking answers and fighting alongside the El until he found a way home.

"Alright, let's do this," Jace said, determination burning in his steel-blue eyes.

"Good, because we'll need every fighter we can get," Forset's voice boomed, echoing across the camp as the captain strode towards them. "The Cambions will not rest, and neither shall we."

"So it begins," Jace responded with an unwavering resolve.

As darkness claimed dominion and stars began their celestial dance overhead, Jace stood amidst the El soldiers, warm illumination from numerous campfires casting long shadows across the plains. He felt an internal glow mirroring those flames—determination kindling within.

"I swear on my love for you, Emma... I will uncover a path home," Jace murmured into the wind, a verbal promise carried away by the night breeze like an unheard prayer.

With this solemn oath hanging in the air, Jace Alexander—a simple youth once—from Glenwood embraced his calling, ready to contribute to the El's cause, prepared for inevitable combat. All this in the hope of returning to those he held dear.

6

Gaians

Jace Alexander walked through the labyrinth of tents, the smell of woodsmoke and earth heavy in the air. His steel blue eyes scanned the area as he searched for Forset, captain of the El army. The sun was setting, casting long shadows that stretched across the fields like fingers grasping at the horizon, and Jace felt a sense of urgency settling into his bones.

He found Forset standing tall among the soldiers, his eyes locked onto the parchment in his hands. The El captain had an ethereal quality; his height and graceful movements made him appear as if he belonged to another world entirely.

"Captain Forset," Jace addressed, his tone firm yet respectful. "May I inquire about Gaian's?"

Forset beckoned for Jace to follow him to his tent and sat at the table inside.

"Unfortunately, I don't have much information to share with you," he admitted. "It's been a long time since we've seen any Gaians, and none of us can remember the last time they were here."

Jace furrowed his brow and asked, "How long ago was that?"

Forset answered, "That was over a thousand years ago, as far as we know. But there have been rumors floating around." He paused momentarily before speaking again with urgency, "We've received word from another tribe that they found a Gaian in a different area of

Nelhelm. However, we have no concrete evidence to support this yet."

"Truly?" Jace asked, his surprise showing on his face. He had always believed himself to be the only one of his kind in these strange lands, so the idea of others like him filled him with hope. But he couldn't ignore the unease in his gut, wondering if their presence might signify something more sinister at work. "How did they end up here? And why now?"

"Those are questions we do not yet have answers to," Forset replied, thoughtfully stroking his chin. "But rest assured, we will not stop until we uncover the truth."

Jace's mind raced with thoughts of the discovered Gaian, wondering if they, too, shared his story of displacement and loss. Even though he had found a home among the El, some of him yearned to know more about his people to understand the true extent of their shared heritage. But with each new revelation, it seemed that only more questions arose.

"Perhaps they, too, have been brought here for a purpose," Jace mused aloud, his eyes fixed on the distant horizon where the shadows were deepening into night. "Maybe we are all meant to find our way to each other and join forces against some greater enemy."

"Perhaps," Forset agreed, a thoughtful expression crossing his face. "But until we know more, our primary focus must remain defending the El and securing Nelhelm." He paused, his gaze holding Jace's. "I understand your desire to learn more about your origins and the fate of your people; however, I must remind you that your journey is far from over. The path ahead is treacherous, and you must be prepared for anything."

Jace nodded, accepting Forset's wisdom with quiet determination. In his heart, he knew the captain was right: there would be time for answers and reflection once the immediate threats had been dealt with. Until then, he would continue to stand beside his newfound allies, supporting them in their fight and learning all he could to ensure their victory.

"Thank you, Captain," Jace said, his voice firm. "I will stay vigilant and do everything I can to help protect our people."

"Good," Forset replied, his tone approving. "Our fates are bound together now, Jace Alexander, and I am confident we will overcome whatever challenges lie ahead."

Forset started to pace back and forth, his long strides creating a steady rhythm as he moved through the dimly lit command tent. His angular face bore the weight of concern, eyes flickering between maps and scrolls scattered across the large wooden table at the tent's center. Jace watched him intently, noting the captain's tall and imposing figure, every movement elegant yet purposeful. The air hummed with anticipation as if charged by the energy coursing through Forset's body.

"Captain," Jace ventured, breaking the silence over them. "What are we waiting for?"

"Word from Malathar," Forset replied, his voice resonant in the confined space. "The nearest El stronghold. They hold the key to determining the next steps."

"Malathar?" Jace repeated, intrigued. "I've never heard of it."

Forset paused, pacing, and turned to face Jace with a small smile. "It is a hidden city where our most skilled and powerful warriors reside, training and preparing for any threat to our people."

Jace's eyes widened in awe at the description of this secret city. He couldn't help but imagine what kind of advanced weapons or tactics they might possess there.

"Is there any news about the Cambions?" Jace asked, steel-blue eyes narrowing as he recalled the fearsome, otherworldly creatures that had appeared that night at the castle.

Forset drew a deep breath, a harbinger of grave news to come.

He spoke with urgency, his voice tinged with worry. "Their aggression is increasing," he informed them. "They've been ambushing our scouting parties; luckily, we haven't lost anyone yet."

Jace stood still, heart pounding in sync with the ticking clock within his mind. The Cambions were more than shadows lurking in the dark. They were nightmares that threatened to consume not only the El but Jace himself and any fellow Gaians who dared live through another day. Yet within him, an unquenchable flame of resolve flickered—the unwavering desire to safeguard those dear to him.

"Captain," Jace asked, his voice as solid as a steel blade despite fear chewing at the periphery of his consciousness, "How might I contribute to our defense?"

"Stay close to us, Jace," Forset instructed, his eyes meeting the young man's with an intensity that promised no room for argument.

"You still have much to learn, and your safety is paramount. We will need you in the coming battles."

"Understood," Jace said, swallowing hard as he acknowledged the gravity of his situation. His emotions were a mix of disappointment and relief. With a heavy swallow, he accepted the reality of his situation.

"Good," Forset replied, a hint of warmth creeping into his voice. "You have already proven yourself resourceful and determined, Jace Alexander. Your upbringing has served you well."

"Thank you, Captain," Jace murmured, feeling a swell of pride at Forset's recognition.

Silence descended upon the tent once more for a moment, punctuated only by the rustling of parchment and the distant sounds of El soldiers preparing for whatever lay ahead. Then, with a sudden flurry of movement, a messenger burst through the tent flaps, breathless and wild-eyed.

"Captain Forset," he gasped, "a message from Reynard!"

As Forest unfurled the missive, Jace couldn't help but feel a shiver of apprehension crawl down his spine. The future was uncertain, but one thing was clear: the fight against the Cambions had just begun, and he would need every ounce of courage and strength to face the dark days ahead.

The piercing sound of the horn sliced through the air like a silken blade, its mournful cry resonating throughout the camp. Jace's heart thundered in his chest as adrenaline coursed through his veins. He knew the El call to battle had been sounded; a Cambion army had been spotted near them in the plains.

"Steel yourselves, my kin!" Forset's voice boomed across the encampment. "The hour of battle is nigh!"

Jace's steel-blue eyes darted from one warrior to another as they armed themselves with ancient weaponry: spears gleaming like moonlight on water, swords as sharp as a serpent's fang, and bows that seemed to hum with eldritch energy. He could feel the primal urge to fight surging within him, the desire to stand shoulder-to-shoulder with these ethereal beings against the darkness that threatened them all.

Jace started to speak, but the tall El captain, Forset, was already standing by his side, closely studying the young man.

"Jace Alexander," Forset's voice was severe yet understanding. "You are not prepared for the chaos of war just yet. It would be best to remain at the camp with Aydis and Ahat. Your journey has only begun, and there is much to learn."

Jace clenched his fists, feeling the sting of disappointment and frustration, but he swallowed his pride and nodded. Forset was right – he had only recently entered this strange new world, and his knowledge and skills were still limited. It would be folly to charge headlong into the fray.

"Understood, Captain," he replied with a nod, trying to hide his frustration. Forset gave him a small smile.

"Good," Forset replied, his gaze softening with understanding. "I know it is difficult to watch without taking part, but trust that your time will come."

A silence fell over the pair as they watched the El warriors gather in formation, their faces etched with grim determination and quiet pride. Jace could sense their unity, the unspoken bond forged by years of shared struggles and triumphs.

"Captain," Jace ventured, his voice barely above a whisper, "Are we going to win this fight?"

Forset gazed out at the assembled ranks of his people, the lines of his face hardening like the bark of an ancient oak.

"Victory is never guaranteed, Jace," he said, his voice heavy with the weight of battles past. "But one thing I know for certain: we will stand together and fight with all our might. That is the way of the El – and soon, it will be your way too."

Twilight descended upon them as the El army readied themselves for battle. Jace observed in awe and excitement, knowing he would join their ranks one day.

He promised himself that he would be fully prepared when that time came.

The morning air around the El encampment hummed with an intensity that resonated deep within Jace's chest. He could feel it thrumming in his blood, calling out to him as if it had always been a part of him. Surrounding him were the El warriors preparing for battle; their movements were precise and fluid, like water flowing over stone.

"Look at them," Ahat murmured, his dark eyes alight with admiration. "Like a well-tuned orchestra, each knowing their part and playing it without hesitation."

Jace couldn't help but agree. The El moved with a unity he had never seen before, even among the most disciplined human soldiers. Their determination was palpable, an almost tangible force that seemed to hover just above the ground, lifting and propelling them forward.

"Your time will come, Jace Alexander," Aydis said softly, her hand resting reassuringly on his shoulder. "You will stand beside us, not just as our ally, but as one of us – a warrior forged in the fires of adversity and tempered by the strength of your convictions."

"But first, you must learn," Ahat added, nodding sagely. "Learn our ways, our traditions, our secrets. Only then can you become one with us and take your place on the battlefield."

Jace looked from one to the other, their words both comforting and challenging. He knew they spoke the truth, yet a part of him yearned to be out there now, fighting alongside the El against the Cambions, who threatened their existence.

"Patience, young one," Aydis said as if reading his thoughts. "There is a time for action and a time for reflection. Now is the time for the latter."

"Watch and learn, Jace," Ahat advised, gesturing toward the El warriors. "See how they move, how they communicate without words. This is the essence of who we are – a people bound by a common purpose, united in our resolve to protect the land and its inhabitants."

Jace nodded, his steel-blue eyes narrowing as he focused on the scene before him. The El warriors were indeed a sight to behold; their grace and agility belied their strength, and there was a fluidity to their movements that seemed almost otherworldly.

"Remember this day, Jace Alexander," Aydis whispered, her breath warm against his ear. "For when your time comes, you will draw upon the memories of what you have seen here, and they will guide you as surely as the stars themselves."

"May the winds of fortune be ever at your back," Ahat intoned solemnly, his gaze never wavering from the tableau before them. "And may the wisdom of our ancestors light your path, now and always."

Jace felt gratitude for their support, knowing he could not face the coming trials alone. With Aydis and Ahat by his side, he would learn, grow, and one day stand shoulder to shoulder with the El, fighting for a cause greater than any of them could have imagined.

As he watched the El continue their preparations, Jace's determination blossomed like a flower reaching for the sun. He would not let them down, he vowed silently. He would do whatever it took to become the warrior they needed him to be – and when his time came, he would be ready.

Forset's voice rang out like the crack of a whip across the camp, his ancient El dialect echoing through the air. "Nárë lerta!" he commanded, his silver eyes blazing with determination. The El warriors, clad in their armor and armed with weapons, formed ranks around him, their faces set in grim lines.

"Is it time?" Jace asked, his hands restless as he watched the scene unfold.

"Indeed," Aydis replied solemnly, her eyes never leaving Forest. "The call to battle has been sounded, and our people will answer."

That placed a reassuring hand on Jace's shoulder. "Pay attention," he advised, "There is much to glean from the war strategies of the El."

Jace nodded, steeling himself for what was to come. He could feel the anticipation thrumming through the air, the moment's weight pressing down upon them like a heavy fog. There was no turning back now - the battle against the Cambions was upon them, and the El would fight with everything they had.

"Alcarë nórë!" Forset cried, raising his arm high above his head. In response, the El warriors lifted their weapons, their voices joining together in a haunting battle cry that sent shivers down Jace's spine. With one final, resounding shout, they began to march forward, their footfalls synchronized and steady.

"May the light guide them," Aydis whispered, her voice barely audible over the din of boots and armor.

"May the stars watch over them," Ahat added quietly, his dark eyes filled with concern.

As Jace watched, the El warriors seemed to blend with the fog that swirled around them, their forms becoming indistinct and ghostly until they were little more than shadows moving through the mist. It was as if the air was embracing them, cloaking them in a protective shroud as they ventured into the unknown.

"They're manipulating the elements," Ahat explained.

"By the gods," Jace breathed, unable to tear his gaze away from the sight. "How do they do it?"

Jace watched in amazement as the fog swirled and shifted, almost dancing at the command of the El.

"Our people have learned to harness the elements themselves, drawing upon the strength of the earth, wind, and water to aid them in their battles," Aydis explained.

"Remember this, Jace Alexander," Ahat reminded him, his voice steady and calm. "For soon enough, you too will walk among them, your powers awakened and your destiny fulfilled."

As the last El warriors disappeared into the fog, leaving Jace, Aydis, and Ahat alone in the now-empty camp, Jace felt awe and anticipation welling inside him. The battle against the Cambions had begun, and there could be no room for doubt or hesitation - only the unwavering certainty that they would emerge victorious.

The sun dipped lower as Jace stood in the now-empty camp, casting its warm glow over the Nelhelm plains. The air was still thick with tension and anticipation, but a sense of urgency also hung in the air.

Aydis was the first to break the tense silence, urgently stating they needed to move quickly. Jace turned towards her, still trying to process everything he had just witnessed.

"But where are we headed?" he asked.

"To gain a better vantage point," Ahat answered. "You will learn the most valuable lessons in preparation for the upcoming battles."

Without wasting time, the three gathered their belongings and set off towards the nearby hills. Jace's heart pounded with anticipation as he followed Aydis and Ahat, his mind overflowing with questions about what awaited them at their destination.

As they reached the top of the highest hill, Jace was struck by the breathtaking view. The Nelhelm plains stretched out below, and the El army stood, their armor glinting in the sun's dying light. In the distance, he could see a dark mass looming ominously on the horizon.

Aydis spoke, her voice akin to a delicate symphony, "Jace, every endeavor sets sail with a solitary act. You have already moved beyond the first obstacles, marching forward on this quest."

Jace met her gaze with his metallic-blue eyes, acknowledging the mutual understanding connecting them—an unyielding chain crucial for surviving the forthcoming trials.

'Indeed,' Ahat added, his words imbued with irrefutable wisdom. 'Don't let apprehension obscure your foresight. Welcome the difficulties that loom before you; they merely form the stones paving your path to greatness.'

With each word spoken, Jace drew strength from their unwavering faith in him. He knew that he must continue to hone his skills, sharpen his instincts, and unlock the secrets of this world if he was ever to stand beside the El in battle against the Cambions.

7

Cambion

Jace Alexander crouched low behind a boulder, Aydis and Ahat flanking him on either side. From their vantage point, they could see the battle raging in the valley below, where the El and Cambions clashed like titans of myth. The air was thick with the stench of burnt flesh and ozone as lightning and flame tore through the sky and scorched the earth.

"By the gods," Jace muttered, his steel-blue eyes wide in awe as he watched the carnage unfold.

He had never seen such a display of raw power before, not even in the countless mythologies he had studied growing up. Aydis nodded grimly, her fingers gripping the hilt of her sword so tightly that her knuckles turned white.

"This is the battlefield, Jace. It's never pretty, but it's where we must stand and fight to protect our world."

Ahat, the more stoic of the two, merely grunted in agreement, his gaze never leaving the fray.

The El, masters of light and nature, were a blur of motion on the battlefield. Their bodies crackled with electric energy as they summoned bolts of lightning from the heavens, splitting the ground and felling trees in their quest to destroy the Cambions.

But the Cambions would not be defeated so easily. They fought back with the fury of the inferno, turning the very air around them into a searing blaze. The forest surrounding the battlefield quickly caught flame, and the once lush greenery was reduced to ash and embers as the two forces collided with terrifying force.

"Look at that one!" Jace exclaimed, pointing to a particularly fierce El warrior who wielded a staff crackling with lightning.

The warrior danced gracefully between the shadows, his movements fluid and precise as he struck down one enemy after another.

"His name is Caelum," Aydis said, her voice tinged with a hint of reverence. "He's one of our greatest fighters."

As Jace watched the battle unfold, he couldn't help but feel a pang of fear for the El, as well as a deep-rooted sense of responsibility. These were the people who had taken him in, who had given him shelter and purpose when he had found himself lost in this strange new world. He owed them everything, and yet he could only watch from the sidelines as they fought and died for their home.

"Look out!" Ahat shouted suddenly, his eyes fixed on a rogue fireball that was hurtling toward their position.

Jace barely had time to react before Aydis leaped forward, summoning a gust of wind to deflect the deadly projectile. The fireball veered off course, exploding harmlessly against a nearby rock face.

"Thanks," Jace breathed, his heart pounding in his chest. "That was close."

"Stay vigilant," Aydis warned, her eyes never leaving the battlefield. "The danger isn't over yet."

And she was right. As the battle raged on, it became increasingly clear that neither side was willing to give an inch. With each clash of power, the destruction grew, the once pristine valley now a scorched wasteland marred by the scars of war.

Jace felt a sinking feeling in his stomach as he watched the El struggle against the relentless tide of smoke. What if they couldn't win? What if they were truly facing an enemy that could not be defeated?

"Stay strong, Jace," Aydis murmured, sensing his doubts. "We've faced dark days before, and we will rise above this one as well. We just need to keep fighting, no matter the cost."

"Right," Jace agreed, steeling himself for what was to come. He had survived countless challenges before, and he would face this one head-on with all the determination and courage that had carried him through his entire life. For El, Emma, and himself, he would not back down.

The air was thick with the scent of charred earth and ozone as the battle raged on, a cacophony of elemental power that seemed to shake the very ground beneath Jace's feet. From his vantage point, he could see the El struggling to hold their ground against the relentless onslaught of the Cambions.

"By the gods, they're being pushed back," Ahat muttered, his eyes narrowed in concern. "I've never seen us falter like this before."

"Neither have I," Aydis admitted, her voice strained with worry. "But we must believe in their ability to overcome this."

Jace watched as light arcing through the sky met with the roaring flames of the Cambions, the clash of elements creating a spectacle that both mesmerized and horrified him. What had begun as a fierce skirmish now teetered on the brink of utter defeat for the El.

"Retreat!" The booming voice of Forset echoed through the chaos, his normally composed demeanor replaced by one of urgency. "Fall back! We cannot win this fight today!"

Jace clenched his heart at the order, his mind racing as the implications of El's retreat settled upon him. He had believed them to be an unstoppable force, a bastion of strength and wisdom that could guide him in this strange new world. But now, as he watched them flee from the battlefield, he was forced to confront the possibility that perhaps they were not invincible after all.

"Are we really... retreating?" Jace asked, his voice barely audible even to himself.

"Sometimes, we must know when to fight and when to step back," Aydis replied solemnly. "Today is not our day, but the war is far from over. We will regroup, and we will come back stronger."

As the El began their withdrawal, Jace felt a mixture of disappointment and fear churning within him. He had placed his faith in the El and trusted their strength to aid him in finding a way back to Emma. With each footfall that took them further from the battlefield, he couldn't help but wonder if he had been wrong to trust so fully in their abilities.

"Jace," Ahat said, placing a hand on his shoulder. "Remember, even the mightiest of warriors can falter. The El is not infallible, but they have endured countless battles before this one. They will regroup, and they will come back stronger."

"Will it be enough?" Jace asked, his words laced with uncertainty.

As the smoke and ash began to clear, revealing the true extent of the devastation left behind by the clash of fire and lightning, his thoughts drifted to Emma and the life they were meant to share together.

"Only time will tell," Aydis whispered, her eyes filled with a quiet determination. "But we must never lose hope, Jace. For as long as hope remains, so too does our chance for victory."

The once lush and verdant battlefield now lay in ruin, a scorched testament to the ferocity of the clash between the El and Cambions. Fallen trees smoldered, their charred limbs reaching toward the sky like the twisted hands of the damned. The earth itself bore the scars of flame and lightning, deep gouges and blackened craters telling the tale of the battle that had taken place.

Aydis let out a quiet gasp, her voice barely audible above the crackling of dying embers. Her eyes were wide with disbelief, as if she couldn't quite comprehend the destruction that lay before them.

"Indeed," Ahat agreed, his voice somber. He cast a glance at Jace, who stood watching the retreating El with a mixture of concern and betrayal etched across his face. "I fear this is a harsh lesson for us all."

"Lesson?" Jace spat, anger flaring through him like wildfire. "Why didn't you tell me the truth about the situation? I thought the El were...unbeatable!" His voice shook, fists clenched at his sides. "I trusted you!"

"Jace, we never intended to mislead you," Ahat said with a pained expression. "We had faith in our cause and the power of our people to overcome the Cambions. But unfortunately, things don't always go as planned."

"Hope and faith won't bring me back to Emma," Jace growled, his heart aching with longing for his fiancée. "What good are your promises when I'm stranded in a world on the brink of destruction?"

"Jace, please," Aydis pleaded, her eyes shimmering with unshed tears. "We will find a way. We will regroup, plan, and fight again. And we will do it together."

The sun began to set, casting a warm orange glow over the devastated battlefield. Jace and Aydis sat on a fallen tree trunk, their heads hanging low in defeat. Ahat had gone to gather the wounded El soldiers, leaving the two of them alone to process the events of the day.

"I just can't believe it," Jace said, his voice heavy with sorrow. "Emma and I were supposed to be starting our lives together, getting married. And now..."

Forset's stern voice cut off Jace's words. The El leader strode towards them, his gaze fixed upon Jace.

"Jace Alexander, I understand your anger. For now, we are dealing with this loss - our pride wounded, our confidence shaken."

Jace fell silent, a mix of shame and fury bubbling up inside him.

Forset looked around at the desolate battlefield, his eyes filled with a steely resolve.

"We will retreat back to the camp, and there we will recover, strategize, and forge ahead. Our losses today have been great, but they will not be in vain."

"Your words are inspiring, Forset," Jace said, his voice still tinged with bitterness. "But I need more than words. I need action. I need results. If we are to fight together, tell me everything – no more secrets."

"Very well," Forset agreed solemnly. "From this moment on, you shall be privy to all aspects of our struggle against the Cambions. You have my word."

"Good," Jace nodded, his heart heavy with disappointment and dread.

He gazed out over the battlefield, the devastation a stark reminder of the life he had left behind and the uncertain future that now lay before him. As the sun dipped below the horizon, casting long shadows across the scarred earth, Jace couldn't help but wonder if he would ever find his way back home to Emma.

Jace stood in silence, watching the El retreat from the scorched battlefield. The once lush and verdant land now lay charred and lifeless, an eerie graveyard of smoldering trees and blackened earth. He couldn't help but think of the Cambions' ruthless power and how easily it had overwhelmed the El's forces.

"Is this what we're up against?" he mused to himself, feeling a wave of doubt wash over him. "If the El, with all their magic and might, can be so easily defeated... then what chance do I have?"

As the remaining El warriors limped back to their camp, their heads hung low, Jace noticed the extent of their injuries; some leaned heavily on their comrades for support, while others nursed deep gashes and burns. He clenched his fists, the anger and frustration building within him. Why hadn't they told him about the true nature of their enemy? Why had they allowed him to believe they were invincible?

"Jace," Reynard approached him, his face etched with exhaustion and grief. "We must tend to our wounded and assess the damage. But do not lose hope; this is but one battle in a long war."

"Hope?" Jace spat bitterly. "I came here seeking help, believing that your people could aid me in finding my way home. Instead, I find myself in the midst of a losing battle against an enemy I never even knew existed."

"Jace, I understand your skepticism and your doubts," Reynard said, his voice calm and measured. "But remember, we are fighting for the same cause – survival. We may have lost today, but we will learn from our mistakes and come back stronger."

"Will we?" Jace asked, his eyes narrowing.

"Every defeat carries a lesson, my friend," Reynard replied, placing a hand on Jace's shoulder. "We will grow from this."

As they trudged back to camp, Jace studied the El warriors. He read the exhaustion on their faces and noticed how their gaze seemed unsure as they murmured among themselves. The once mighty, confident race now appeared undermined, their faith in their skills visibly shaken.

"Reynard," Jace broached quietly, unable to dismiss the creeping doubt nesting in his thoughts. "Can I count on you to support me when it's evident you're struggling for survival?"

"Earning trust is a painstaking process, Jace," Reynard replied gravely. "My assurance is that we are committed to standing by your side until the end, whatever it entails."

Jace nodded, his spirit burdened with the enormity of uncertainties looming ahead. As they stepped into the camp, an oppressive air of despair and defeat was palpable. Jace couldn't help but question if he'd ever return to Emma – or was destiny chaining him in this peculiar, perilous world.

The somber gray sky mirrored the mood in the El camp as they returned from the battlefield, defeated and weary. Jace walked alongside Reynard, observing the wounded warriors who stumbled and leaned on one another for support. The once vibrant colors of their armor were dulled with soot and blood, radiant leaves charred by the Cambions' flame. Sobs echoed through the air, punctuated by the occasional anguished cry, as they mourned their fallen comrades.

"By the roots of Yggdrasil..." whispered one warrior, cradling her injured arm. "We've never faced such a devastating loss before."

"Indeed," murmured another, his gaze distant as he stared at the smoldering remains of the forest beyond the camp. "It's as if the very world has turned against us."

"Silence your doubts!" snapped Forset, striding amongst the disheartened warriors. "We must regroup and prepare for the coming storm. Our enemy will not rest, and neither shall we."

The El leaders gathered together in Forset's tent, discussing their next steps. Jace stood outside, listening intently, as Forset stood in a circle with his officers, all of them gathered around a gold bowl filled with liquid. He appeared to be conversing with somebody called Mitra through this pool as though it were a form of telecommunication.

"Malathar is your only hope now," Mitra said firmly. "We cannot afford to lose any more of our people in these futile skirmishes."

"Abandon the plains? How can you even suggest such a thing?" Forset countered, his voice tight with anger. "We have fought for centuries to protect these lands. We cannot abandon them now!"

"Enough," commanded Mitra, silencing the growing cacophony of voices. "Our situation is dire, but we must not let fear guide our actions. A strategic retreat to Malathar will allow you to regroup, gather your strength, and prepare for the battles to come. We must not be hasty, but neither can we afford to let pride cloud our judgment."

"Very well," said Forset begrudgingly. "We shall retreat to Malathar. But know this: I will not abandon our struggle against the Cambions. They will pay for the destruction they have wrought upon our people."

"Of course," Mitra replied, her tone softening. "Our fight is far from over, but we must be wise in our approach. We will endure, and we will prevail."

As the El leaders dispersed, Jace found himself torn between his desire to trust the El and the doubts that continued to gnaw at him. He couldn't shake the image of the fallen warriors, their faces twisted in pain and despair. Was it selfish to still hope for a way back to Emma when so many lives were at stake?

"Jace," Reynard called out as he exited the tent. "Walk with me."

Together, they wandered through the camp, observing the wounded and heartbroken El as they tended to one another. Even in their darkest hour, there was a resilience in their eyes, a determination to endure.

"Remember this moment, my friend," Reynard said softly. "For in the depths of despair, we find the true measure of our strength."

Jace stared at the flickering embers of a dying fire, the orange glow casting shadows across his troubled face. The camp was eerily quiet, the hushed whispers and muted sobs of the El the only sounds to break the silence. Reynard's words echoed in his mind, gnawing at him like a restless wind through the trees.

"Betrayal" - the word seemed too heavy, too dark for what he felt. But still, it clung to him, a whispering serpent that coiled around his heart. They had not told him of their vulnerability, of the true might of the Cambions.

Jace clenched his fists, nails digging into his palms. His desire to return home, to find Emma again, burned like an unquenchable fire within him. And yet, as he watched the El tending to their wounded, their eyes filled with sorrow and determination, he couldn't help but feel a pang of guilt. Was it selfish to want to leave these broken people behind?

"Jace," a familiar voice called out gently. It was Aydis, her eyes searching his face with concern. "Are you alright?"

"I don't know," he admitted, his voice cracking. "I thought the El was invincible, but... I've never seen such devastation."

"Neither have we," she confessed softly. "This battle has shaken us all to our very core."

"Can we still defeat the Cambions?" Jace asked, desperation creeping into his tone. "Can you still help me find a way back to Emma?"

Aydis hesitated, her gaze meeting his.

"We will do everything in our power to aid you, Jace. But first, we must ensure the survival of our people."

"Of course," he murmured, his heart heavy. "I understand."

The wounded were tended to, and plans were made to fortify their defenses. Jace did his best to assist wherever he could, but his mind was consumed with thoughts of Emma and finding a way back to her. He couldn't shake the feeling of guilt and selfishness that clung to him.

"By the Ancients," Ahat murmured, his voice barely audible above the distant crackle of flames. "I have never seen such wanton destruction."

"Nor did I," Aydis agreed solemnly, her emerald eyes downcast as she surveyed their fallen brethren. "The Cambions' rage knows no bounds."

"Will they come back?" Jace asked, an uneasy shiver crawling down his spine.

"Unlikely," Ahat replied, his gaze flickering towards the darkening sky. "They've inflicted enough damage for one day. They'll regroup, lick their wounds, and plan their next attack."

"Then we must do the same," Aydis declared, her jaw set in grim resolve. "We cannot let this loss break us. We must rise from the ashes and face our enemies with renewed strength and purpose."

"Agreed," Ahat nodded, clenching his fists at his sides. "The El shall not falter."

Jace watched the determination in their eyes and tried to summon a similar resolve within himself. But as he looked upon the shattered remains of the El's once indomitable force, he couldn't help but feel a nagging sense of doubt. How could they hope to defeat an enemy capable of such devastation? And even if they managed to prevail, would there be anything left worth saving?

"Jace," Aydis said gently, placing a comforting hand on his shoulder. "I know that you're afraid. We all are. But fear can either cripple us or drive us forward. The choice is ours."

"I understand," Jace replied quietly, his gaze lingering on the wounded El being tended to by their comrades. "It's just...hard to see a way back from this."

"Sometimes we must lose everything in order to rebuild anew," Ahat offered, his voice heavy with sorrow. "But we cannot do it alone. We must stand together, united against the darkness."

Jace nodded solemnly, knowing that their words held truth. As much as he longed to return to Emma and the life they had planned, he couldn't abandon the El in their time of need. They had shown him kindness and offered their aid, and he would not turn his back on them now.

"Alright," he said, steeling himself for what lay ahead. "I'm with you. Whatever it takes, we'll find a way to stop the Cambions. Together."

As the shadows of the night deepened, Jace found himself lost in thought. He couldn't help but think of Emma, of the life they had planned together. And then it struck him, a bolt of lightning searing through his very soul: today was the day they were supposed to be married.

He imagined her standing at the altar, a vision of beauty bathed in sunlight, surrounded by friends and family. And here he was, in a world torn apart by war, consumed by darkness and despair. The contrast was almost too much to bear.

"Emma," he whispered into the night, hoping against hope that, somehow, she could hear him. "I will find my way back to you. I promise."

Jace Alexander walked through the labyrinth of tents, the smell of woodsmoke and earth heavy in the air. His steel blue eyes scanned the area as he searched for Forset, captain of the El army. The sun was setting, casting long shadows that stretched across the fields like fingers grasping at the horizon, and Jace felt a sense of urgency settling into his bones.

8

The Guests

The small mountain town of Glenwood was shrouded in a thick mist as if the very air shared in the collective anxiety over Jace's disappearance. The search effort had reached a fever pitch, with volunteers scouring every last inch of the surrounding wilderness for any sign of the missing young man.

Through the fog, the wedding guests began to arrive, their expressions somber and determined. With Emma and Jace's nuptials called off indefinitely, one would have expected them to be disappointed or upset; instead, they seemed eager to lend their aid in finding Jace. Allen and Sarah exchanged puzzled glances as they watched the Williams' friends and relatives gather. The sheer number of willing participants struck them as odd, considering most people would find it difficult to abandon their day-to-day lives at a moment's notice.

"Strange bunch, aren't they?" Sarah mused, her voice low and uncertain.

"Definitely," Allen replied, his brow furrowed in thought. "Most people wouldn't be able to drop everything like this. Makes you wonder..."

Sarah nodded solemnly, her gaze never leaving the crowd that had amassed before them. She picked out faces she recognized—colleagues from work, family friends, acquaintances—but many more were strangers to her. They carried themselves with an air of authority and discipline, their chiseled features and toned bodies hinting at years of training and experience. Clear, purposeful strides and efficient movements gave off an intimidating presence.

"Jace would appreciate their help," she said finally, her voice laced with a quiet resolve. "We need all the support we can get."

Allen placed a reassuring hand on her shoulder, feeling the weight of responsibility settle upon him in his role as deputy. He looked out at the gathering, his heart pounding in his chest.

"Emma's really done right by him," he murmured, watching the young woman intently. She stood amidst the throng of people, her eyes filled with a fierce determination that only fueled the fire within him.

Allen felt a surge of pride as he watched Emma address the crowd, her voice ringing out with steely determination.

"Thank you all for coming," she said, her words carrying weight and purpose. "I know that Jace would be grateful for your support."

The crowd responded with murmurs of agreement and nodding heads, their attention fully focused on Emma's every word.

"Find my son," Sarah whispered, her voice barely audible in the crisp mountain air. "Bring Jace home."

As Allen took in the scene before him, the fog seemed to thicken, shrouding the search party in an eerie silence. The unknown faces peering through the mist became ghost-like, their expressions shadowed by the uncertainty of what lay ahead.

"Let's find him," he said quietly, his voice resolute. "No matter what it takes."

Emma, undeterred by the wedding being called off, focused her energy on finding Jace. Her lack of upset was noticeable to those around her, but it only served to emphasize her commitment to locating her fiancé. She moved through the crowd, organizing search parties and disseminating information about Jace's last known location.

"Jace means everything to me," she told Allen, her brown eyes shining with determination. "I won't rest until he's found."

In contrast, Emma's parents, Liz and Nicholas Williams, had a different approach to the situation. Rather than continuing to participate in the search efforts, they focused on attending to the wedding guests who had traveled to Glenwood.

"Make sure everyone has enough to eat," Liz directed the catering staff as she bustled around the room, arranging table settings and adjusting floral bouquets. "We mustn't have anyone going hungry during this search."

"Of course, Mrs. Williams," the caterer responded, observing her with a mixture of admiration and confusion.

Nicholas, too, was occupied with keeping up with what his guests were learning about the ongoing search.

He quickly apologized to one of Emma's aunts, who had just arrived and was caught off guard by the sudden change in plans. Then, he turned his attention to another man. The man stood tall and fit, his muscular frame noticeable even under his tactical gear. He had short hair styled almost like a military cut, and his eyes were intense and observant as he scanned the area.

"Allen," Nicholas called out, flagging down the deputy. "Let me introduce you to Rick Waters. He's a friend from Philadelphia who has experience with these types of situations."

"Good to have you here, Rick," Allen responded, extending his hand. "I'm Allen Walker, and over there is Sheriff Callahan."

"Good to meet you, Allen," Rick said, shaking his hand firmly. "A few of us from Philadelphia would like to band together and conduct some searches."

Allen's face lit up with gratitude.

"That would be incredibly helpful. We have teams heading out in different directions, but more manpower is always welcome."

Rick motioned towards the two men standing behind him.

"This is John and Mark. They're part of our team as well."

John was tall and muscular, dressed in tactical gear like Rick. His dark eyes were sharp and observant. Mark, on the other hand, had a strong and compact build with a bald head and thick beard. He stood confidently, with the posture of someone who had undergone rigorous military training.

"We're happy to join forces," Allen said warmly as he began organizing their efforts.

Allen let out a sigh as he began to assign new search teams for the day. Glancing over at Emma, he couldn't help but admire her determination in finding Jace. Her unbreakable resolve was infectious, and it motivated him to keep going despite the increasing challenges they faced each day.

"Jace is out there somewhere," Sarah said softly, joining Allen as they watched Emma work. "He's strong, resourceful, and determined. Just like Emma. We will find him."

Despite the wedding being called off and her parents' shift in focus to entertaining guests, Emma remained undeterred in her quest to find Jace. The guests, however, were not what one might expect for a wedding celebration.

"Strange company you keep," Allen remarked as he surveyed the crowd.

The guests appeared to be, like John and Mark, more suited to a military ball than a wedding gathering. Their athletic builds and rigid posture exuded an air of discipline, while their eyes conveyed a sense of purpose that surpassed mere social pleasantries. They wore formal attire, but it was clear they would be more comfortable clad in armor or tactical gear.

"Indeed," Emma replied, her gaze lingering on a particularly imposing figure with a buzzcut and chiseled features. "But they are precisely the type of people we need right now."

"Are you sure about this?" Allen asked, his voice laced with concern. He couldn't shake the nagging feeling that something was off with these newcomers.

"Absolutely," she said, her voice firm. "They may be unconventional wedding guests, but I trust them implicitly. They're here to help, and that's all that matters."

As Emma walked away, Allen couldn't help but notice the subtle tension in her body language. She didn't seem completely at ease.

As the search efforts continued, the Sheriff decided to lock down the area around the Old Chimney, declaring it a crime scene.

"I don't like the looks of this," he announced, addressing the assembled group. "We found fresh tracks near the chimney and bullet holes. Until we know more, I want everyone to stay away from that area."

The announcement sent a ripple of unease through the group. Emma's jaw tightened as she exchanged a worried glance with Allen. She knew that area was their best bet for finding Jace, and now it was off-limits.

"What do you think happened?" Sarah whispered to Allen, her brows furrowed in concern.

"I don't know," he replied, his own worry etched on his face. "But I am pretty certain it's connected to Jace's disappearance."

As the group dispersed, Emma approached the Sheriff.

"Can I at least go in and take a look around?" she asked, trying to keep her voice calm despite the building frustration inside her.

The Sheriff shook his head.

"I'm sorry, Ms. Williams, but we can't risk compromising any evidence."

Emma nodded reluctantly and turned to walk away.

There was a murmur of discontent among Rick Water's team, who had hoped to scour every inch of the surrounding woods in their quest for Jace. But Emma's guests did not question the Sheriff's decision; instead, they merely exchanged knowing glances and nodded in agreement.

"Emma," Allen whispered, pulling her aside. "I know your friends are eager to help, but we have to be careful. We don't know what happened to Jace, and bringing in outsiders could complicate matters."

"Jace is one of us," Emma replied with a steely determination. "And my friends are here to help find him, nothing more. They're loyal and skilled, Allen. I trust them with my life – and Jace's."

"Very well," he said reluctantly, his instincts still at odds with her confidence. But for now, they needed all the support they could get.

As the day wore on, the tension within the group grew. Rick and his team had taken to patrolling the perimeter of the Old Chimney, searching for any clues that might lead them to Jace.

Allen and the Sheriff, accompanied by a small group of deputies, made their way through the dense forest towards the Old Chimney. The ancient structure stood like a weathered sentinel, its stone and mortar scarred by the passage of time. It was all that remained of a once-grand Alexander house, long abandoned to the encroaching wilderness.

"It has been a while since I saw this chimney," muttered Allen, his eyes scanning the surrounding area for any signs of Jace. "It makes sense that Jace would run this way."

As they approached the chimney, Allen felt a sinking sensation in the pit of his stomach. He had hoped that the search would lead them to Jace, safe and sound, but the reality seemed far more sinister. The evidence before him spoke volumes: fresh bullet holes pockmarked the chimney's crumbling stones, and several footprints were clearly visible in the soft earth around it.

Anxiety tinged Allen's voice as he spoke, "I hope Jace wasn't here when these bullet holes were made."

The group cautiously made their way closer to the chimney, Allen leading the way with his gun at the ready. He couldn't shake off the feeling of unease that had settled over him like a heavy cloak.

The Sheriff's face mirrored his own worry as he responded solemnly, "I can't say for certain. But we must locate him quickly either way."

"Dammit!" Allen exclaimed quietly through gritted teeth, clenching his fists in frustration. "What the hell happened here? Who did this?"

"Stay composed, Deputy," the Sheriff advised calmly, scanning the area with a trained eye. "Losing our temper won't bring us any closer to answers. We need to gather every piece of evidence we can find."

"Right," Allen nodded, swallowing his anger and focusing on the task at hand.

He searched the ground for shell casings or any other valuable clues while the Sheriff documented the bullet holes and footprints, his seasoned hands moving deftly over the rough, charred stones.

"Find anything?" the Sheriff asked after a few minutes of silence.

"Nothing yet," Allen answered, his voice tight with barely contained fury. Every moment they spent uncovering evidence was another moment Jace remained missing. He couldn't help but feel as though they were failing him. "Whoever was here must have been careful not to leave much behind."

Allen crouched behind the chimney and noticed a set of footprints leading down an old, neglected trail. He called for his deputies to come take photos of the prints. As he followed the tracks, they became harder to follow until they suddenly disappeared without a trace.

The sheriff turned to Allen and asked, "Did you find something?"

Allen nodded, saying, "Yes. There are footprints leading down this path."

"Excellent work," the sheriff praised. "With these footprints and the bullets we found in the Chimney, we might have a chance at figuring out what's happening here."

Sarah Alexander stood at the edge of the crime scene, her eyes locked on Allen and the Sheriff as they investigated the Old Chimney.

The weight of her concern for Jace was etched into the lines of her face, but she remained resolute in her faith that he would return unharmed.

"Jace is strong," she murmured to herself, clutching her hands together. "He can survive this. He will survive this."

"Mom, are you okay?" Emma asked gently, joining Sarah at the perimeter.

Her own expression was a mix of determination and worry, but she refused to let it consume her. She had seen Jace face countless challenges over the years, and what she'd learned from him was that resilience could make all the difference in the world.

"Emma, my dear, I'm just worried about Jace," Sarah said, her voice trembling slightly. "But I know he'll make it through this. He's got the heart of a lion, that one."

Emma nodded, knowing it was her turn to be strong—for both Jace and his mother.

"I agree. And we're going to do everything we can to find him and bring him home."

"Of course," Sarah whispered, her gaze never leaving the sight of the Old Chimney. "I just wish we could do more."

"Speaking of which," Emma said, her tone resolute, "have you heard anything new? About the evidence they've found?"

"Nothing yet," Sarah replied, watching the Sheriff and Allen carefully examine the area. "But they seem to be taking it very seriously. That has to count for something."

"Absolutely," Emma agreed, her jaw clenched with determination. "We'll support them any way we can. We'll find Jace, and we'll help him through whatever he's facing."

"Emma," Sarah began, her eyes filling with tears. "You truly are a treasure. Jace is blessed to have your love."

"Thank you, Sarah," Emma said, her own eyes glistening with emotion as she wrapped an arm around the older woman. "And he's blessed to have a mother like you. We'll be strong together, for him."

Together, they stood and watched the investigation unfold, their unwavering faith in Jace's survival driving them to support the search efforts with every fiber of their being. In the face of uncertainty and fear, they found solace in their shared determination to bring Jace back home, no matter what it took.

Allen approached Sarah and Emma with a worried expression on his face.

"We discovered new bullet holes in the chimney, and there are footprints leading into the forest."

Sarah's mind raced as she asked aloud, "Who would want to shoot at Jace?"

"We can't jump to conclusions just yet," Allen said, trying to soothe the nerves of both Sarah and Emma. "First, we have to examine those footprints."

Allen's words hung heavily in the air as Sarah and Emma exchanged worried glances. Their minds raced with questions, but they both knew that no answers could be found until the investigation progressed further.

The sun dipped lower in the sky, casting long, eerie shadows across the mountain landscape. Emma and Sarah stood side by side, their eyes fixed on the Sheriff as he addressed the small army of volunteers assembled before him. Among them was-/* Rick Waters's team, their once pristine attire now stained with the dirt and sweat of countless hours spent searching for Jace. The Old Chimney loomed in the background, a dark sentinel guarding secrets yet to be uncovered.

"Listen up!" the Sheriff bellowed, his voice hard with resolve. "We're opening up the area around the Old Chimney for searches again. Stay clear of the Chimney until we can get the bullets excised. We need to comb through every inch of this place and analyze any new evidence we might find. I want teams working together, covering every possible angle. You all know the drill."

He paused, his gaze sweeping over the faces of the gathered crowd.

"I want to thank you all for your continued dedication to finding Jace. This ain't gonna be easy, but I believe we can find him if we work together."

As the search parties began to fan out, Emma's thoughts raced, her heart pounding in her chest. She knew that Liz and Nicholas Williams had withdrawn from the search efforts. Their focus shifted to entertaining their friends who had stayed behind. However, the absence of her parents did little to deter her determination to find Jace.

"Emma," Sarah murmured, her voice trembling with emotion, "I can't help but worry about what we might find. What if...?"

"Sarah," Emma interrupted gently, placing a comforting hand on her future mother-in-law's arm. "We have to stay positive. Jace is strong, and he has all of us looking for him. I truly believe he'll come out of this alive."

"Y-yes," Sarah stammered, taking a deep breath. "You're right. Thank you, dear."

"Stay close to me," Emma whispered, her grip tightening on Sarah's arm as they joined the throng of searchers.

The Waters team moved with a sense of precision and purpose that verified their athletic and military appearances, their eyes scouring the terrain for any sign of Jace.

The air grew colder as dusk approached, the shadows lengthening around them. Emma glanced back at the Old Chimney, its crumbling form a stark reminder of the mysteries hidden within the mountains. A chill ran down her spine, and she knew in her heart that they were close to uncovering the truth.

"Let's find him," she said, her voice barely audible over the sound of rustling leaves and crunching footsteps. "Let's bring Jace home."

As they disappeared into the wilderness, a sense of anticipation hung heavy in the air. Uncertainty gnawed away at the edges of their resolve, but they pressed on, driven by love, loyalty, and the unshakeable belief that Jace was still out there, waiting for them.

And so, beneath the watchful eye of the Old Chimney, the search continued.

9

Retreat

The sun dipped low in the sky as Jace and his companions strode along the dusty road to Malathar. The light cast a warm orange glow on their faces, highlighting the determination in their eyes. Forset, the towering captain of the El army, led the group at a steady pace. His long grey hair flowed behind him like a cape, and his piercing eyes scanned their surroundings.

"Why don't we use the fog to travel to Malathar?" questioned Jace.

"Using the fog would be too risky," Forset explained, his deep voice resonating through the air. "The Cambions have learned our tricks over time. They can track us through the mist. In the old days, just the sight of the El's fog of war would cause any Cambion army to retreat."

"Then we'll have to rely on our wits and skill," Reynard quipped, his red hair striking against the fading sunlight. He glanced at Jace with a wry smile. "And I suppose our Gaian friend here will have to learn fast if he wants to survive."

Jace clenched his fists and nodded, steel-blue eyes unyielding. "You can count on me," he said firmly. "I won't let you down."

As they continued along the road, the camaraderie between them was evident. Despite their different backgrounds, they were united by a shared sense of purpose: to defeat the Cambions and protect

Nelhelm. Their laughter echoed through the stillness, their voices blending into a harmonious chorus.

"Jace, you must tell us more about your world," Aydis urged, her eyes twinkling with curiosity. "What is it like to live among the Gaians?"

"Life back home is... different," Jace replied, pausing to gather his thoughts. "There's peace, for the most part. But there are also struggles and challenges to overcome. We don't face supernatural threats like the Cambions, but we still have our own battles."

"Sounds like a pleasant place," Ahat mused, his playful demeanor never wavering. "I'd love to see it someday."

"Who knows?" Jace responded with a faint smile. "Maybe you will."

As they walked, Reynard sidled up to Jace and slung an arm around his shoulders, the familiarity between them growing stronger with each passing day. "You've got quite the spirit, my friend. I must admit, I'm impressed."

"Thanks, Reynard," Jace said, returning the grin. "But I couldn't do any of this without all of you. You've shown me what it means to fight for something greater than myself."

"Ah, humility!" Reynard exclaimed, feigning shock. "Truly a rare trait among heroes."

Jace rolled his eyes, though his smile remained. "Just trying to keep up with you lot, that's all."

"Indeed," Forset interjected, his tone serious once more. "We must all rely on one another if we are to succeed in our mission."

With a collective nod, they pressed onward, their footsteps a steady rhythm in the twilight. Together, they faced the uncertain road ahead, bound by their shared determination and the unbreakable bonds of friendship.

The vastness of Nelhelm's plains stretched out before them, a tapestry of vibrant greens and golds that seemed to go on forever. Rolling hills rose and fell gently beneath the azure sky, dotted with bursts of wildflowers that swayed in the breeze. It was truly a sight to behold, unlike anything Jace had ever experienced back in Gaia.

As they continued their journey, their conversations turned to the legends of Gaians who had come to Nelhelm in the past. These tales of heroism and sacrifice served as a beacon of hope, a reminder of the strength that could be found even in the darkest of times.

"Did you know," Forset began, his voice carrying the weight of ancient knowledge, "that there were once three Gaians who fought side by side with us against the Cambions? They were known as the Triumvirate, and their deeds are still sung about in our halls."

"Really?" Jace asked, his curiosity piqued. "What did they do?"

"Ah, young one," Forset replied, a hint of a smile playing at the corners of his mouth. "Their story is one of great courage and determination. The Triumvirate was instrumental in turning the tide of battle, for they possessed powers the likes of which we had never seen."

"Each of them had a unique gift," Reynard chimed in, his eyes alight with excitement. "One could command fire, another could manipulate the very earth beneath their feet, and the third... well, they say she could bring the dead back to life."

"Remarkable," Jace murmured, thinking of the abilities he'd discovered within himself since arriving in Nelhelm. "And they made a difference?"

"More than you can imagine," Aydis added, her face full of admiration. "The Triumvirate pushed the Cambions back and helped us reclaim our lands. Their bravery inspired others to rise up, and their legacy lives on in the hearts of our people."

"Who knows?" Ahat teased, nudging Jace gently with his elbow. "Maybe someday they'll be singing songs about you too, huh?"

Jace chuckled, but deep down, he wondered if he could ever live up to such a storied legacy. As they continued onward, the shadows of the past seemed to walk alongside them, reminding him that he was part of something much larger than himself.

In those moments, as they traversed the breathtaking landscape and shared stories of legendary heroes, Jace couldn't help but feel both humbled and empowered. Though the path before him was fraught with danger and uncertainty, he knew that he did not walk it alone.

With his newfound friends by his side, he would face whatever challenges awaited them – and together, they would write their own chapter in the annals of Nelhelm's history.

As the sun dipped below the horizon, casting a warm golden glow across the vast plains, Jace couldn't help but be struck by the haunting beauty of this world. He felt an odd mixture of awe and melancholy, knowing that such a place could harbor danger and conflict just as easily as it inspired wonder.

"Reynard, Forset," Jace ventured cautiously, his voice almost a whisper in the gentle breeze that rustled the tall grasses around them. "Do you think Mitra will have more answers for me about my purpose here? As a Gaian, I mean."

Reynard glanced at him with a thoughtful expression before exchanging a look with Forset. "Mitra is wise, Jace," Reynard finally answered. "If there are answers to be found, she'll know where to find them."

"Still," Forset added, his deep voice resonating with authority, "do not forget that ultimately, it is you who must uncover your own purpose. Mitra can guide you, but the path you walk is yours alone."

Jace nodded, his eyes focused on the distant horizon, where the first stars of the evening began to sparkle against the darkening sky. He knew they were right – the responsibility was his to bear. But he clung to the hope that Mitra would offer some guidance, a beacon to light his way through the darkness.

"Speaking of paths," Aydis interjected, her playful tone breaking the somber mood, "how about we focus on the one right in front of us? Jace, it's time for more archery practice."

"Ah, yes," Ahat chimed in, grinning broadly. "The art of turning sticks into deadly weapons. I've seen children with better aim than our dear Gaian friend here."

Jace rolled his eyes good-naturedly but accepted the bow Aydis handed him. He knew the teasing was all in good fun, and it helped to ease the tension that had been building within him.

"Alright then," Jace said with a smile, drawing an arrow from his quiver. "Let's see if I can manage not to embarrass myself too much this time."

"Remember, focus on your target and let your instincts guide you," Aydis instructed, watching intently as Jace took aim at a small rock some distance away.

"Instincts?" Ahat scoffed playfully. "If we're relying on his instincts, that rock is safe. I'll be amazed if he even hits the ground."

"Quiet, you," Jace retorted, grinning despite himself. "I'm trying to concentrate."

"Of course, of course," Ahat conceded, raising his hands in mock surrender. "Concentrate away, oh mighty Gaian."

Jace took a deep breath, letting the stillness of the moment settle over him as he focused his attention on the rock, feeling the weight of the bow in his hands, the tension of the string against his fingers. A sudden chill washed over Jace. Without hesitation, he swiftly and seamlessly released the arrow from his bow.

With a graceful trajectory, it flew through the air and landed perfectly on target.

"See? You're improving already!" Aydis exclaimed, clapping Jace on the back. "At this rate, you might just become a halfway decent archer someday."

"Or maybe even a full-fledged, marginally competent one," Ahat added with a wink.

"Thanks for the vote of confidence," Jace replied dryly, but his heart swelled with warmth and gratitude.

As they continued their journey across the plains, Jace couldn't help but feel that a great adventure lay ahead. And with each arrow, he lost, and every step he took toward Malathar, the bonds of friendship and trust that had begun to form between them only grew stronger.

The sun dipped below the horizon, casting long shadows across the vast plains of Nelhelm. A chilling wind whispered through the tall grass, carrying with it a sense of foreboding that settled deep in Jace's bones. He glanced around at his companions, each one alert and watchful as they picked their way carefully across the uneven terrain.

Jace tightened his grip on his bow, feeling the familiar weight of it in his hands. He knew better than to underestimate the danger they faced, but still, a part of him couldn't help but wonder if he was truly prepared for the battle that lay ahead.

"Remember what we've taught you," Aydis murmured, sidling up beside him. "Trust your instincts, and don't be afraid to take risks."

"Easy for you to say," Jace muttered under his breath, though he appreciated her encouragement.

As they continued onward, the landscape grew steadily more treacherous. The earth beneath their feet became rocky and unstable, forcing them to navigate a maze of jagged outcroppings and narrow ravines. Insects buzzed in the twilight, drawn by the scent of sweat and fear.

It was then that they came upon them – a Cambion party.

"By the gods…" Ahat breathed, staring wide-eyed at the swirling dark storm that seemed to appear out of nowhere. It loomed before them like an inky black cloud, its edges churning and roiling as if alive.

"Keep your wits about you," Forset warned, his voice steady despite the growing tension. "This is only the beginning."

Through the thick smoke, the Cambions emerged, their large muscular forms barely distinguishable. Though they resembled humans, they were much larger and more imposing.

"Jace," Reynard hissed, his eyes never leaving the approaching enemy. "You have to help us fight."

"Protect Jace!" Forset ordered Aydis and Ahat, who nodded grimly, moving into position around the young Gaian.

"Okay, Jace," Aydis said, her voice surprisingly gentle. "It's time. Remember what we practiced."

He nodded, swallowing hard as he nocked an arrow and took aim. The bowstring hummed as he loosed it, sending the projectile arcing through the air toward the nearest Cambion. It struck true, taking down the creature with a satisfying thud.

"Good shot!" Ahat called out, grinning fiercely as he dispatched another foe. "Keep it up!"

Jace felt coldness course through him as he continued to fire, each arrow finding its mark with deadly precision. Around him, Aydis and Ahat fought valiantly, their blades flashing in the dim light as they kept the Cambions at bay.

But it was Forset who truly captured Jace's attention. The El captain moved with a grace and ferocity that seemed almost otherworldly, every strike a testament to his prowess on the battlefield. Jace couldn't help but feel awestruck as he watched him cut through the enemy ranks with ease.

"Reynard!" Jace shouted suddenly, realizing his red-haired friend had disappeared from sight. Panic seized his chest as he scanned the chaos for any sign of him.

"Focus, Jace!" Aydis snapped, parrying a blow aimed at his head. "We can't afford to lose you too!"

Shaking off his fear, Jace forced himself to concentrate, losing another volley of arrows into the fray. He couldn't think about Reynard now; he had a job to do, and he would not let his friends down.

"Keep pushing forward!" Forset roared, driving the last of the Cambions back into the darkness from which they had come. "We will not be defeated!"

And so, with gritted teeth and clenched fists, they fought on, united in purpose and determination against an enemy that threatened to consume them all.

The battle was over. The Cambions lay defeated, their dark forms crumpled upon the blood-soaked earth. With a final puff of smoke, they disappeared from sight. Warily, Jace surveyed the battlefield, his heart racing with the residual rush of battle.

"Reynard!" he called out, scanning the hazy aftermath for his red-haired companion. His voice echoed in the stillness of the clearing, a stark contrast to the cacophony of moments before.

"Over here!" Reynard replied, emerging from behind a fallen foe. Relief washed over Jace at the sight of him, unscathed and grinning triumphantly.

"By the gods, that was exhilarating! But we mustn't linger," he said, glancing at Forset, who leaned heavily on his sword, his powerful form visibly depleted from the strain of battle. Aydis and Ahat stood nearby, their breaths ragged but their spirits high.

"Agreed. Let's move forward," Forset rasped between labored breaths. "Malathar awaits."

As they continued their journey, Jace found himself walking beside Reynard, drawn to his warmth and humor despite the horrors they had just faced. They spoke of their homes, their families, and the worlds they knew, finding comfort in their shared humanity.

Jace's face was heavy with concern as he spoke. "I've been away for months now, and I can't help but wonder what my family back home must think."

"Time is fickle here in Nelhelm," Reynard explained gently. "In truth, it has only been a few months since you arrived. When you return, you may find that even less time has passed."

Jace sighed, a mixture of relief and disbelief. "It's difficult for me to fully grasp. It feels like I've lived a lifetime already."

"Strange as it may be," Reynard agreed, "it's a reminder that this world is full of wonders beyond our understanding."

As they trudged on, the landscape seemed to take on an ethereal beauty, the stark plains of Nelhelm stretching out before them like an ancient tapestry. The companionship between Jace and Reynard deepened with each step, their bond forged in both laughter and steel.

"Tell me, Jace," said Reynard, his voice tinged with curiosity, "what do the people of your world think of ours? Do they believe in the legends?"

"Many see them as mere stories," Jace replied thoughtfully, "but others, like my father, held fast to the belief in their truth. I suppose I stand somewhere in the middle now – unable to deny what I've seen but still struggling to comprehend it all."

"Ah, well," Reynard mused, "the best stories always hold a grain of truth, don't they?" He flashed a sly grin at Jace, who couldn't help but smile back.

"Indeed they do," Jace agreed, his heart swelling with gratitude for the friendship he had found in this strange and wondrous land.

Together, they walked on, their footsteps echoing across the vast expanse of Nelhelm's plains, each mile bringing them closer to the mysteries of Malathar that lay ahead.

The sun sank towards the horizon, casting long shadows that reached out like grasping fingers across the plains of Nelhelm. Jace stood atop a small rise, taking a moment to survey the land around him. He felt the cool breeze on his face and listened to the distant calls of unfamiliar birds. The world seemed so vast, and yet, it was but a mere fraction of the mysteries he had yet to uncover.

"Quite a view," Reynard remarked, joining him on the hilltop. His gaze followed Jace's, sweeping across the horizon with an appreciation born from years of traversing this world.

"Indeed," Jace replied, a sense of awe filling him. "But as beautiful as it is, I can't help but wonder what my purpose here truly is. And whether I'll be able to return to Emma."

"Ah, your betrothed," Reynard said thoughtfully. "It's only natural that you'd wish to return home. But we must believe that our fates are intertwined for a reason. Perhaps there is some greater purpose yet to be revealed."

"Perhaps," Jace murmured, his thoughts turning inward. As much as he longed for the familiar comforts of home, there was something about this world that resonated within him. A whisper of destiny, perhaps, or the echoes of a story yet untold.

The days passed, marked by the relentless march of the sun across the sky. Each night, they made camp beneath a blanket of stars that seemed to stretch into infinity, their shared laughter and camaraderie warming the chill air. Slowly, inexorably, Malathar drew nearer.

"Jace, do you ever think about what awaits us in Malathar?" Aydis asked one evening as they huddled around the fire, her eyes reflecting the dancing flames.

"Every day," Jace admitted, his grip tightening around the bow that had become a constant companion. "I can't help but hope that I'll find answers there. About my purpose, about how to get home."

"Malathar holds many secrets," Ahat added, his eyes narrowing as he stared into the fire. "But it is also a place of great power. I have no doubt that you will find what you seek."

"Thank you," Jace said, touched by their faith in him. But deep down, a small kernel of doubt remained, gnawing at him like a persistent itch.

As they traveled, Jace found himself growing more and more accustomed to the rhythms of Nelhelm. The landscape seemed to unfold before him with each passing day, revealing hidden depths and nuances that he might once have overlooked. And yet, despite the beauty that surrounded him, his thoughts kept drifting back to Emma – her smile, her laughter, the warmth of her embrace.

"Your heart is heavy," Reynard observed one evening, his keen eyes missing nothing. "It's not easy being so far from the ones you love."

"No, it isn't," Jace admitted, his voice barely audible above the sigh of the wind. "But I have to believe that there's a reason for all of this. That somehow, this journey will lead me back to her."

"Sometimes, the most difficult paths are the ones that lead us to where we truly belong," Reynard said softly. "Remember, Jace, you are not alone in this. We walk beside you, ready to face whatever challenges await us in Malathar."

"Thank you, Reynard," Jace said, clasping the older man's shoulder in gratitude. "I won't forget that."

And so, as the sun dipped low once more, casting its golden light across the plains of Nelhelm, Jace and his companions pressed on toward Malathar, their hearts filled with hope and determination.

The Mountains of the Stars rose majestically in the distance, their peaks covered in a golden hue that glowed in the sun. From afar, they appeared to be a mirage, an otherworldly landscape that beckoned the wanderer to come and discover its secrets. The sun cast a golden glow across the distant mountains, making them appear as if they were made of pure gold. The light danced and shimmered against their rocky peaks, creating a mesmerizing sight that Jace couldn't look away from.

"Beautiful, aren't they?" Aydis murmured, her voice soft with wonder. "In all my years, I've never grown tired of this view."

For a moment, the group fell silent, each lost in their thoughts as they drew closer to their destination. Jace could feel the weight of expectation settling heavily upon his shoulders, a burden that threatened to crush him beneath its inexorable force. But alongside the fear, there was something else – a flicker of hope, faint yet undeniable, that whispered to him of possibilities yet unexplored.

Malathar rested in the valley, nestled next to the towering Mountains of the Stars.

"Are you ready for this, young Gaian?" Ahat asked, clapping a strong hand on Jace's back and jolting him from his reverie. "Your training has come a long way, but now the real test begins."

Jace nodded, steeling himself for the challenges ahead. He knew that his journey was far from over and that the path before him would be fraught with danger and uncertainty.

"Let's go," he said quietly, his voice steady and resolute. "It's time to find the answers I've been searching for – and to fulfill my destiny as a Gaian."

With that, Jace and his companions pressed onward, their resolve unwavering as they crossed the threshold into the Valley of Malathar.

10

Malathar

Jace Alexander led his group down the rugged path. The anticipation building within him was almost palpable, like a fire that grew hotter with every step they took toward Malathar. The landscape unfolded before them—a tapestry of rolling hills and verdant fields speckled with the occasional grove of trees. Birds sang their twilight melodies, their voices joining the whispers of the wind through the grasses.

"Is it far now?" Jace asked, his steel-blue eyes scanning the horizon. "Patience, Jace," chided Aydis, a teasing smile playing on her lips. "You'll see it soon enough."

As if on cue, the grand city of Malathar revealed itself to them, nestled in the heart of the valley. From a distance, it seemed an ethereal vision, its walls shimmering like a mirage. But as they drew closer, the details sharpened, and Jace could scarcely believe his eyes.

Malathar's walls stood proud and tall, their surfaces gleaming with a deep, cerulean hue. Their imposing height and thickness spoke not only of the craftsmanship that had gone into their construction but also of the powerful magic that reinforced them. It was said that these walls had never fallen, and Jace could well believe it.

"By the gods," he breathed, captivated by the sight. "It's magnificent."

"Indeed," agreed Aydis, her own eyes alight with pride. "And just wait until you see what lies beyond."

The buildings within the city shared the same striking palette as the walls—shades of blue from the darkest midnight to the palest azure, punctuated by vivid splashes of crimson. This gave the city an air of regality, befitting its status as the last bastion against Belloch's dark forces in Nelhelm.

Through the city's gates, Jace could glimpse more fortifications—towers and battlements that seemed to defy gravity, soaring high above the streets and squares. He felt as if he were peering into another realm, one where the impossible was made real, and he knew that the adventure they had embarked upon was only just beginning.

As they entered the city, Jace was struck by the unique architectural feature of rectangular-shaped columns that adorned many of the buildings. These columns seemed to defy logic, their sharp edges and flat planes contrasting starkly with the traditional rounded pillars he had seen in other cities. Yet there was a strange beauty to them, an elegance that spoke of both strength and artistry.

"Look at those columns," Jace marveled, his gaze tracing the lines of one such structure. "I've never seen anything like them."

"Ah, yes," said Aydis, following his gaze. "It's a distinctive feature of Malathar architecture. It's said that the El themselves designed them, drawing inspiration from the geometry of crystals and gemstones."

Jace nodded, intrigued by the idea of a city built by beings who could manipulate the very fabric of reality. He felt a newfound respect for the El, as well as a growing curiosity about their enigmatic culture.

As they made their way deeper into the bustling streets of Malathar, Jace's attention was drawn to the warriors who patrolled the city. Tall and imposing, clad in gleaming armor that caught the sunlight, these soldiers were a formidable sight. Their eyes burned with fierce determination, and the weapons they carried—swords, spears, and bows—were as finely crafted as any he'd ever seen.

The warriors' armor glinted in the sunlight, reflecting the vibrant colors of the city around them. Their sharp features and intense gazes held a sense of otherworldly power, making them both fearsome and fascinating to behold.

"Those warriors," Jace murmured, unable to tear his gaze away from a group of them passing by. "They appear powerful, relentless... almost otherworldly."

Aydis nodded, her voice filled with admiration. "These warriors dedicate their entire lives to protecting Malathar from Belloch's forces. They are just as fierce and skilled as the legends describe, if not more so."

Jace could only nod, awestruck by the sight of such powerful beings dedicated to the city's defense. As he continued to take in the wonders of Malathar, his sense of wonder and excitement only grew, and he knew that he had much to learn from this ancient, mysterious place.

"Stay close," Aydis cautioned as they navigated the bustling streets, her voice a reminder of the challenges that lay ahead. "There is more to Malathar than meets the eye, and we must be prepared for anything."

With that sobering thought, Jace steeled himself for the journey ahead, knowing that the fate of the city and its people rested on their shoulders. And as they ventured deeper into the heart of the grand city of Malathar, he felt an unshakeable resolve take hold—a determination to protect this place at all costs, no matter what dangers awaited them.

"Wait, so these warriors are also El?" Jace asked, almost breathless, as he tried to keep up with Aydis through the throngs of people. The sounds of merchants hawking their wares filled the air, melding with the clatter of hooves and the murmur of countless conversations.

"Indeed," Aydis replied, her eyes scanning their surroundings with a keen alertness. "They are among the deadliest of our kind, possessing strength and skills far beyond that of ordinary El."

Jace felt a shiver course down his spine at her words, the gravity of the situation sinking in.

The city itself seemed to pulse with a vibrant energy, making Jace feel as though he were merely a speck within a vast, living tapestry. The streets were lined with buildings of varying heights, their walls adorned with intricate carvings that told stories of battles won and lost. Above them, the sky was a brilliant azure, providing a stunning backdrop to the interplay of reds and blues that characterized the architecture of Malathar.

"Extraordinary," Jace murmured, taking in the sights and sounds with wide-eyed wonder. The scent of exotic spices wafted through the air, mingling with the aroma of freshly baked bread and roasting meats from nearby food stalls.

"Malathar has always been a place of great beauty," Aydis said, her voice tinged with pride. "But do not let its splendor fool you. Beneath this veneer of tranquility lies a deadly struggle, one that we have waged since time immemorial."

As they continued their journey through the heart of Malathar, Jace couldn't help but feel a sense of awe at the sheer scale of the city and its breathtaking beauty. Yet beneath it all, he knew that danger lurked, ready to strike at any moment. As he walked alongside Aydis, the weight of their mission bore down upon him, a sobering reminder of the challenges that lay ahead.

The group ventured further into Malathar, the city's vibrant pulse quickening around them. They came upon a bustling marketplace, teeming with life and color. Traders called out their wares, hawking everything from shimmering silks to exotic fruits and spices that filled the air with heady scents.

"By the gods," Jace murmured, his eyes wide as he took in the scene before him. "I've never seen anything like this."

"Malathar is truly a wonder," Aydis agreed, a note of pride in her voice. "But there is still much to show you."

As they navigated through the market, Jace couldn't help but be drawn to an ornate fountain that dominated the square. Water cascaded from the mouths of intricately carved creatures, sparkling in the sunlight like liquid diamonds.

"Amazing," he mused aloud, reaching out to touch the cool, wet stone.

"Many believe that the waters of this fountain have healing properties," Aydis explained, watching Jace's fascination with interest. "Whether there is truth to that claim or not, it has become a symbol of hope for our people."

"Hope is something we all need right now," Jace acknowledged, his thoughts drifting momentarily to the loved ones he'd left behind.

"Indeed," Aydis said softly, her gaze lingering on the fountain a moment longer before she led them away.

Jace's attention was soon caught by a group of performers, their fluid movements set to the beat of a hypnotic drum. He watched in awe as they spun and leaped, their bodies twisting in ways that seemed almost unnatural.

"Is this a form of dance?" he asked, unable to tear his eyes away.

"More than just dance," Aydis replied. "It is an ancient martial art practiced by some El warriors. It helps to sharpen their senses and strengthen their connection to the divine."

"Remarkable," Jace breathed, filing away the information for later. "There's so much to learn here."

"Indeed," Aydis agreed, her eyes twinkling with amusement at his enthusiasm.

They continued their exploration, each new sight and sound further testament to the city's cultural richness. Jace couldn't help but be swept up in the atmosphere, his curiosity piqued by every little detail.

"Malathar is truly a marvel," he exclaimed, his excitement infectious as the group exchanged smiles.

"Wait until you see the Hall of Records," Aydis teased, her eyes sparkling with anticipation. "It houses centuries of knowledge, some predating even the founding of Malathar itself."

"Then there's no time to waste!" Jace declared, caught up in the moment.

As they made their way through the winding streets, laughter and friendly banter flowing easily between them, Jace felt a sense of camaraderie that he had not experienced since leaving home. It was a welcome respite from the heavy burden of their mission, and for a brief moment, he allowed himself to forget the darkness that lay ahead.

But as the sun dipped lower on the horizon, casting long shadows over the brilliant blue walls of the city, Jace knew that their time was running out. And as the group pressed on, the looming threat of Belloch's forces cast a shadow over the beauty of Malathar, reminding them all of the challenges yet to come.

As Jace and his companions ventured deeper into the heart of Malathar, they were met with a dizzying array of sights and sounds that seemed to assault the senses. The streets were a labyrinth of cobblestone paths flanked by towering buildings adorned with intricate mosaics and carvings depicting scenes from El history. The city's layout was like an artist's canvas, each stroke of genius meticulously placed to create a symphony of color and form.

"By the gods," Jace breathed, eyes wide as he took in the grandeur around him.

Reynard nodded in agreement, the fox-like smirk ever-present on his face. "Malathar is one of the jewels in the crown of El civilization," he remarked confidently.

The group passed through bustling market squares where vendors hawked their wares, the air filled with the enticing scents of exotic spices and sweet confections. Jace could hear the cacophony of voices, each vendor vying for attention.

"Care for some miraj fruit?" Aydis offered, holding out a strange purple fruit towards Jace. He hesitated for a moment before taking a bite, the taste of an explosion of tangy sweetness that left him wanting more.

"Delicious!" Jace exclaimed, devouring the rest of the fruit eagerly, juice running down his chin. His friends chuckled at his enthusiasm, and he couldn't help but join in their laughter.

"Come," Forset beckoned, guiding them along a narrow alleyway that opened up onto a vast courtyard dominated by an enormous fountain, its waters cascading down tiers of intricately carved stone. As they drew closer, Jace could make out the figures of mythical creatures and El heroes adorning the fountain, each seeming to come alive under the shimmering water.

"Behold the Fountain of Legends," Aydis announced, her voice a mixture of pride and reverence. "A tribute to our ancestors and our enduring legacy."

"Truly magnificent," Jace murmured, awestruck by the sheer scale and artistry that had gone into the creation of such a monument.

As they continued their journey through Malathar, Jace found himself falling deeper under the city's spell, his senses overwhelmed by the sights, sounds, and smells that surrounded him. He could hear the rhythmic pounding of metal on metal as blacksmiths forged weapons in the glow of their forges while the scent of roasting meats mingled with the earthy aroma of freshly baked bread.

"Are all El cities like this?" Jace asked Aydis as they walked side by side.

"Each city has its own unique charm," she replied, her eyes reflecting the wonder that filled his own. "But Malathar... there's something truly special about this place."

"Indeed," Jace agreed, his heart swelling with a newfound appreciation for the rich tapestry of life that thrived within these ancient walls.

Yet amidst the beauty and vibrancy of Mahathir, he couldn't quite shake the nagging feeling that danger lurked just beyond the horizon, waiting to shatter the city's tranquil façade. But for now, he would revel in the magic of this extraordinary place, allowing the sensory feast to envelop him like a lover's embrace.

Jace felt as if he were walking through the pages of an ancient, illuminated manuscript, with each step forward revealing a new wonder. The exotic plants that lined the streets seemed to sing beneath the touch of the sun's warm rays, their vibrant colors casting kaleidoscopic patterns onto the cobblestone paths.

"Look at this," Jace said in awe, pointing towards a towering statue of an El warrior, its intricate details so lifelike that he half-expected it to come alive any moment. "The craftsmanship is incredible."

Aydis nodded, her eyes shining with pride. "Our people have always been skilled artisans. But there's more to Malathar than just beauty and art. We've managed to survive countless threats over the centuries, including Belloch's forces."

"Really?" Jace asked, his curiosity piqued. "But how have you managed to defend yourselves against such a powerful enemy?"

"Malathar has never fallen for a reason," Aydis said, her voice taking on a solemn note. "Our warriors are some of the fiercest in the realm. But we also have something else—something that no other city can claim."

"And what's that?" Jace inquired, his interest growing by the second.

"Unity," Aydis replied, her gaze sweeping across the bustling marketplace where El of all ages and backgrounds mingled together in harmony. "We stand together, not just as families or clans, but as a people united in purpose. That's what gives us strength."

Jace couldn't help but admire the conviction with which she spoke, and he found himself wishing that his own world could learn from the lessons of Malathar. Perhaps if they could find a way to put aside their differences and work together, they too might stand a chance against the encroaching darkness.

As they continued their exploration of Malathar, Jace found himself captivated by every aspect of the city—its people, its history, and its enduring spirit. And though he knew that the road ahead would be fraught with danger and uncertainty, he couldn't help but feel a sense of hope stirring in his heart, fueled by the knowledge that such a place could exist in this world.

As they made their way through the winding streets, Jace noticed a group of El warriors gathered around a large map, their faces etched with concern. The tension in the air was palpable, hinting at the challenges that lay ahead for him and his companions. He could feel a growing unease within himself as if he were being watched by unseen eyes.

Aydis led Jace through the streets of Malathar, her steps quick and purposeful. As they weaved through the bustling marketplace, Jace couldn't help but notice the growing tension in the air. Everywhere he looked, there were pockets of El warriors deep in discussion or training; all focused on one thing: preparing for an inevitable attack.

Jace thought back to his own world and how wars were often waged over greed and power. He couldn't imagine what it must be like for the people of Malathar to constantly live under the threat of invasion.

Jace sensed the weight of the situation pressing down on her, and he couldn't shake the nagging suspicion that there was more to it than anyone realized. Aydis seemed to be hiding something, and Jace couldn't ignore the looming danger they were facing. As they strolled through Malathar, he tried to focus on its breathtaking beauty, a temporary distraction from the ominous cloud hanging over the city.

"Tell me more about your customs," Jace suggested, his curiosity piqued by the unique aspects of El culture he had observed thus far.

"Very well," Aydis replied, seemingly grateful for the distraction. "One of our most sacred rituals involves the bonding of magic between individuals. It's a deeply personal and meaningful connection that strengthens both parties."

"Could such a bond be formed between an El and a human?" Jace wondered, his heart racing at the thought.

"Perhaps," Aydis mused, her eyes meeting his with an intensity that sent shivers down his spine. "But it would require a level of trust and understanding beyond anything you've ever known."

Jace couldn't shake the thought of what it would be like to bond with another, his mind reeling at the possibilities. He had always felt like an outsider in his own world, never quite fitting in with others. But here, in Malathar, he felt a sense of belonging and acceptance that he had never experienced before.

Jace leaned against the moss-covered wall of the ancient library, his eyes fixed on Aydis as she offered her response. A flicker of hope ignited within him, and he found himself captivated by the possibilities that lay before him.

As they were about to continue their discussion, a messenger appeared and handed Aydis a note. After reading it, Aydis said, "Jace, you must ready yourself. You have been summoned to the palace to meet with Mitra."

11

Mitra

As Jace approached the entrance to Malathar's palace, his eyes widened in awe at the grandeur of the building before him. The palace was a masterpiece of otherworldly architecture, with spiraling towers that seemed to defy gravity as they reached towards the heavens. The walls and structures of the palace were adorned in various hues of red, from the deepest crimson to the faintest blush, giving the palace an almost ethereal quality.

Intricate carvings of mythical creatures and ancient symbols decorated the façade, each one telling a story of its own. "By Gaia," Jace muttered under his breath, his steel blue eyes scanning the surroundings with curiosity. His heart raced with anticipation as he took in the sights and sounds of this new world. He had never seen anything quite like it back home in his small town, where the only buildings that came close to rivaling this were the modest church and the town hall.

"Welcome to Malathar, Jace Alexander," called out a deep, melodic voice. Jace looked up to see a tall, regal-looking woman with flowing silver hair standing on the palace steps. She was dressed in shimmering robes that reflected the colors of the setting sun.

Though her appearance was striking, Jace couldn't help but notice the air of authority that surrounded her, as if she commanded the very essence of the palace itself.

"Thank you, my lady," Jace replied, bowing his head slightly in respect.

As he did so, he caught sight of a stern-faced man standing at attention beside her. The man's posture suggested military discipline.

"Please, come inside," the lady beckoned as she turned and led the way into the palace.

The doors swung open, revealing a bustling interior filled with beings of all shapes and sizes going about their duties. Jace marveled at the variety of El warriors, each with unique abilities and appearances.

As he followed his hosts through the grand hall, Jace couldn't help but feel a sense of wonderment. He thought back to his days spent in the woods with his father studying ancient texts, never imagining that one day, he would find himself in the center of a world unlike anything he had ever experienced.

"I am Anna," the woman began. "News of your arrival has already reached every corner of Malathar, Jace Alexander."

"Is that so?" Jace replied.

"Yes, word travels fast in Malathar," Anna said with a smile. "And it has been a long time since we received visitors from the human realm."

Jace couldn't help but feel a twinge of unease at the thought of being an outsider in this new world. Would he be accepted by its people? Would he be able to adapt to their customs and ways?

The echoes of footsteps resonated throughout the palace's vast chambers as Jace was guided further by his hosts. The walls were adorned with intricate carvings and tapestries that seemed to shimmer with life, retelling stories of an ancient world. He felt a shiver of awe coursing through him as if he had stepped into a realm where time itself stood still.

"Your arrival at Malathar is most timely, Jace Alexander," said a deep, commanding voice. It reverberated through the hallway, causing Jace's heart to quicken in anticipation.

As they entered a large chamber, Jace laid eyes upon Mitra for the first time. A majestic figure, she appeared both fierce and regal, her dark hair cascading over her shoulders like a waterfall of night. Her penetrating gaze held a hint of agelessness as though she had seen the rise and fall of countless empires.

"Welcome, Jace Alexander," Mitra greeted him, her voice resonating with power. "I am Mitra, leader of Malathar. I have been expecting you."

"Thank you, my lady," Jace replied, his voice wavering slightly under the weight of her presence. He couldn't help but feel humbled standing before her, sensing the great wisdom and authority that surrounded her like a palpable force.

"Please, tell me about your journey," Mitra said, gesturing for Jace to sit down on a nearby cushioned seat.

He hesitated for a moment, taking in the grandeur that filled every corner of the chamber, before finally obeying her command.

Jace recounted his tale, describing how he found himself transported from his familiar world into one of myth and legend. As he spoke, he noticed Mitra listening intently, her eyes never leaving him. She seemed to absorb each word, weighing them carefully before responding.

"Your presence here is no coincidence, Jace," Mitra said, her voice containing a hint of gravity. "I have sensed a disturbance in the balance of our world. Your arrival may well be the key to restoring the harmony that has been lost."

Jace pondered her words, his thoughts racing with questions and uncertainties. How could he, an ordinary man from a small town, possibly play a role in saving this fantastical realm? In the presence of such power and grandeur, he felt insignificant – like a single drop of water in the midst of a vast ocean.

Yet as he looked into Mitra's eyes, he saw within them a glimmer of hope - a belief that he held the potential to change the course of destiny. And in that moment, he found himself filled with a newfound sense of purpose, fueled by a desire to protect both his own world and this one from the darkness that threatened to consume them all.

As Jace stood before Mitra, he couldn't help but steal glances at the imposing figure that stood beside her. Mitra's second-in-command was like a statue carved from black marble, his broad frame adorned with armor that appeared to be made of the same material as the palace walls. His black eyes were cold and unyielding, boring into Jace with an intensity that sent shivers down his spine.

"Jace," Mitra began, her voice soft yet powerful. "Allow me to introduce you to my trusted advisor, Kane."

"An honor," Jace murmured, extending his hand. Kane stared at it for a moment as if contemplating whether or not to accept the gesture before finally giving in and shaking it firmly. Jace could feel the strength in Kane's grip, and he knew that this man was not one to be trifled with.

"Kane," Mitra continued. "Has been by my side in the fight against the Cambions since the beginning. He is a skilled strategist and warrior, but his true value lies in his loyalty and devotion to our cause."

"Your presence here intrigues me, Jace Alexander," Kane said, his voice a low rumble. "I hope that you will prove yourself a worthy ally in the battles to come."

"Speaking of allies," Mitra chimed in, her gaze shifting towards the entrance of the great hall.

A tall young woman entered, her athletic form wrapped in light armor. Her long blonde hair cascaded down her back, framing steel blue eyes that seemed to match Jace's own.

"Jace, I would like you to meet Raina," Mitra said, gesturing towards the newcomer. "She is another Gaian who found herself in Nelhelm, much like yourself."

Raina nodded curtly, her eyes never leaving Jace's as they sized one another up. There was a shared understanding in that brief moment, a recognition of the strange circumstances that had brought them both to this place. Intrigue mingled with caution, and Jace wondered what experiences Raina had faced since her arrival.

"Raina," Mitra continued. "Has proven herself a valuable member of our forces, using her unique talents to help us gain an advantage over our enemies."

"Nice to meet you," Jace said, still holding Raina's gaze.

He could feel an undercurrent of tension between them, but there was also a spark of curiosity - a desire to learn more about each other and their shared connection to their home world.

"Likewise," Raina replied, her voice carrying the same guarded tone that permeated their interaction.

She was a stranger to him, and yet, she represented a link to earth and to everything he had left behind.

As Jace turned his attention back to Mitra and Kane, he knew that even amidst the grandeur and strangeness of this new world, he would not be alone in facing the challenges that lay ahead. With the wisdom of Mitra guiding them, perhaps they could find a way to restore balance to both Nelhelm and Gaia - and protect those they loved from the encroaching darkness.

The sun dipped low in the sky, casting a golden glow over the courtyard where Jace and Raina found themselves. They stood side by side, watching the intricate dance of shadows play across the red stone walls and ancient statues that lined the periphery. In this quiet moment, the tension that had surrounded their initial meeting slowly ebbed away, replaced by a growing sense of camaraderie.

"I hear your archery skills are impressive," Raina said, breaking the companionable silence. Her voice was soft but carried a note of genuine admiration. "I've been practicing since I was a child, but from what I hear, you seem to have a natural talent for it."

Jace glanced at her, surprised by the compliment.

"Thank you," he replied, his cheeks warming with a hint of pride. "My father taught me everything he knew about hunting and survival. It's been a big part of my life back on Earth."

"Same here," Raina said, smiling as she brushed a strand of blonde hair from her forehead. The last rays of sunlight illuminated her features, highlighting the gracefulness of her athletic build and the intensity of her steel blue eyes - eyes that seemed to mirror Jace's own. "I grew up in the wilderness, learning how to track, hunt, and live off the land."

As they continued to share stories of their past, Jace couldn't help but feel a sense of comfort and familiarity in this strange world. Despite their differences, he and Raina shared common ground - a connection rooted in their love for nature, their resourcefulness, and their determination to persevere against all odds.

"Have you ever encountered anything like the Cambions before?" Jace asked, curious about Raina's experiences since her arrival in Nelhelm.

"Nothing quite like them," Raina admitted, her gaze darkening as she recalled the monstrous creatures. "But I've faced my share of dangers back on Earth - wolves, bears, even mountain lions. You learn to adapt and develop new strategies to survive."

"Exactly," Jace agreed, feeling a surge of kinship with the woman beside him. They were both Gaians - warriors forged by the trials of their homeland and brought together by fate in this fantastical realm.

As dusk swallowed up the last rays of the sun, they remained standing side by side. Their mutual understanding was unspoken – life's hurdles would be tackled individually; human resilience resonated strongly within each of them.

As they left the confines of the courtyard and stepped into the grand corridor, Jace was once again struck by the sheer scale and vibrancy of Malathar's palace. The walls seemed to breathe with life as the crimson hues danced and reflected the light from the torches lining the hall. It was a stark contrast to the muted colors of their surroundings, but it only served to heighten the sense of wonder that had taken root in Jace's heart.

The palace was a bustling hive of activity, with El warriors rushing past, their armor glinting, and their boots echoing against the stone floor. Servants scurried about, carrying trays laden with food or various tools, each one intent on their task at hand. Amidst the throng, Jace couldn't help but feel both overwhelmed and invigorated - this place was alive like no other he had ever seen before.

"Quite a sight, isn't it?" Raina said, her eyes sparkling as she took in the spectacle around them. "It took me some time to get used to all this."

"Indeed," Jace admitted, his thoughts swirling with images of his own world, of Emma waiting for him back home.

"Jace, there is something I must ask you," Mitra's voice rang out, drawing his attention away from the bustling scene before him. She stood with Kane at her side, both radiating authority and power.

"Of course, my lady," Jace replied, trying to maintain his composure despite the sudden weight of their gazes upon him.

"Tell me," Mitra began, her voice steady and deliberate. "How did you come to Nelhelm?"

They walked together through the majestic corridors of the palace, with Kane and Raina following behind.

Jace hesitated for a moment, memories of his arrival in this strange land flooding his mind. He remembered Emma, their love, and the promise of a life together. The pain of their separation still clawed at his heart, but he knew he had to push forward.

"I was brought here against my will," Jace confessed, his voice tinged with a simmering portal that took me from my home and left me stranded in Nelhelm.

"Is there any indication as to why you were chosen?" Kane's deep voice rumbled, his black eyes scrutinizing Jace closely.

Jace couldn't stop thinking about the word "chosen" as it hung in the air. He had always believed that he ended up here by pure coincidence.

"None that I know of," Jace replied, feeling a sense of vulnerability beneath Kane's unwavering gaze. "I come from a simple life - hunting and spending time with my family and Emma, my fiancée. I am no one special."

"Yet here you are," Mitra said softly, her eyes shining with wisdom. "In a world foreign to your own, standing among us with strength and conviction."

"Perhaps it's because of your connection with Raina," Kane suggested, casting a sidelong glance at the young woman beside him.

Jace considered it, his mind still lingering on their previous conversation.

"Maybe," he finally said. "But regardless of the reason, I can't give up on my mission to return home and make things right."

Mira nodded in understanding, her posture exuding grace and approval.

"Understood," she stated, "Jace Alexander of Gaia, we stand with you. Together, we will face whatever challenges await us."

As Mitra guided them back to her throne room, Jace couldn't help but admire its grandeur. The walls were adorned with beautiful tapestries, illuminated by flickering torches. At the end of the room sat a massive throne on a raised platform adorned with velvet cushions and intricate gold and jewel designs. Mitra took her place on the throne.

Mitra's gaze swept across the room, pausing for a moment on Jace. She leaned forward on her throne, the golden fabric of her gown cascading around her.

"Jace, I sense that you are troubled," she began, her voice resonating with authority and wisdom. "I believe it is time for you to fully understand the gravity of the situation we face."

"Indeed," Kane interjected, his piercing eyes taking in the scene before him as El warriors moved about the palace with purposeful strides. "The war with the Cambions has raged for millennia, but Belloch's ultimate goal has always remained the same: power."

"Power?" Jace asked, his steel blue eyes narrowing in concentration as he sought understanding. His heart pounded in his chest, and an inexplicable urge to protect both Gaia and Nelhelm took hold of him.

"Absolute dominion over all realms," Mitra elucidated, her voice like the calm at the center of a storm. "Belloch craves the obliteration of our world, the subjugation of yours, and the creation of a new order where he reigns supreme."

"His corruption spreads like a blight, seeping into every corner of our worlds," Kane added, his grip tightening on the hilt of his sword, betraying a rare flicker of emotion.

"Is there no way to stop him?" Jace inquired, his mind racing with thoughts of Emma, his family, and the people of Earth, who had no knowledge of the imminent threat they faced.

"Defeating Belloch will not be easy," Mitra admitted, her eyes betraying a hint of sorrow. "But it is not impossible. We have fought many battles against his forces, and though the cost has been great, we remain resolute."

"Then we must find a way to stop him," Jace declared, feeling the weight of responsibility settle upon his shoulders. "I will do whatever it takes."

"Your determination is admirable," Mitra acknowledged, her voice softening. "But you must understand that this journey will test you in ways you cannot yet fathom."

"Let it test me," Jace replied fiercely, clenching his fists at his sides. "I refuse to stand idly by while those I care are in danger."

"Very well," Mitra acquiesced, a knowing smile gracing her lips. "We shall aid you in your quest, Jace Alexander of Gaia, but be prepared for the trials that lie ahead."

"Thank you," Jace said with a bow, his mind already racing with plans and strategies.

Regardless of the trials he would face, he knew one thing for certain: he would not falter in his mission to save both worlds from the darkness that threatened to consume them.

As the sun dipped below the horizon, casting an ethereal blend of crimson and gold across the sky, Jace found himself standing beside Raina on one of Malathar's palace balconies. They leaned against the intricately carved railing, their eyes taking in the breathtaking view of Nelhelm's landscape stretching out before them.

"Hard to believe this is real, isn't it?" Raina mused softly, her steel blue eyes reflecting the last rays of sunlight. "I mean, one moment, we're living our lives on Gaia, and the next, we're here, in a world only imagined in stories."

Jace nodded, his thoughts echoing Raina's sentiments, "It's all so surreal. But at least we have each other to navigate through it all."

"True," Raina agreed with a smile, tucking a strand of blonde hair behind her ear. "Having someone who understands what it's like to suddenly be thrust into this strange world – it helps, you know?"

"Definitely," Jace murmured, finding solace in the knowledge that he was not alone in this bewildering journey.

"Look!" Raina pointed excitedly towards a flock of creatures soaring gracefully through the twilight. Their iridescent wings shimmered as they danced in the air, weaving intricate patterns above the palace grounds.

"Amazing," Jace breathed, marveling at the sight. He turned to look at Raina, their gazes locking for a moment before they both broke into grins.

"Feels like a dream, doesn't it?" Raina asked, her voice barely more than a whisper.

"An incredibly vivid one," Jace replied, his mind still reeling from the magnitude of their shared situation. "But I'm determined to make the most of it while we're here. Belloch won't stand a chance."

Raina chuckled, her laughter tinged with a hint of nervousness, "I have to admit, I'm scared. But knowing that you're here, fighting alongside me – it gives me hope."

"Same here," Jace admitted, his steel blue eyes meeting Raina's gaze once more, their shared fears and determination intertwining like the very vines that adorned the palace walls.

As they stood there on the balcony overlooking a world so vastly different from their own, Jace and Raina found comfort in each other's presence. They had been brought together by fate, bound by a common goal and shared experiences, and in that moment, they knew they were not alone.

Together, they would face whatever challenges Nelhelm threw their way, united by a bond forged in adversity and strengthened by the camaraderie between them. And as the last embers of daylight flickered across the horizon, the two Gaians steeled themselves for the trials that lay ahead – determined to protect both their worlds from the darkness that threatened to consume them.

12

Questions

The sun was rising, casting long shadows across the courtyard as Jace and Raina were escorted separately through the towering gates of the palace in Malathar. They could sense the tension in the air, the whispered rumors that Mitra had received orders from none other than Mount Myra itself. These orders demanded answers from the two Gaians in their custody.

The palace loomed above them, its spires and turrets reaching for the heavens like a symphony of stone and magic. Its walls were adorned with intricate carvings depicting ancient battles and mythical creatures. The grandeur and regality of the palace were unmistakable, an opulent testament to the might and majesty of those who ruled within.

As they stepped into the main hall, Jace couldn't help but marvel at the sheer scale of it all. He had never seen anything so grand, not even in his wildest dreams. The ceiling soared high overhead, supported by massive columns of polished marble. Tapestries hung from the walls, vibrant and alive with depictions of heroes and legends. The floor beneath their feet was made of countless intricately laid tiles, each one a masterpiece in its own right. A feeling of awe and reverence settled over him as he took in his surroundings.

Raina, on the other hand, remained cautious, her steel blue eyes darting around the room, taking in every detail. She was acutely aware of the power that resided within these walls, and she knew that it could be wielded as easily for ill as for good. There was no telling what lay ahead for her and Jace, and the uncertainty gnawed at her.

Mitra stood regally in the center of the hall, her posture straight and confident. Her long, dark hair was intricately braided and adorned with jewels, cascading down her back like a waterfall. She wore a gown of shimmering gold with intricate details that seemed to catch the light from every angle. Her sharp features and piercing gaze exuded power and grace. Standing next to her was Kane, whose formidable stature loomed over them both like a dark cloud.

"Step forward," Mitra commanded, and Jace complied, feeling the weight of countless eyes upon him as he did so.

In the meantime, Raina was escorted to a different chamber by Kane for questioning. She could sense the chill in the air and couldn't help but shiver. The room was cloaked in darkness, intensifying the already tense ambiance with a sense of foreboding.

"Raina," Kane said, his voice barely more than a whisper. "We have much to discuss."

She nodded, steeling herself for the questions that were to come. She wouldn't give anything away, not without knowing Kane's true intentions. The game was afoot, and the stakes were higher than ever before.

"Tell me again how you came to be here," Mitra's voice cut through the air like a blade, her eyes fixed on Jace with an intensity that made him feel as though she could see straight through him. The grandeur of the palace seemed to press down upon him, the weight of its history and power bearing down on his shoulders.

Jace stammered, trying to stay calm as he explained, "I found myself in Nelhelm. I have no idea how I got there. I'm actually from Gaia--or as we call it, Earth."

Despite his unease, Jace also felt a strong urge to uncover the truth behind Mitra's change in behavior towards him.

"Gaia. Yes," Mitra raised an eyebrow as if the name itself were unfamiliar. "Can you describe your life in Gaia and how you ended up in Nelhelm?"

Jace hesitated, unsure of how much he should reveal. He knew nothing of Mitra's intentions, but at the same time, he needed her help if he had any hope of getting back home. He decided to take a chance.

"Glenwood is my home. I don't know why I was brought to Nelhelm or even how I crossed over into this realm," Jace explained, trying to keep his voice steady. "I was hiking in the woods near my hometown when I was attacked. I ran to get away and then I saw a symbol floating in front of me. It was like pitchforks in a circle. Everything went dark when I came to; I was in Nelhelm."

"Where did you wake up in Nelhelm?" Mitra asked, her voice filled with intensity.

"I woke up in a castle on the far side of Nelhelm," Jace replied. "Reynard said it was an old garrison fort that the El occasionally use."

"So your portal led you to Zeven castle, then?" Mitra clarified.

"No, actually," Jace corrected.

He went on to explain how he had seen the plains of Nelhelm before passing out and how Reynard had found him and brought him to the castle for shelter.

"Interesting," Mitra mused, her gaze never wavering from Jace's face. "And what were you doing before you found yourself in our world? What is your purpose in Gaia?"

"I'm just a regular guy," Jace said, frustration seeping into his words. "I have a fiancée, Emma, and I work as a mechanic. My life is simple. I don't know why any of this is happening to me."

Mitra offered, cloaked in cryptic words.

"Maybe you were meant to be here," she said. "Or maybe not. Only time will reveal."

"Or maybe there's some way to undo whatever brought me here in the first place," Jace replied stubbornly. "I need to find a way back home. My family, my friends... they're all waiting on me."

"Very well," Mitra said after a moment, her expression softening ever so slightly. "We will do what we can to assist you in your quest. But first, we must uncover the truth behind your presence in Nelhelm."

Jace nodded, grateful for Mitra's willingness to help but still wary of the secrets that lay hidden within the palace walls. He knew that his journey was far from over and that each step he took would bring him closer to the heart of the mystery that had torn him from his world and thrust him into the unknown. Jace was still reeling from Mitra's sudden change in attitude, but he chose to set that aside for now as there were more pressing matters at hand.

As the guards escorted Raina into the chamber, she gave Jace a brief nod before taking her place before Mitra and Kane. Her posture was rigid, her eyes darting around the room as if searching for any sign of danger.

"Raina," Kane began, his deep voice echoing throughout the chamber. "You have been in Nelhelm longer than Jace. Tell us what you know about this place and its inhabitants."

Raina paused, considering her words carefully, "Nelhelm is a harsh and unforgiving terrain controlled by Mitra and her armies. The El and Cambions who live there are locked in an eternal battle." She glanced at Mitra, who showed no emotion. "I don't know much else beyond that. My main concern has been staying alive and finding a way back to Gaia."

The sound of Jace's own heartbeat filled his ears, drowning out the low murmurs of others in the room from Raina's unexpected answer.

"Have you encountered the Cambion's?" Kane asked, his gaze sharp and probing.

Raina hesitated before responding, "I haven't encountered them directly, but I've heard rumors of their plans to conquer Nelhelm."

"Indeed," Kane said, his eyes narrowing as he assessed her response. "It seems we have much to learn from one another if we are to uncover the truth behind your presence here."

The air in the chamber hung heavy with tension, as if the very walls were holding their breath. Raina studied Kane's face, trying to read his expression as he continued to scrutinize her. His black eyes were like bottomless pits, depths that seemed impossible to plumb. She did not trust this man or his intentions, and she knew she must tread carefully.

"Tell me," Kane said, his voice a low rumble that sent shivers down Raina's spine. "Why do you think you were brought here to Nelhelm? What purpose could your presence serve?"

Raina paused, her mind racing as she considered her response. She had learned long ago that revealing too much could be dangerous, especially when dealing with those who held power over her.

"I cannot say for certain," she replied slowly, her steel blue eyes never leaving his obsidian gaze. "Perhaps it was fate, or perhaps there is some unknown reason that only time will reveal."

"Interesting," Kane murmured, stroking his chin thoughtfully. "You speak as though you believe there is some grand design at play here."

He paced slowly around the room, his footsteps echoing ominously off the high ceiling and ornate walls of the chamber. The grandeur of the palace, with its gold leaf and intricate carvings, served as a stark reminder of the power Mitra wielded – and, by extension, her second-in-command.

"Isn't there always some grand design when it comes to matters such as these?" Raina countered, careful to keep her tone neutral. She dared not give him any reason to suspect her true feelings about the situation they found themselves in. "In any case, I have no way of knowing what brought me here or why."

Kane stopped in his tracks, turning to face her once more.

"Your skepticism is noted, Raina," he said, the corners of his mouth lifting ever so slightly in a cold smile. "But I wonder if perhaps there is more to your story than you are letting on."

Raina swallowed hard, her heart pounding in her chest. She knew she had to maintain her composure, and yet it felt as though the very air in the room was pressing down upon her, threatening to suffocate her.

"If there is," she said quietly. "I am not aware of it."

"Very well," Kane replied, his voice betraying a hint of frustration. "We shall see if time reveals the truth of your words or if there are deeper secrets hidden within you."

He turned away from her, striding towards the door of the chamber.

As he departed, Raina allowed herself a moment to breathe. The interrogation had been exhausting, both mentally and physically, but she had managed to navigate it without giving too much away. And that, she knew, might just be the key to her survival.

"Tell me," Mitra began, her voice echoing through the opulent chamber like a peal of thunder. "Do you two know of the Emmon Fields?"

Jace hesitated, his mind racing to recall anything that might be relevant. The walls of the room seemed to close in on him, their intricately carved murals depicting scenes both beautiful and terrible. He studied Mitra's eyes as if they held the answers he sought.

"I... I've heard of them, yes," he replied cautiously.

"Then allow me to enlighten you further," she paused, letting the weight of her words hang heavy in the air. "The El's are divided into three factions: the Sha of Nelhelm, the Raka of Takama, and the Drakyns of Etna."

"The three realms are separated by three mountain ranges," Mitra continued. "The Mountains of the Stars, which you have seen here. The Mountains of the Sun and the Mountains of the Moon."

Jace's brow furrowed as he considered this information. It was clear that this information was integral to the workings of this place, and yet he could not shake the feeling that there was more to be revealed.

"And what makes Mount Myra so important?" he asked, unable to keep the curiosity from his voice.

"Mount Myra is the central point of the plains, the pinnacle from which all El power flows," Mitra explained, her eyes glinting with a mixture of reverence and determination. "It lies in the middle of all the plains."

"However, Mount Myra is not only a source of power but also the key to our survival in the ongoing war against Belloch," she said, her voice tinged with bitterness. "He seeks to corrupt all that is pure and good on Gaia by desecrating the mountain's sanctity. The factions of the El's must protect Mount Myra from his grasp, lest he bring about the end of us all."

The gravity of Mitra's words struck Jace like a hammer blow, and he found himself reeling from the implications. The world he had known was now far beyond his reach, replaced by a realm fraught with danger and intrigue. And at the heart of it all lay a single, immutable truth - this war would determine the fate of not just Nelhelm but Gaia itself.

Jace's heart raced as Mitra's words echoed in the chamber. A new fire burned inside him, one he had never felt before. He refused to be a mere pawn in this cosmic game, standing by helplessly. Whatever lay ahead, he would face it with unwavering resolve and determination. He glanced at Raina, hoping to see the same fierce determination reflected in her eyes.

Raina remained composed, taking everything in with a serious expression.

"Thank you for sharing this knowledge with me, Mitra," he said, clenching his fists in resolve. "I will do whatever it takes to protect both Nelhelm and my home, Gaia. I know not what role I am meant to play in this struggle, but I will face it head-on, no matter the cost."

Mitra regarded him with a mixture of admiration and caution as if gauging the depth of his conviction.

"Very well, Jace," she replied, her voice heavy with the burden of responsibility. "Be prepared for the challenges that lie ahead, for they will test you in ways you never imagined possible."

Mitra's eyes flickered with a mixture of fear and determination as she began to unravel the darkest aspects of their enemy.

"Belloch's ultimate goal is far more sinister than we could ever have imagined," she said, her voice barely above a whisper. "He seeks not only to rule Nelhelm but also to corrupt Gaia - your beloved Earth."

Jace felt his heart clench at the thought of his home being threatened by this malevolent force.

He looked into Mitra's eyes, searching for answers, "How does he plan to do that?"

"Through the creation of the Cambions," she replied, gritting her teeth. "Belloch has discovered a way to twist and corrupt human souls, transforming them into the monstrous beings who serve him unquestioningly."

As Mitra spoke, Jace envisioned his family, his friends, and all the people of Gaia, their souls ripped apart and reassembled in grotesque forms. A cold sweat prickled across his skin, and he clenched his fists, struggling to control the rising anger within.

"Every time a Cambion emerges victorious on the battlefield, another soul is lost to Belloch's corruption," Mitra continued, her voice trembling with the weight of her words. "And with each corrupted soul adding to Belloch's Army when they die."

Jace's mind raced with thoughts of resistance as he exclaimed in shock, "We must stop them! This cannot continue!"

"Indeed, we must," Mitra agreed, placing a hand on Jace's shoulder. "But it will require all our strength, cunning, and courage. For Belloch is no ordinary foe; he is a master manipulator, a wielder of shadows, and a destroyer of worlds."

At that moment, Jace understood the gravity of the situation. He felt the weight of responsibility on his shoulders, and a determination surged through him like lightning. His thoughts turned inward as he contemplated the enormity of the task that lay before them.

"Is there no hope for those who have been corrupted?" he asked quietly, unable to shake the image of lost souls from his mind.

"Before they die? Only if we defeat Belloch," Mitra replied, her gaze solemn. "For as long as he reigns, their souls will remain shackled in darkness."

"Then we cannot fail," Jace declared, steeling himself for the battle to come. "I will fight alongside you, Mitra. I will do everything in my power to protect Nelhelm and Gaia from this unspeakable evil."

Mitra's eyes sparkled with a newfound sense of hope as she praised Jace's bravery. "You are truly courageous," she exclaimed. "Together, we will fight against the forces of darkness and reclaim the light that has been taken from us."

The room seemed to shrink around Jace and Raina as the weight of Mitra's revelations settled upon them. Raina glanced at Jace, her steel-blue eyes searching his for any sign of doubt or fear. He met her gaze, his own eyes resolute, and briefly squeezed her hand as if to say, "We will face this together."

"Very well," Mitra nodded. "But let us not forget that Belloch and his Cambions are cunning adversaries."

"Then we must be one step ahead of them," Jace said, a fire burning within him. "We cannot afford to falter, not when so much is at stake."

"Agreed," Raina added, her eyes flashing with determination. "I will do everything in my power to help you, Jace. Together, we can make a difference."

"Your resolve is inspiring," Mitra said, looking between the two Gaians. "May it guide you through the darkest of days and the most treacherous of battles."

As the trio stood there, a fleeting moment of unity and purpose washed over them. But even as it did, they could not shake the sense of dread that lingered in the air. For they knew that the path ahead would be fraught with danger and uncertainty, their fates intertwined with those of countless others who would rise or fall in this epic struggle between light and darkness.

"Let us begin," Jace said quietly, his voice barely more than a whisper. "For every moment we delay, another soul is lost to corruption."

"Indeed," Mitra agreed, her eyes filled with a steely determination. "Let us wage war against the shadows and reclaim our world from the clutches of evil."

As they stepped into the dimly lit corridor, leaving behind the chamber where the weight of their destiny had been revealed, the door clicked shut with an ominous finality. A chill ran down Jace's spine, and he couldn't help but wonder if this was the beginning of the end or merely the end of the beginning.

As Jace and Raina moved deeper into the dimly lit corridor, they couldn't help but feel that the walls seemed to close in around them. The air was heavy with a sense of foreboding as if the very stones were whispering secrets from the past.

"Jace," Raina murmured, her voice taut with an unspoken question. "Do you really think we can change the course of this war?"

The doubts echoed in his own mind, gnawing at the edges of his resolve. But he couldn't afford to entertain such thoughts now. There was too much at stake. He focused on the goal ahead, drawing strength from the memory of Emma's face - the love and determination he saw there.

"Raina," he replied, steeling himself against the uncertainty that threatened to consume him. "I have to believe we can. We owe it to our loved ones - and to ourselves - to try."

They continued in silence, navigating the twisting passageways, their footsteps echoing ominously in the vast emptiness. The palace was a labyrinth, its grandeur almost oppressive in the cold, unyielding stone that encased them.

With a deep breath, Jace took the first step towards an uncertain future, his heart heavy with the knowledge of the sacrifices that would be demanded of them all. As the torchlight flickered behind them, casting long shadows that seemed to reach out like grasping fingers, he couldn't help but wonder if they would ever find the light amidst the darkness that lay ahead.

"Emma," he whispered under his breath, drawing strength from her memory. "I promise I will find my way back to you."

And with that vow, he strode forward, determined to face whatever challenges fate had in store.

13

Training

Jace's muscles screamed in protest as he swept his sword in an arc, sending a shower of sparks into the air as it collided with Aydis' blade. Sweat dripped from his brow, stinging his eyes as he quickly sidestepped another strike. Steel blue eyes locked on his opponent; Jace lunged forward, only to find himself parrying yet another attack.

"Good!" Aydis exclaimed, her voice tinged with approval. "Your reflexes are improving, Jace."

Beside him, Raina's blonde hair whipped around as she ducked under Ahat's swing, countering with a thrust of her own that the El warrior narrowly evaded. Her steel blue eyes glinted with fierce determination, reflecting the same fire that burned within Jace.

"Focus, Jace," Aydis said, her tone shifting to one of reprimand. "You're not here to watch Raina."

"Right," Jace muttered, redoubling his efforts and driving Aydis back with a series of rapid strikes. He found solace in the rhythm of combat, leaving his thoughts behind as he immersed himself in the dance of swords.

As their training session came to a close, Jace marveled at how far they had come since arriving in this strange land. At first, the El warriors had seemed untouchable, their skills honed by centuries of practice. Yet, day by day, he and Raina had pushed themselves to their limits, driven by the need to survive and protect their people.

"Enough," Ahat called out, signaling the end of their sparring. Jace lowered his weapon, panting heavily. He shared a nod with Raina, acknowledging their progress and mutual respect.

"Your skills have grown considerably," Aydis admitted, wiping the sweat from her brow. "You may stand a chance against Belloch's forces yet."

"Thank you," Jace replied, his chest swelling with pride. "We couldn't have done it without your guidance."

"Indeed," Raina agreed, her voice betraying a hint of exhaustion.

As the El warriors departed, Jace glanced around the training grounds, taking in the various structures designed to test and hone their abilities. He felt a sense of camaraderie with Raina as they pushed themselves both physically and mentally, striving to adapt to their new reality.

Reynard appeared out of nowhere and discreetly signaled for Jace and Raina to come with him, away from the bustling crowd. In a hushed tone, he revealed that he had heard rumors that the message Mitra received from Mount Myra came from scholars studying the Gaians. The information they had discovered seemed to have sparked the curiosity of Jace and Raina.

"I may need to talk to Mitra about this," Jace responded, equally hushed in tone.

"Jace," Raina said, her hand on his arm, "remember why we're here. Our priority is to gather all the information we can to help the El and devise a plan to return home."

His gaze hardened with determination as he responded, "I am aware. There is something I must discuss with Mitra. It may provide insight on ourselves and the predicament we find ourselves in."

"Be careful," Raina advised, her eyes filled with concern.

"Always," Jace assured her, patting her hand before setting off towards Mitra's chambers.

The winding corridors of Malathar's palace felt like a labyrinth to Jace, but he had committed every turn and corner to memory, ensuring that he would never lose his way. As he approached Mitra's door, he hesitated for a moment, gathering his thoughts before knocking softly.

"Enter," came Mitra's voice from within.

Stepping inside, Jace found Mitra hunched over a desk littered with parchment and inkwells; her attention focused on the delicate task of translating the ancient texts.

"Jace," she greeted him, glancing up from her work. "What brings you here?"

"News has reached me that there's ongoing communication with Mount Myra regarding the scholars' efforts to learn more about us," Jace began, his curiosity piqued. "I was hoping you could share any insights or discoveries that might aid us in our quest to return home."

"Indeed," Mitra replied, her expression thoughtful as she set her quill down. "The scholars have been working tirelessly to unravel the mysteries of the Gaians. While I cannot divulge everything just yet, I assure you that progress is being made."

"Every bit of information helps," Jace said, grateful for any crumbs of knowledge they could glean from their ancestors' legacy. "We'll do whatever it takes to protect our people and find a way back home." Jace's response carried a double meaning.

Mitra's chambers, dimly lit by flickering candles, cast shadows on the ancient scrolls strewn about the room. The air was thick with the scent of old parchment and lingering incense. She looked up from her work, gesturing for Jace to come closer.

"Jace, I must impress upon you the urgency of our situation," she said; her tone carried a sense of urgency and foreboding as she spoke to Jace. The war against Belloch was rapidly intensifying, and they needed answers. "It is crucial to be certain of all those involved in the conflict now more than ever."

Jace nodded solemnly, his steel-blue eyes reflecting the dancing flames. He knew the stakes were high, and he felt the weight of responsibility pressing down on him. As he opened his mouth to speak, the door to Mitra's chamber swung open, revealing the imposing figure of Kane, Mitra's second-in-command.

Kane stood tall and broad, his muscular frame filling the doorway. He had a stern, chiseled face with sharp, hawk-like features. His dark hair was cropped short, and his piercing eyes sparkled with intelligence and determination.

"Apologies for the interruption, Mitra," Kane said, his black eyes betraying no emotion. "But I must insist that Jace and Raina's movements within the city be limited. It is for their own safety, as well as ours."

Jace bristled at the insinuation, his fists clenching unconsciously. He fought to keep his voice steady as he replied, "Kane, we have done nothing to warrant suspicion. Restricting us will only breed tension between us and the El."

"Your presence here is unprecedented, Jace," Kane countered, unmoved by Jace's plea. "I must ensure the security of Malathar, even if it means placing restrictions on you and your fellow Gaian."

Mitra, sensing the tension between Jace and Kane, interjected, "Kane, I understand your concerns, but we must confer about this. Jace, can you excuse us?"

"Very well," Kane conceded, his voice cold and unyielding. "But know this, Jace: my eyes will be ever watchful. Should you or Raina pose any threat to our city, I will not hesitate to take action."

Jace's heart raced as he locked eyes with Kane, the unspoken challenge hanging heavy in the air. The room seemed to grow colder as if the frost of Nelhelm itself had crept into Mitra's chamber.

"Understood," Jace finally said through gritted teeth, forcing himself to maintain a level tone. He turned back to Mitra, desperation flickering in his eyes like the dying embers of a fire. "We will continue our training and do all we can to aid in this fight."

Mitra nodded her expression a mixture of sympathy and determination. With determination in her voice, she assured Jace, "We will not stop searching for a solution, I promise you." She then signaled for him to leave her chambers and be escorted to his own. As the door shut behind them, it sealed away the tension and secrets that were discussed within.

In the dimly lit chamber, Jace and Raina sat huddled together, their backs pressed against cold, ancient stone. The flickering glow of a solitary torch cast shifting shadows upon the intricate carvings that adorned the walls, telling tales of battles long past and heroes forgotten. Jace's steel blue eyes stared into the dancing flames, his mind racing as he replayed the events of the day.

"Kane asked me about our people," Raina whispered, her voice barely audible above the distant echoes of footsteps in the corridor beyond their door. "He wanted to know about our strengths, our weaknesses... Everything."

Jace furrowed his brow, his fingers absently tracing the patterns on the hilt of his sword as he considered her words. "Odd," he murmured, "Mitra asked me something similar, but she focused more on who I was in Gaia. It was as if she was trying to focus on how I got here and why."

Raina's eyes flashed with a mixture of anger and fear. "Do you think they mean us harm?" she asked, her voice wavering ever so slightly. "Could they be plotting against us?"

Jace hesitated, his heart heavy with the weight of his suspicions. "I don't know," he admitted, his eyes meeting hers. "But there is something about this situation, Raina... Something I cannot quite put my finger on."

"Kane's loyalty to Mitra seems almost... forced," Raina said, her expression darkening. "As if he serves her out of obligation rather than genuine devotion."

"True," Jace agreed, his gaze returning to the fire. "And I can't help but wonder what would happen if that obligation were to... shift."

The silence that settled between them was heavy, laden with doubt and unease. Jace knew that in times like these, trust was a scarce resource, and yet he could not shake the feeling that Kane held secrets beneath his stoic facade - secrets that could prove dire for both the Gaians and the El.

"Jace," Raina said softly, breaking the silence. "We need to be careful. Whatever Kane's intentions may be, we cannot allow him to jeopardize our mission or our safety."

He nodded, his resolve hardening. "You're right. We must be vigilant and prepared for whatever may come."

With a shared glance, they understood the path before them. It would be one filled with uncertainty and danger, but they would face it together as Gaians and allies to the El. And within the cold, stone chamber, their bond burned brightly, a beacon of hope in the dark shadows of Nelhelm.

Reynard's nimble fingers tapped an irritated tattoo against the worn stone of Malathar's ancient walls. The shadows of the evening danced around him as if conspiring to hide his intentions. He couldn't abide by Kane's restrictions any longer; he couldn't watch Jace and Raina being treated like caged animals.

"Enough," Reynard muttered under his breath, his voice barely audible over the distant cries of night birds. With a flourish of his red hair, he strode purposefully through winding corridors until he found himself before Mitra's chambers.

He hesitated for a moment, his thoughts churning like storm waves. Reynard knew that speaking out could be dangerous, but it had to be done. Swallowing hard, he raised a hand and knocked on the heavy door.

"Enter," came Mitra's voice, muffled by the thick wood.

Reynard pushed open the door, stepping into a room bathed in the golden glow of candles. Mitra sat at a large table, her brow furrowed as she studied an ancient scroll. She looked up, her eyes narrowing slightly as she regarded Reynard.

"Reynard," she said, her tone guarded. "What brings you here?"

"Apologies, Mitra, but I must speak with you about Jace and Raina," Reynard began, his voice tight with anxiety. "Kane's restrictions are stifling their growth, and I fear they're beginning to doubt our intentions."

"Go on," Mitra urged, her expression softening into one of concern.

"Jace and Raina need the freedom to move about Malathar," Reynard continued, his words quickening as his passion took over. "They are allies, not prisoners. How can we expect them to trust us if we cannot trust them?"

Mitra replied, "The reports from the scholars in Mount Myru are concerning. It has been over a thousand years since we last encountered Gaians, and what we have discovered is not exactly what we had anticipated."

Mitra's gaze drifted to the flickering shadows cast upon her chamber walls, her thoughts a whirlpool of emotion. "But, you make a valid point, Reynard," she conceded after a moment. "I will address the issue with Kane."

"Thank you, Mitra," Reynard said, relief washing over him like a cool breeze. "We must remember that we are all fighting for the same cause."

"Indeed," Mitra agreed, her voice tinged with determination. "Now that we have uncovered more about their world from Mount Myra, it is imperative that we work together as one."

"Your wisdom and leadership are invaluable, Mitra," Reynard said earnestly, bowing his head in respect. "We are fortunate to have you guiding us through these tumultuous times."

"Thank you, Reynard," Mitra replied, her eyes softening as she regarded him. "Now, go and rest. We have much to do on the morrow."

Nodding his agreement, Reynard turned and left the chamber, feeling lighter as if a great weight had been lifted from his shoulders. The night air greeted him once more, its cool embrace a balm to his troubled soul. He knew there was still much to be done, but for now, he had fought for what he believed was right - and had emerged victorious.

Reynard exited the chamber, and soon after, Kane entered. "Are you seriously considering releasing the Gaians?" he asked.

"Yes," Mitra answered. "Reynard made a convincing argument."

"Why do you think Reynard is so invested in this?" Kane questioned.

Kane paced the length of the chamber, his mind racing with thoughts. He couldn't shake off the feeling that there was more to Reynard's sudden concern for Jace and Raina than just wanting them to have more freedom.

"I don't trust him," Kane muttered under his breath, more to himself than to Mitra, who was watching him with a careful gaze.

"You always think people have hidden agendas like you do," Mitra replied, her tone laced with concern.

"But sometimes, people's motives are simply what they claim them to be."

Kane stopped in his tracks and turned to face Mitra. "And what of the information that came from Mount Myra?"

Mitra responded to Kane without hesitation, her gaze meeting his with confidence. "There is no certainty in the information."

Kane's dark eyes narrowed as he studied Mitra. There was a reason why she was their leader - her unwavering faith in their allies and her willingness to see the best in others even when he couldn't.

The sun had barely risen above the horizon, casting a golden glow over the training grounds as Jace and Raina sparred with Aydis and Ahat. The rhythmic thud of wooden swords meeting their marks filled the air, punctuated by the occasional grunt of exertion or hiss of frustration. Sweat beaded on their brows, dampening their hair and soaking into their tunics, but they refused to relent. They knew that every strike, every parry, and every evasion counted in honing their skills for the inevitable battles to come.

"Focus, Jace," Aydis barked, his eyes narrowing as he deftly blocked an overhead swing from Jace and countered with a swift jab to the ribs. "Each blow must carry purpose."

"Understood," Jace grunted, gritting his teeth against the pain in his side and launching into another series of quick slashes. He could feel the weight of his past training sessions heavy on his shoulders, but there was no time for weariness – not when the fate of his people was at stake. His mind echoed memories of Emma and the life they had envisioned together; it fueled his determination to become a worthy warrior.

Raina danced around Ahat's powerful swings, her agility allowing her to evade the El warrior's brutal strikes. Though she lacked Jace's physical strength, her speed and cunning compensated for it. She had learned to read her opponents, anticipating their moves before they made them. As she ducked under a wide arc, she saw an opening and landed a solid hit on Ahat's thigh.

"Good," Ahat praised, wincing slightly. "You're learning."

"Thank you," Raina replied, panting slightly. She stole a glance at Jace, locking eyes with him for a brief moment before returning her focus to Ahat. They were in this together, bound by their shared destiny as Gaians, and she found strength in their connection.

Meanwhile, Mitra stood at the edge of the training grounds, her eyes flitting between Jace and Raina's progress and the stern figure of Kane, who had approached her. The air between them was tense, heavy with unspoken grievances and concerns.

"Kane," Mitra began, her voice calm but firm, "I have considered Reynard's proposal about the restrictions you've placed on Jace and Raina. It is time for us to trust them and allow them the liberty they need to become true allies."

Kane's dark eyes narrowed, his jaw tightening. "The scholars from Mount Myra may provide us more valuable knowledge about the Gaians, but we cannot forget that our enemies are cunning and relentless. We must not let down our guard."

"Of course," Mitra conceded, "but unity and trust within our ranks are paramount. You know this. We cannot afford divisions or suspicions."

"Indeed." Kane's voice was cold and unyielding, like the iron of a freshly forged sword. "I will consider your words, Mitra."

"Make haste in your consideration, Kane," Mitra urged, her gaze fixed on the young warriors who continued to spar with unrelenting determination. "We may not have much time left before Belloch strikes again."

As Kane turned to leave, Mitra's thoughts drifted back to the scrolls recounting the history of Nelhelm and the Gaians' connection to it. Her heart swelled with pride and hope, her faith in the abilities of Jace and Raina unwavering. She knew they held the key to unlocking the secrets needed to defeat Belloch once and for all.

Kane's black eyes flickered with frustration as he watched Jace and Raina from a distance. Despite his reservations, he knew better than to question Mitra's wisdom. He clenched his jaw and muttered to himself before approaching the young warriors.

"Jace, Raina," Kane called out, his voice low and gravelly. "Mitra has spoken, and I am to grant you access to all of Malathar."

Jace exchanged a glance with Raina, a flicker of surprise in their steel blue eyes. Raina arched an eyebrow but said nothing, her stance guarded.

"Very well," Jace replied cautiously, a hint of suspicion lingering in his voice. "We appreciate the trust."

"See that you do not squander it," Kane warned, his gaze never leaving theirs. He turned on his heel and strode away, leaving them to ponder their newfound liberty.

Jace and Raina were both simultaneously shocked and elated that Kane had finally given in and allowed them their freedom once again.

As they left the training grounds and ventured deeper into Malathar, Jace and Raina marveled at the city's architecture. Ancient stone buildings towered overhead. The streets were alive with activity, El warriors sparring and merchants peddling their wares. The air was thick with the scent of roasting meats and sweet spices, stirring their appetites and curiosity.

"Such a beautiful city," Raina murmured, her fingers brushing against a carved pillar. "But there's so much we don't understand."

"True," Jace agreed, his gaze following the flight of a hawk circling high above. "But now we have a chance to learn more about this place and its people. Perhaps we'll find some answers."

As they moved through the city, Jace and Raina spoke with several El warriors, exchanging tales and knowledge about their respective homelands. Though most were friendly and welcoming, they couldn't shake the feeling that some hidden agendas lurked beneath the surface.

"Captain Zorath," Raina greeted one warrior, extending a hand in friendship. "We've heard much about your prowess on the battlefield. Can you tell us more about how you train for combat?"

Zorath's eyes narrowed, studying the two Gaians with keen interest. "Indeed, I can," he replied after a moment, his tone guarded. "But first, tell me about your own methods. I'm curious to learn how the fabled Gaians prepare for battle."

As they spoke, Jace couldn't help but feel a growing sense of unease. It was as if every conversation was laced with veiled intent, each El warrior seeking something from them – information, perhaps, or leverage. He shared his concerns with Raina in hushed whispers, his instincts urging caution.

"Trust no one but ourselves," he said softly, his words a vow. "Until we know more about what we're up against, we must rely on our own strength and cunning."

Raina nodded in agreement, her steel blue eyes reflecting both determination and worry. Together, they continued their exploration of Malathar, determined to uncover the secrets of Nelhelm and their place within it.

Jace's heart quickened as he noticed the shadows of Mitra's guards flitting about the towering stone walls that encircled Malathar, their vigilant eyes tracking his and Raina's every move. The city's grandeur was breathtaking, yet the sense of being watched gnawed at him like a persistent itch. He could almost feel the weight of their gazes as they walked along the cobblestone paths beneath the archways adorned with intricate engravings of mythical beasts and ancient heroes.

"Raina," Jace murmured, keeping his voice low. "We're being watched."

Her steel blue eyes flicked to the guards' silhouettes and then back to him, her expression guarded. "I know," she whispered, her words barely audible. "But we mustn't let them see that we're aware."

"Indeed," Jace agreed, forcing a smile as they continued their stroll through the city. The El warriors they encountered eyed them with a mix of curiosity and suspicion, each interaction a delicate dance of diplomacy and deception.

As they navigated the complexities of their new world, Jace found solace in Raina's presence. Their shared experiences had forged a bond between them that transcended their individual pasts – a connection that provided comfort amidst the doubts and uncertainties that plagued them.

"Remember the first time we trained with Aydis and Ahat?" Raina asked, attempting to lighten the mood. "I thought I'd never master their techniques."

"Ah, yes," Jace chuckled, recalling the memory fondly. "The way you fumbled with the sword, I feared you might lose a limb."

"Hey now," Raina protested, feigning offense. "I improved quickly, didn't I?"

"Indeed, you did," Jace conceded, his grin broadening. "You've become a formidable warrior in your own right."

"Thank you," she replied, a hint of pride in her voice. "And so have you."

As they reminisced, Jace felt the knot of tension in his chest begin to loosen. Despite the watchful eyes of Mitra's guards and the ever-present sense of unease, he knew that they faced these challenges together – united by their determination to succeed.

"No matter what is thrown our way," Jace proclaimed, his voice resonating with resolve, "we need to face it head-on."

"And we will," Raina concurred, her eyes staring back at him with unyielding trust. "We can conquer anything."

The sun dipped below the horizon, casting a warm glow across the ancient stone buildings of Malathar. Jace and Raina stood at the edge of the city's training grounds, their breaths heavy from another long day spent honing their skills.

Raina's gaze hardened as she looked out at the bustling city. "I fear that time may be running out with all these distractions. The longer we wait, the stronger Belloch becomes."

Jace nodded, his steel blue eyes taking in the sight of El warriors sparring in the dusky light. "You're right, Raina. We can't let Kane distract us ."

As they spoke, the clang of swords and the rhythmic thud of footfalls filled the air around them. Their own training with Aydis and Ahat had been rigorous, pushing them both to their physical and mental limits. Yet as the days turned to weeks, they began to see progress: their movements growing more fluid, their strikes more powerful.

Raina's gaze met Jace's, and he could see the fire burning within her – a fierce passion that mirrored his own. With a nod of agreement, they turned their attention back to the training grounds.

"Tomorrow," Raina whispered, her voice resolute, "we will face whatever challenges come our way. We are ready."

"Ready and determined," Jace echoed, his heart swelling with anticipation and pride. "For Gaia, for Nelhelm, and for our very survival."

As night fell upon Malathar, the city's ancient stones seemed to hum with a newfound energy. High above, the stars shone bright, bearing witness to the resolve that now burned within Jace and Raina, Gaians who would stop at nothing to protect both worlds from the darkness of Belloch. There was no turning back now, only forward – toward the trials and tribulations that lay ahead.

14

Spies

"Raina," Jace said quietly as they strode through the grand streets of Malathar, "I can't help but think of the ancient cities from Earth when I see these buildings."

"Me too," Raina agreed, her voice soft but full of wonder. "Look at the different hues of red in the bricks – it's as if they've captured the essence of a setting sun."

They marveled at the intricate details of the architecture. The stone walls were adorned with stunning bas-reliefs depicting scenes from a time long past. Rectangular columns rose majestically from the ground, supporting towering structures that seemed to scrape the sky itself.

"Have you ever seen anything so awe-inspiring?" Raina asked, her steel blue eyes reflecting the rich colors of the city.

"Never," Jace admitted, his own eyes wandering over the magnificent landscape before them. "It's like stepping into a world that should have been lost to history."

"Indeed," Raina replied, her voice tinged with a sense of longing. She seemed to be searching for something within the ancient stones – some connection to her own past, perhaps.

As they wandered through Malathar, Jace couldn't help but admire Raina's determination and resourcefulness. Though she remained guarded about her past, he knew that the skills she possessed had been hard-earned. Together, they were a formidable pair, and Jace couldn't deny the spark of excitement that ignited within him at the thought of unraveling the enigma that was their current situation.

"Freedom," Raina thought, feeling the weight of responsibility on his shoulders. "With this comes an opportunity to learn more about Mitra and Kane's true intentions and what they want with us."

"Are you thinking what I'm thinking?" Raina asked, her voice barely audible above the din of the city.

"Spying on them?" Jace whispered back,

"Something like that," she replied, a smirk playing at the corners of her mouth. "But we'll need to work together if we hope to uncover the truth."

Jace's head shook from side to side, his expression resolute and protective. "We have Mitra's trust now," he stated with conviction.

Raina couldn't help but admire Jace's resolve. He was right – they had just been granted a measure of freedom and trust by Mitra. It would be foolish to jeopardize that by sneaking around and potentially getting caught.

But she also couldn't shake the feeling that there was something off about their situation. Why were they suddenly brought to this ancient city? And what did Mitra and Kane want with them?

"We can't just blindly trust them," Raina whispered back, her voice laced with urgency. "We need to know what we're dealing with."

"And if we get caught?" Jace whispered.

"We'll have to be careful," Raina replied, her mind already working on a plan. "We can't let them know what we're up to."

They continued walking through the bustling streets of Malathar, taking in the sights and sounds of this wondrous city. But their minds were preoccupied with thoughts of uncovering the truth about Mitra and Kane.

With a reluctant nod, he agreed, and they began their journey into the heart of Malathar.

As Jace and Raina meandered through the city, they took in the sights and sounds of Malathar. The sunlight filtered through the tall rectangular columns, casting a warm glow on the red-tinged stone. The atmosphere was electric, pulsating with life and energy that both excited and overwhelmed them.

"Raina," Jace began as they sat down on a bench beneath a towering tree, its leaves rustling gently above them. "You never told me much about your past. How did you become so skilled at surviving in this world?"

Raina hesitated for a moment, her steel blue eyes gazing into the distance as if lost in memories she had long kept buried. She sighed, then gave Jace a small smile. "I guess it's time I shared my story with you."

"Take your time," Jace reassured her, his genuine curiosity apparent.

"Growing up, my mother and I lived in the north of the Czech Republic, near the border with Germany. It was a beautiful place, a tranquil haven, with lush green trees lining the rolling hills and crystal clear streams weaving through the landscape. The majestic sandstone valleys towered overhead. Nature was our playground, and my mother taught me everything she knew about survival," Raina began, her voice tinged with nostalgia.

"Your mother must have been an incredible woman," Jace said, admiration clear in his voice. Thinking of his father.

"She was," Raina nodded. "But there's more to our story. You see, we didn't move there by choice. We left Prague because my mother was involved in a secret organization, one that most people didn't even know existed."

"Really?" Jace raised an eyebrow, intrigued. "What kind of organization was it?"

"I don't know much about it," Raina admitted, frowning. "My mother never spoke of it, but I could tell it haunted her. The things she taught me – stealth, evasion, how to defend myself – it all came from a dark place in her past."

"Sounds like she was trying to protect you," Jace observed, his steel blue eyes reflecting concern.

"Indeed, she was," Raina agreed. "But it always felt like there was more to it than just protection. There was a sense of urgency in her teachings as if time was running out."

"Did you ever ask her about it?" Jace inquired, his curiosity piqued.

"Once," Raina replied, her face clouding with emotion. "She told me it was best I didn't know, that the less I knew, the safer I would be. I never brought it up again. But now..." She paused, looking around at the mysterious world they found themselves in, so far from their home. "Now I can't help but wonder if her past has anything to do with us being here."

"Maybe," Jace said thoughtfully. "My father loved studying ancient texts and hunting down secrets, but he never mentioned any secret organizations. Still, there might be a connection we're not aware of yet."

Raina's eyebrows rose in surprise. "I assumed your father would have been involved in something like that, considering how well-prepared you are for this new world."

"Seems like our parents both had their secrets," Jace mused. "But right now, I think it's important that we focus on figuring out what Mitra and Kane's true intentions are."

"Agreed," Raina nodded, determination settling on her features. "We need to learn everything we can if we want to survive and find our way back home."

Together, they continued exploring Malathar, seeking answers to the mysteries surrounding them but also finding solace in each other's company. Unbeknownst to them, the shadows of their past and the enigmatic leaders of the El would continue to shape their journey in ways they could never have anticipated.

Jace leaned against one of the towering red columns, his steel-blue eyes scanning the bustling square as merchants and shoppers alike swarmed around them. Raina stood beside him, her blonde hair tied back and her gaze just as keen, watching the people of Malathar with a mixture of curiosity and wariness.

"Mitra and Kane do seem to be hiding something," Jace murmured, his voice barely audible over the cacophony of voices.

"Agreed," Raina whispered, her eyes narrowing as she observed the two leaders in the distance, engaged in a hushed conversation. "I can't quite put my finger on it, but their intentions don't line up with what they've told us."

"Then let's find out the truth," Jace stated, determination igniting within him. "We'll try your idea and spy on them, gather whatever information we can."

A hint of a smile tugged at the corners of Raina's lips, and she nodded. "Alright. But we must be careful not to arouse any suspicion."

They moved stealthily through the throngs of people, using the chaos of the marketplace to their advantage. Jace's resourcefulness and adaptability shone through as they slipped into shadowy alleys or ducked behind stalls when necessary to avoid being seen.

Raina, too, displayed her own cunning, her childhood experiences in the wilds of the Czech Republic serving her well in this unfamiliar environment. Her keen senses allowed her to pick up on the subtlest of sounds, alerting them to any potential threats.

Raina and Jace crept silently along the palace walls, their eyes scanning for any sign of guards.

"Did you hear that?" Raina asked softly, pausing as they neared an ornate building adorned with intricate carvings.

As they neared Mitra's chambers, they heard hushed voices coming from within. Raina motioned for Jace to join her on a nearby balcony, where they could listen in without being seen.

Together, they discovered a small alcove hidden behind a cluster of potted plants. Crouching low, they peered out from their hiding spot as Mitra and Kane spoke.

"…the two newcomers are proving to be more resourceful than I anticipated," Kane's deep voice rumbled, the words just barely reaching Jace and Raina's ears. "But I still have my doubts."

"Patience, my friend," Mitra replied smoothly. "They have much to learn, but their potential is undeniable. We must nurture that potential and guide them on the path we have chosen."

Raina and Jace exchanged a glance, both realizing that they were the ones being referred to. They listened intently as the two leaders discussed their plans for them.

"Once they have proven themselves, we will reveal the truth about our role in their journey," Mitra continued. "And then, we will see if they are truly worthy of our guidance."

Jace's jaw tensed at the mention of hidden agendas, but Raina held up a hand to stop him from interrupting. She could sense there was more to be learned.

Kane chuckled darkly. "I'm not sure I trust these outsiders yet. They could pose a threat to our people."

"They may also bring great benefits," Mitra countered. "We must keep an open mind and observe their actions before jumping to conclusions."

As Mitra and Kane exited the chambers, Jace couldn't help but shudder at their words. He shared a worried glance with Raina, who appeared just as unnerved. Their suspicions had been confirmed – Mitra and Kane's intentions were not what they seemed.

"Come," Jace whispered, his hand brushing against Raina's as they prepared to slip away unnoticed. "We need to find answers, to know what they're planning."

"Agreed," Raina murmured, her eyes meeting his for a brief moment before she turned her attention back to the task at hand. "Let's go."

As they moved further into the heart of Malathar, Jace couldn't help but feel a growing sense of unease. He knew that they were treading dangerous ground, but there was no turning back now. They needed to uncover the truth, and together, they would face whatever challenges lay ahead.

Under the crimson sky, Jace and Raina crept through the narrow alleys of Malathar, their steps muffled by the deafening sound of the bustling city. The shadows cast by the towering rectangular columns seemed to twist and morph with each passing moment as if they were alive.

"Damn," Jace muttered under his breath as they rounded a corner only to find a pair of guards stationed at the entrance to a courtyard. "We'll need to find another way."

Raina glanced at him, her eyes narrowing in determination. "Leave it to me," she whispered, and without another word, she scaled the wall that bordered the alleyway. With the grace of a cat, she traversed the rooftop and disappeared from Jace's sight.

"Raina..." he breathed, concern furrowing his brow. He couldn't help but worry about her, even though he knew she was more than capable.

A short while later, Raina reappeared, signaling for Jace to follow her. As he scaled the wall and reached the rooftop, he found himself in awe of her resourcefulness. From this vantage point, they could observe Mitra and Kane without being detected – or so they thought.

"Look, there they are," Raina murmured, pointing at the figures standing in a far-off courtyard. Their voices carried faintly through the air, though not enough for them to decipher the conversation.

"Can you make out what they're saying?" Jace asked, his eyes fixed on Mitra and Kane.

"Only fragments," she replied, frustration evident in her voice. "Something about...plans and power."

As they continued to spy on the two leaders, Jace couldn't shake the feeling that they were being watched. He glanced around, searching for any signs of guards or potential observers. That's when he noticed them – black-clad figures lurking in the shadows, their eyes never straying from Jace and Raina.

"Raina," he whispered urgently, "we're being watched."

Her eyes widened, and she scanned the area before locking onto one of the shadowy figures. "They must be Mitra and Kane's personal guards. We need to be more careful."

"Agreed," Jace nodded, his jaw clenched in determination. "But we can't give up. We have to find out what they're plotting."

"Of course," Raina replied, her voice resolute. "We've come this far, and we won't let a few guards stand in our way. We'll find a way to get closer."

As they continued their efforts to spy on Mitra and Kane, the obstacles seemed to multiply, with each attempt proving more challenging than the last. And with every step, the ever-watchful eyes of the guards weighed heavier, a constant reminder of the stakes at hand.

Yet despite the mounting tension and uncertainty, Jace and Raina persevered, driven by an unwavering resolve to uncover the truth. Their connection, forged through shared experiences and an innate understanding of one another, only served to strengthen their determination.

For now, however, the secrets of Mitra and Kane remained shrouded in mystery, leaving Jace and Raina to navigate the treacherous path that lay ahead.

As they walked through the bustling city, they couldn't help but feel overwhelmed by the sheer magnitude of life teeming within its walls. The air was perfumed with the scent of spices and fragrant oils, while the cacophony of voices from merchants hawking their wares and children laughing filled the atmosphere with vibrant energy.

"Jace," Raina murmured, her face drawn in frustration as they hid behind a corner, watching Mit

ra and Kane from afar. "We're getting nowhere. We've been trailing them for hours, and yet we know nothing more than when we started."

Jace clenched his fists, anger bubbling beneath his calm exterior. "I know. It's maddening. The bloody guards are always there, watching us like hawks."

"Maybe we should call it a day," she suggested, biting her lip. "We're just putting ourselves in danger at this point. There must be another way."

"Perhaps you're right," Jace admitted, the weight of disappointment settling heavily on his shoulders. "But if we don't uncover the truth soon, I fear for what might become of us."

"Jace" - her voice was soft, yet determined - "we're resourceful and adaptable. We've survived this long in Nelhelm, and we'll find a way to get the answers we seek. But first, let's get some rest. Tomorrow is another day, and we need to be at our best."

"Alright," he agreed reluctantly, his mind churning with unanswered questions and simmering frustration. As they retreated from the marketplace, Jace couldn't shake the nagging feeling that something far more sinister lay beneath the surface of Malathar's beauty.

As the sun dipped behind the horizon, casting its final rays upon the ancient city, Jace and Raina knew that their quest for truth was far from over. In the shadows, danger loomed, and their determination to uncover it would test the limits of their resilience and cunning.

"Tomorrow," Jace vowed, steeling himself for the challenges ahead, "we will find the answers we seek, no matter the cost."

Jace stood at the edge of the balcony, his eyes scanning the cityscape below. The first stars of twilight began to appear, casting a shimmering glow over the ancient structures of Malathar. He clenched his fists, feeling the cool night air on his face as he struggled to contain the whirlwind of emotions within him.

"Jace," Raina murmured, stepping up beside him. "We cannot let this defeat us."

"I know," he replied, his voice barely more than a whisper. "But if we cannot find the truth, how can we hope to survive in this world?"

"Sometimes the path to survival is not a straight one," Raina said, placing a hand on his shoulder. "We must adapt to the circumstances we find ourselves in."

"Trust and adapt..." Jace repeated, his steel blue eyes reflecting the determination that burned within him. "I can do that." He paused, looking deeply into Raina's eyes. "And I know you can too."

"Of course," she answered with a small smile, her own resolve shining through. "Together, we will find the answers we seek."

As they stood there, united in their purpose, Jace couldn't help but wonder if Mitra and Kane were watching them, aware of their every move. The thought sent a shiver down his spine.

"Raina," he whispered, keeping his voice low. "Do you think they know what we're trying to do?"

"Perhaps," she admitted, her gaze shifting toward the shadows that danced across the buildings. "But that only means we have to be more cunning, more careful, and even more determined."

"Agreed," Jace nodded, his heart racing at the thought of the challenges that lay ahead. "We need to be ready for anything."

Their voices seemed almost swallowed by the encroaching darkness, and Jace felt a growing sense of unease as the night closed in around them. It was as if Malathar itself were conspiring against their quest for truth, hiding its secrets behind a veil of mystery and deceit.

"Raina," he said abruptly, "I have an idea. Tomorrow, we'll split up. That way, we can cover more ground and avoid drawing too much attention to ourselves."

"Alright," she agreed, her voice tinged with uncertainty. "But we need to be careful. Stay alert and trust your instincts. If something doesn't feel right, get out of there."

"Same goes for you," Jace replied, his concern for Raina evident in his eyes.

They stood there for a moment longer, staring out at the city that held so many secrets yet to be uncovered. And as the darkness deepened, they knew that their pursuit of answers would lead them down a dangerous and uncertain path.

"May the stars guide us," Raina whispered, squeezing Jace's hand.

"May the stars guide us indeed," he echoed as if he knew what that meant.

With that, they turned away from the balcony and retreated to their rooms, each lost in their own thoughts as they prepared for the trials and tribulations that lay ahead. The shadows lengthened, the night deepened, and the city of Malathar seemed to slumber, but within the hearts of Jace and Raina, anticipation and determination burned bright.

15

Homesick

Jace Alexander sat on the edge of a stone bench, his eyes scanning the unfamiliar landscape of Nelhelm. The once vibrant colors that used to amaze him now felt like a cruel mockery of the life he had left behind. He clenched his fists and shook his head, trying to clear away the doubts that gnawed at the corners of his mind. Jace and Raina had been unsuccessful in their attempt to gather information through spying. Luckily, they were not caught in the process.

"Is this my fate?" he wondered. "To be forever trapped in this strange land? To never set foot in my hometown again and hold Emma in my arms?"

With every passing moment, his determination to fulfill his mission seemed to grow weaker, as if it were being consumed by the shadows that haunted his thoughts. It was a battle he fought each day, and sometimes, he wasn't sure which side would emerge victorious. The weight of his responsibility pressed down upon him, testing the limits of his resolve.

"Damn it all," Jace muttered under his breath, the frustration boiling over. "Why me? Why did I have to be the one chosen for this godforsaken task?"

He slumped forward, resting his head in his hands. The memories of his loved ones crept into his mind's eye – his father teaching him the art of hunting, the first time he held Emma close, and the laughter they shared with their friends. These memories, once a source of comfort, now served only to intensify his longing to return home.

"Emma, what I wouldn't give to see your face again, to hear your voice," he whispered into the stillness. His chest tightened as he imagined her waiting, unknowing and afraid, while he struggled through this strange world.

"Will I ever find a way back?" Jace asked himself, his voice barely audible. "Or am I destined to remain here, alone and forgotten?"

The silence that followed his question seemed to stretch out infinitely, punctuated only by the distant rustle of leaves in the wind. It was as if Nelhelm itself were taunting him, reminding him of his isolation and the seemingly insurmountable odds he faced.

"Enough," Jace finally said, his voice firm and resolute. "I cannot give in to despair."

He forced himself to stand, his muscles aching from hours of inactivity. He knew that he had a duty to protect Gaia and Nelhelm from the darkness that threatened to consume them. This knowledge burned within him, fueling his determination and driving him forward.

"Emma would want me to succeed," he told himself, taking a deep breath and filling his lungs with the crisp Nelhelm air. "She would want me to be strong and see this through."

With renewed vigor, Jace began to consider his options. He knew he couldn't simply wander aimlessly through this foreign land, hoping to stumble upon a solution. There had to be a way to achieve his mission and find a path back home – he just needed to discover it.

As Jace contemplated his next move, a faint glimmer of hope began to flicker in the depths of his heart. The weight of his doubts and fears seemed to lessen ever so slightly, replaced by a steadfast resolve.

"Perhaps there is a way," he thought, a small smile tugging at the corners of his lips. "Perhaps I can conquer this challenge, as I have conquered countless others."

And so, with a newfound sense of purpose, Jace Alexander set forth on his journey once more. His love for Emma and his family and his duty to Gaia and Nelhelm propelled him into the unknown, where he would face whatever trials lay ahead.

"Let them come," he whispered to the wind, the words carrying both a promise and a prayer. "I will not falter. I will not fail."

Jace's heart pounded like a hammer against his chest, each beat echoing through him like the distant memory of happiness. The cold, unforgiving terrain of Nelhelm seemed to stretch out endlessly before him, a prison forged from jagged mountains and twisted forests. His surroundings were as foreign and unyielding as the emotions that gripped him – an impenetrable cage of doubt and despair.

"Emma," he whispered, her name a prayer escaping his lips. The sudden ache in his chest was almost unbearable, as if his very soul longed for the warmth of her embrace, the solace of her presence. "I wish you were here."

The wind sighed mournfully through the trees, its whispered lament mirroring the turmoil in Jace's heart. How had he come to this place, so far from home and all he held dear? He had left with such determination, filled with the unshakable belief that he could protect Gaia and Nelhelm from the darkness that threatened them. And yet, now, that resolve seemed to crumble beneath the weight of his doubts, leaving him adrift in a sea of uncertainty.

"Is it worth it?" he asked himself, the question tearing at the fabric of his conviction. "Am I sacrificing everything I love for a cause that may be beyond my reach?"

He found himself remembering the days spent hunting with his father, the warmth of the sun on his face as they tracked their prey through the familiar woods near their home. The lessons learned during those outings – patience, resourcefulness, adaptability – had served him well in his journey thus far. But now, as he stood on the precipice of an abyss of doubt, he couldn't help but wonder if those skills were enough to see him through the trials ahead.

"Father always said that courage was the key to overcoming any challenge," he mused, the memory of his father's smile a bittersweet comfort. "But what if that courage is not enough? What if it leads me down a path from which there is no return?"

As the weight of his thoughts threatened to crush him, Jace felt the chill of Nelhelm seep into his bones, as though the land itself sought to claim him as its own. He shivered, wrapping his arms around himself in a futile attempt to stave off the cold and the creeping sense of isolation.

"Is this my fate?" he wondered, the question gnawing at the edges of his mind like a ravenous beast. "To be forever trapped in this forsaken land, a prisoner of my own choices?"

And yet, even as despair threatened to consume him, a flicker of defiance began to burn within Jace's heart. It was a stubborn ember, fueled by the love he held for Emma and his family, refusing to be extinguished by the darkness that loomed overhead.

"Neither doubt nor despair shall claim me," he vowed, gripping the hilt of his sword with renewed determination. "For I am Jace Alexander, son of the mountains, and I will find a way to triumph."

In that moment, Jace found the strength to push back against the tide of uncertainty, reclaiming his resolve with every beat of his heart. Though the road ahead was fraught with peril, he knew that he must continue onward – for the sake of those he loved and the world he sought to protect.

"Let the shadows come," he whispered, his voice defiant and unwavering. "I will face them, and I will prevail."

"Emma...," Jace whispered, his voice barely audible above the wind that whipped through Nelhelm's desolate landscape. The name felt like a prayer upon his lips, conjuring an image of her radiant smile, the warmth of her embrace. "Will I ever see you again?"

His thoughts meandered down an increasingly dark path, and he found himself imagining life in this unforgiving realm - an eternity spent wandering these barren lands, never to return to the comfort of home. He shuddered at the thought, feeling the weight of his isolation bearing down upon him.

"Is there even a way back?" he muttered to himself, his steel-blue eyes scanning the horizon for any sign of hope. Yet all he saw was an endless expanse of gray, the jagged mountains looming in the distance like the shattered teeth of some ancient, slumbering beast. It was a sight that stirred a primal dread within him, filling his heart with the chilling realization that he may well be trapped here forever.

"Jace, keep moving," he told himself sternly, his breath misting in the cold air as he forced his legs to carry him forward. "You can't afford to lose hope now."

But try as he might to cling to his determination, he couldn't shake the gnawing sense of loneliness that had settled within him like a heavy stone. In Nelhelm's harsh wilderness, he was utterly alone - cut off from everything and everyone he held dear. And with each step he took, the ache of longing grew more acute, threatening to consume him completely.

"Am I destined to walk this path alone, without so much as a glimpse of home?" he wondered, the question echoing through his mind like a mournful lament. "Is this the price I must pay for my decision?"

"Jace Alexander!" a voice cried out suddenly, breaking through his reverie. He whipped around, his sword at the ready, but there was no one to be seen - only the wind, howling its mournful dirge through the desolate land.

"Was that... my own voice?" he thought, his heart pounding in his chest. "Am I truly so alone that I have begun to hear things?"

As the silence stretched on, unbroken save for the whispers of the wind, Jace felt a growing sense of despair take root within him. He knew that he had made a choice - to protect Gaia and Nelhelm from danger, even at great personal cost. But now, as fear and isolation threatened to consume him, he couldn't help but question if that choice had been worth the sacrifice.

Crouching in the cold, dark corner of an abandoned ruin, Jace's breath came out in ragged gasps as he tried to steady himself. His fingers grazed the crumbling stone walls as he struggled to regain control over his thoughts. "This... this isn't me," he whispered, his voice barely audible.

"Stay focused, Jace," he told himself, squeezing his eyes shut, desperately hoping to find some semblance of inner strength. But instead of the calm, collected resolve he sought, memories of home and loved ones surged forth unbidden.

"Jace, you're going to be late for school!" his mother's voice rang through his mind, accompanied by the scent of freshly baked bread wafting from their cozy kitchen. He could see her warm smile and hear the laughter that filled their home on lazy Sunday afternoons.

"Remember our first date?" Emma's soft, lilting voice echoed in his ears, her beautiful face appearing in his mind's eye. They had been just sixteen, walking hand-in-hand through the woods near their hometown. The sunlight filtered through the leaves, casting dappled patterns on the forest floor, and they had spoken of their dreams and fears beneath the ancient trees.

And there was his father, strong and silent, teaching him the art of tracking prey and reading the signs of nature. Those lessons – both spoken and unspoken – had shaped Jace into the man he had become, instilling within him a deep love for the wild places of the world.

"Please... I need your strength now," Jace pleaded silently, tears pricking at the corners of his eyes. He knew, with a certainty that chilled him to his core, that if he allowed these memories to consume him, he would be lost.

"Focus, Jace," he urged himself again, gritting his teeth and clenching his fists. "You have a mission to complete, a purpose to fulfill. You are not alone."

"Then why does it feel like I am?" he cried out in anguish, the sound echoing through the empty ruin.

"Jace!" a voice called out again, this time accompanied by the faintest rustle of movement. His heart leaped into his throat as he scrambled to his feet, sword at the ready.

"Who's there?" he demanded

"Show yourself!" The tension in his voice was palpable, betraying the vulnerability he felt deep within.

A figure emerged from the shadows, its form shrouded by the dim light of the ruin. Jace's heart pounded in his chest, his grip on the sword tightening as he prepared for a potential threat.

"Easy, Jace," the figure spoke, stepping into the light and revealing a familiar face. It was Reynard.

As he stepped closer, the scent of earth and leather reached Jace's nose. Reynard's cloak was made of worn leather, and it seemed to hold the essence of the wild places he loved so much. Relief washed over him, but it was short-lived as the isolation and loneliness returned.

"Thought I'd find you here," Reynard said, walking towards Jace with a concerned expression. "You've been spending a lot of time alone recently. Are you alright?"

Jace hesitated before responding. "I'm just...struggling," he admitted, his voice cracking slightly. "I thought I could handle this mission – that I had the strength to face whatever challenges awaited me. But now...I don't know if I can do it."

"Everyone has doubts, Jace," Reynard said gently, placing a hand on his shoulder. "It's what makes us human. But we're not meant to face them alone. We're here for you."

"Thank you," Jace whispered, feeling a small spark of hope ignite within him. He knew he could not allow his memories to consume him, but perhaps he could draw strength from them instead. His loved ones, though far away, were still a part of him, and he could honor their memory by continuing to fight for the greater good.

With renewed determination, Jace looked into the eyes of his comrade, steeling himself for the battles to come. He would not let fear and doubt control him any longer. For Emma, for his father, and for the world he left behind, he would find the strength to persevere and protect Gaia and Nelhelm.

"Let's get back to the others," he said, his voice steady and resolved. "We have a mission to complete."

As the two of them walked away from the ruin, Jace felt that glimmer of hope grow within him. The road ahead would be difficult, but he was no longer alone in his struggle. And with each step, he moved closer to finding a way back to those he loved.

As Jace trudged through the dense forest, the weight of his mission bore down on him like a crushing wave. Shadows intermingled with the sunlight filtering through the canopy of leaves above, casting eerie patterns on the ground beneath his feet. The air was thick with the scent of decay and the distant cries of unknown creatures, reminding him that he was far from home.

"Are we any closer to finding a way home?" Jace asked, his voice barely audible above the sounds of the forest.

"Patience, Jace," his Reynard replied. "We must trust in our journey."

Jace clenched his fists, frustration bubbling within him. He longed for the comfort of Emma's embrace, her gentle touch soothing his tormented soul. The memory of their last moments together - the way her brown eyes glistened with unshed tears - haunted him relentlessly.

"Emma," he whispered as if saying her name aloud could bring her closer. A sudden pang of guilt washed over him. How could he have left her behind? What if his quest ultimately led him further away from her?

"Is there something troubling you, Jace?" his companion asked, concern etching itself upon his face.

"Emma," Jace admitted, struggling to keep the tremor out of his voice. "I can't help but feel that I'm failing her, that this mission is tearing me apart."

"Sometimes our duty conflicts with our personal desires," his companion said softly. "But remember, you are here to protect not only her but countless others. You carry the weight of their lives on your shoulders."

Jace stared into the distance, lost in thought. He knew his companion spoke the truth, but the desire to reunite with Emma gnawed at him, making it difficult to focus on his task at hand. As much as he wished to fulfill his mission, the fear of never seeing her again tugged at his heartstrings, threatening to unravel him.

Jace's heart clenched at the thought of Emma in pain, wrestling with her own demons just as he was. He realized then that it wasn't just his own fate that hung in the balance - it was hers as well. The weight of his mission seemed to grow heavier with each passing moment, and he felt the crushing pressure of fear and doubt bearing down upon him.

"Promise me," Jace said, his voice cracking with emotion. "Promise me that I'll find a way back to her."

"Nothing is certain in this world," his companion replied gently. "But I promise you this: as long as you remain true to your purpose, we will do everything in our power to see you reunited with her."

It wasn't the unequivocal assurance Jace had hoped for, but it was enough to quell the storm raging within him. With each step forward, he knew he was inching closer to fulfilling his duty and, perhaps, to finding a way back to Emma. But the shadows of doubt still lingered, casting their chilling tendrils over his heart, and he knew that the battle within had only just begun.

Jace stood at the edge of a cliff, staring out into the vast expanse of Nelhelm, the wind whipping through his dark hair. The cold air bit at his face like jagged needles, but it was not the chill that made his heart shudder. It was the realization that he was far from home and even further from Emma's warm embrace.

"Damn this place," Jace muttered under his breath, tightening his fists as if to anchor himself against the torrent of emotions threatening to sweep him away.

"Every step we take brings us closer to our goal, Jace," Reynard said, the wise scout who had guided him thus far. "Remember, you are here for a purpose."

"Is it worth it?" Jace asked, blue eyes glistening with unshed tears. "Protecting Gaia, saving Nelhelm when all I want is to be back in her arms?"

"Your love for Emma is a testament to your humanity," Reynard replied, placing a reassuring hand on Jace's shoulder. "But you cannot let it blind you to the greater good you can achieve."

Feeling the weight of responsibility upon him, Jace stared down at the swirling mists below, wondering if they held any answers. As he watched, a memory surfaced - one of Emma. They stood together by the river near their hometown, her laughter like sunlight on water. She turned to him, her hazel eyes full of love, and whispered, "I believe in you."

"Emma believes in me," Jace murmured as if saying it aloud could make it real. "She believes I can do this."

"Then use her belief as fuel for your courage," Reynard urged. "If you cannot find strength within yourself, draw it from those who love and support you."

Jace nodded, resolute. With a deep breath, he turned away from the edge of the cliff and faced the path that led deeper into Nelhelm. Each step felt like a battle, but with every stride, Jace could feel his resolve growing stronger.

"Reynard," Jace said, his voice steady and determined. "You're right. I cannot allow my love for Emma to compromise the fate of Gaia and Nelhelm."

"Good," Raegar replied, a hint of pride in his voice. "Remember, Jace, you are not alone in this journey. We walk together, united by our common purpose."

As they continued on their perilous quest, Jace felt something flicker within him - a spark, a glimmer of hope. It was fragile and fleeting, but it was enough to carry him forward. It whispered promises of a future where he could protect both the world and the woman he loved, a future where doubt would be nothing more than a distant memory.

And so, with renewed determination, Jace Alexander took a step closer to fulfilling his destiny, armed with the knowledge that love and hope were powerful allies in the face of darkness.

16

Wallace Clan

The sun was setting over the small town of Glenwood, casting a golden hue on the trees and houses. Emma, Rick Waters, and the teams had been searching tirelessly for Jace since his disappearance. The once-festive atmosphere had turned somber as days passed without any news of Jace's whereabouts. The search parties combed through every inch of the nearby woods, retracing Jace's steps back to the Old Chimney – the place where he was last seen.

Emma stood on the porch, her brown eyes scanning the horizon with determination. She clenched her fists, feeling the weight of the secret she carried within her. A gust of wind carried the distant voices of the searchers, who were growing more desperate with each passing hour.

"Miss Williams!" Sheriff Callahan called out, startling Emma from her thoughts as he approached the porch. He tipped his hat, trying to hide his own concern behind a professional demeanor. "We've got some new information that might help us find Jace."

"Please, tell me," Emma begged, her voice cracking with emotion.

"Well," the sheriff hesitated, glancing towards the house where Emma's parents were watching them from the window. "We found a match for one of the bullets at the Old Chimney. It belongs to a member of the Wallace clan."

"Those mountain people?" Emma's heart raced in her chest. Her mind raced, piecing together fragments of stories about the mysterious Wallace clan – notorious for their fierce loyalty to one another.

"Seems so," the sheriff confirmed, his steely gaze meeting Emma's. "We're gonna question them further, see if they know anything about Jace's whereabouts."

Emma's apprehension was evident as she responded, "Sheriff, are you certain that's a wise decision? They have a reputation for being dangerous."

"Miss Williams, we need to explore every option," Sheriff Callahan replied firmly. "We owe it to Jace and his family."

"Please, do whatever you can to find him," Emma implored, her eyes pleading with the sheriff.

"Of course, Miss Williams. That's what we're here for." He tipped his hat again before heading back to his car, leaving Emma and her parents to digest this new information.

As the sun dipped below the horizon and darkness enveloped Glenwood, Emma could not help but feel a growing sense of dread. What if they never found Jace? The thought was unbearable, and she knew she had to do everything in her power to uncover the truth about his disappearance, regardless of the consequences.

"Jace, where are you?" she whispered into the wind, praying that he was still alive and that they would be reunited once more.

Emma stood near the search party, the cold mountain wind biting at her cheeks. She looked to her parents and Rick Waters, their hushed whispers a palpable undertone to Allen's mounting frustration. She could see it in the way he clenched his jaw; his hands balled into fists as he shot them a glare.

"Emma," Allen called out, his voice seething with irritation. "Can we focus on finding Jace, please?"

"Of course," she replied, stung by his tone but knowing that he was just as worried about Jace as she was. They all were.

Sheriff Callahan led them up the winding path towards the Wallace clan's compound, flanked by Allen and a few other deputies. As they approached the rickety wooden fence surrounding the property, Emma's heart began to race. The Wallaces were an enigmatic group notorious for their run-ins with the law and their insularity from the rest of Glenwood.

"Stay back," Sheriff Callahan instructed the others, his voice low and stern. He and Allen stepped forward, and together, they pushed open the creaking gate.

The Wallace patriarch, a gruff man with a permanent scowl etched on his face, emerged from the cabin and eyed the sheriff with suspicion. Behind him, two younger men peered out from the shadows, their faces hardened and untrusting.

"What's all this about?" Mr. Wallace growled, crossing his arms over his chest.

"We've been investigating the disappearance of Jace Williams," Sheriff Callahan explained. "And we have reason to believe that someone from your family may be involved."

The atmosphere turned tense as Mr. Wallace's eyes narrowed in anger. "My family ain't got nothin' to do with that boy goin' missing," he spat.

"We have evidence that suggests otherwise," Allen interjected, the impatience evident in his voice. "Your bullet matched one found at the Old Chimney. So, someone here is involved in Jace's disappearance."

"You're accusing us based on some damn bullet?" one of the younger men snarled, stepping forward with clenched fists.

"I'm just stating facts," Allen replied evenly. "We have reason to believe that you shot at Jace trying to make it look like an accident."

"That's ridiculous," Mr. Wallace scoffed. "We don't take kindly to false accusations around here, Sheriff."

"We'll let a court decide what's true and what's not," Sheriff Callahan said firmly.

"Enough!" A woman's voice suddenly cut through the tension as she emerged from another cabin nearby. She was tall and strikingly beautiful, with piercing blue eyes and fiery red hair pulled back into a braid. Emma recognized her as Kiera Wallace. Kiera used to date Allen, but that was a long time ago. They used to go on double dates with Emma and Jace.

"Kiera," Allen breathed out in surprise. He thought she had moved away years ago.

Kiera gave Emma a small shake of her head before turning back to face her family and the sheriff.

"If you're going to accuse anyone, accuse me," Kiera spoke calmly but forcefully. "I was the one who had my cousins chase Jace."

Allen's tone was almost shocked as he asked, "Kiera, why did you do that?" His mind flashed back to their high school days, hanging out all four of them.

"I have my reasons," Kiera replied firmly.

"Alright, Kiera," the sheriff interjected. "You and your cousins will need to come with us."

As the party retreated from the Wallace homestead, with the Wallace's in toe. The sun dipped below the horizon, casting eerie shadows across the landscape. Allen's determination to uncover the truth about Jace's disappearance grew stronger with each passing moment.

Emma walked a few paces behind her parents, their disapproving glances weighing upon her like the mountains that loomed around them. The shadows of the towering peaks stretched out across the landscape, concealing secrets within their darkened folds.

"Emma, dear," her mother sighed, her voice brittle as autumn leaves, "you know we're only trying to help you."

"Help me?" Emma scoffed, her eyes narrowing. "Or just find Jace so he can save your reputation?"

"Your father and I are worried about you," her mother insisted, but the words felt hollow, echoing emptily through the crisp mountain air.

"Enough," her father grumbled, his voice rumbling like distant thunder. "We've got bigger problems to deal with right now."

The tension between them crackled like the dry twigs beneath their feet, but Emma refused to let their disapproval deter her. She knew Jace's life was at stake, and she wouldn't rest until she'd uncovered the truth.

As the party made its way back toward Glenwood, the air grew colder, the wind whispering mournful secrets through the trees.

At the police station, Sheriff Callahan had the three Wallace men in an interrogation room, but Kiera remained silent. As a result, she was placed in a cell while Allen and the Sheriff continued to question the men for more information.

"All right, folks," Sheriff Callahan began, taking a seat at the head of the table. "We need answers. How were you involved in Jace's disappearance?"

The room fell silent, only broken by the sound of shifting chairs and nervous coughs.

"Wallace clan ain't no snitches," one of the men growled, his voice scraping like stone against steel. "We ain't got nothing to do with that boy's disappearance."

Sheriff Callahan raised an eyebrow. "Yet we know Kiera was the ringleader."

The man's expression hardened even further, but he remained silent.

"Come on now," the sheriff pressed, leaning forward in his chair. "Jace is missing, and we know that your family was involved."

Allen watched the Wallace's closely, noting how they shifted uncomfortably beneath the weight of the lawman's scrutiny. She could feel the unease that buzzed through them, a disquieting hum that hovered in the air like static electricity.

"Look," one of the younger Wallace's finally spoke up, his voice shaky. "We didn't want no part in this, but we ain't got much choice. Livin' up here in these mountains ain't easy, and when someone offers you money, you take it."

"Who offered you the money?" Allen pressed, his heart pounding with desperation.

"Can't say," the young man replied, his eyes downcast. "Kiera handled that, and all I know is it wasn't one of us."

"Someone paid you to help kidnap Jace," Sheriff Callahan said, his voice rising with fury. "You're all going to tell me who, or so help me, I'll make sure you never see the light of day again."

"And where is Jace now?" Allen interjected.

"We don't know," the older Wallace responded. "He got away from us and disappeared behind the chimney."

"We had him pinned down," another Wallace spoke up, his voice shaking with fear. "But then he just...vanished."

"Vanished? What do you mean?" Allen asked, his mind racing with possibilities.

"He was there one minute, and the next, he was gone," the man explained, his eyes darting nervously around the room.

As the realization slowly spread throughout the room, it became clear that Jace had successfully escaped. He was out there somewhere, but no one had any idea where he could be.

Emma clenched her fists, her heart heavy with the weight of guilt and secrecy. Through the one-way mirror of the interrogation room, she watched intently as if communicating in a secret code known only to them. Her gaze shifted back and forth between the three Wallaces, studying their faces for any sign that could lead her to Jace.

The door to the observation room opens. "Emma," Allen's voice was soft, placing a hand on her shoulder. "We'll get to the bottom of this, I promise."

She shook off his touch, anger bubbling beneath the surface like water in a boiling pot. "I know you mean well, Allen, but every second we waste is a second closer to losing Jace forever."

Allen sighed, his eyes clouded with concern. "We're all worried about him, Em. But aggravating the Wallaces won't help us find him any sooner."

"Then what do you suggest?" she snapped, her frustration spilling over. "Should we just sit idly by while Jace goes missing?"

"Enough!" Sheriff Callahan barked from inside the interrogation. "Let's focus on the task at hand. If you can't give us a name, at least tell us how you received the money."

The young Wallace who had spoken earlier hesitated, glancing nervously at his family. "It was...it was left for Kiera in a hollow tree. Wrapped in a cloth with instructions."

"Instructions?" the sheriff repeated, his pulse quickening. "What kind of instructions?"

"Can't remember exactly," he said, his voice shaking. "Something about keepin' quiet and layin' low with Jace. Not to ask questions."

Suspicion gnawed at Emma's insides, threatening to consume her. She knew the truth - that it was she who had paid the Wallaces, desperate to postpone the wedding and buy herself more time to come to terms with her feelings for Jace. But her plan had gone horribly awry, and now Jace was missing, his life hanging in the balance. Shortly after Jace's disappearance, Kiera sent word to Emma that the Wallace family did not have him.

"Emma, let's take a break," Allen suggested, sensing her distress. "You're not doing yourself any favors by getting so worked up."

"I won't stop until I find him, Allen," she said through gritted teeth. "I don't care what it takes or who I have to confront - I'll tear this mountain apart if I have to."

"Your determination is admirable," Sheriff Callahan interjected, coming into the room, "but we must tread carefully. We cannot risk alienating the Wallaces further and losing our only lead."

"Fine," Emma conceded, her voice barely a whisper. "But we can't afford to waste any more time."

As they regrouped, Emma's thoughts swirled like leaves caught in a whirlwind. She couldn't shake the feeling that the answer lay hidden in the shadows, waiting to be uncovered like a buried treasure long forgotten. As the sun dipped lower in the sky, casting long fingers of shadow across the mountainside, she knew that she had no choice but to face the darkness within herself and confront the lies that threatened to unravel everything she held dear.

"Jace," she whispered, her voice carried away by the wind, "I will find you, even if it means exposing my own secrets."

The sun sank lower in the sky, casting a blood-red hue over the mountains. Sheriff Callahan's brow furrowed as he paced the edge of the cliff, his eyes pinned on the vast, desolate landscape below. The Wallace clan's vague answers burned like coals in his mind, hinting at truths that danced just out of reach.

"Damn it!" he muttered, slamming his fist against a nearby tree. "The search of the Wallace's homestead turned up nothing." "Kiera didn't give us anything to go on. Can't they see a young man's life hangs in the balance?"

"Be patient, Sheriff," Emma urged softly, her voice quivering with emotion. She stared down at her trembling hands and clenched them into fists. "We'll find Jace. We have to."

"Patience is a luxury we can ill afford," the Sheriff grumbled, his frustration mounting. "Every moment that passes is another moment closer to losing him forever."

"Then let's not waste any more time," Allen interjected, his gaze shifting between Emma and the Sheriff. "We need to gather everyone and intensify our efforts. Nothing else matters until we find Jace."

Rick Waters's men, huddled together like a team, exchanged glances and murmured in agreement. Their tactical attire now appeared worn, serving as a stark reminder of the urgency at hand.

"We must leave no stone unturned," Emma declared, her brown eyes ablaze with determination. "I don't care if we have to search through the night; I will not rest until Jace is found."

"Nor will I," Allen added, his voice steely. "He's family, after all."

"Very well," Sheriff Callahan sighed, running a hand through his graying hair. "Let's split up and cover more ground. Time is not on our side."

As the group dispersed into the fading light, Emma's thoughts raced with the urgency of a wild river, desperate for any clue that might bring her closer to Jace. The wind whispered through the trees, its haunting melody a reminder of the secrets she bore.

"Jace," she murmured, her voice barely audible above the rustling leaves. "Hold on, my love. We're coming."

As they journeyed deeper into the mountains, the darkness seemed to envelop them. Every step they took was a daring act of resistance against the encroaching shadows. They were determined to reach the old Alexander homestead on their return trip.

Trudging through the thick underbrush, Emma's heart pounded as fiercely as her footsteps. The gnarled roots of ancient trees reached out like grasping hands, attempting to hinder their progress. But she would not be stopped; her love for Jace propelled her forward with an inexorable force.

"Emma," Allen called out from behind, his voice strained. "Slow down. You'll wear yourself out."

She ignored him, focusing on the rhythmic crunch of leaves beneath her boots. Her breaths came in ragged gasps, mirroring the turmoil within her heart. In that moment, doubt crept into the dark recesses of her mind, threatening to overwhelm her.

"Jace," she whispered, a tear tracing its way down her dirt-streaked cheek. "What if I never find you? What if you're already…"

"Emma!" Allen shouted, grabbing her arm and pulling her back just as she was about to stumble over a hidden root. He steadied her, his eyes filled with worry. "You need to stay focused. Jace is out here somewhere, and we have to believe he's still alive."

"Alive?" she echoed, a bitter laugh escaping her lips. "And what if he's not? What if I've already lost him?"

"Then we'll find whoever did this," Allen said, his jaw set. "But you cannot give up hope. Not now. We must continue searching."

Allen's words hit her with full force as she realized that it was her who caused this situation. She had to figure out a way to communicate with Kiera somehow, but it would be difficult since the Sheriff had detained her.

As they pressed on, the sun dipped below the horizon, casting eerie shadows across the forest floor. The air grew colder, chilling Emma to her bones, but she refused to shiver. Fear had no place in her heart. Only determination remained.

"Wait," Sheriff Callahan called out suddenly, holding up a hand to halt their progress. "I found something."

The group gathered around a small clearing, illuminated by the pale moonlight that filtered through the treetops. In the center lay a piece of torn fabric – the same color as the shirt Jace had been wearing when he disappeared.

"Is it…?" Emma's voice trembled, her eyes never leaving the scrap of cloth.

"Could be," Sheriff Callahan replied, his face grim. "Stay here. I'll take a closer look."

As they held their breaths, the sheriff examined the area around the fabric, his flashlight casting eerie shadows upon the trees. A heavy silence settled over the group, broken only by the distant cry of a lone wolf.

"Any luck?" Allen asked, his voice barely audible.

Sheriff Callahan shook his head, disappointment etched on his weary features. "Nothing else here. But this could still be a clue. We'll keep searching."

Emma's heart clenched at the thought of what might have happened to Jace. She knew she couldn't let her fear consume her; she had to stay strong and find him – no matter the cost. But as the night wore on, the truth seemed to slip further away, shrouded in darkness like the forest that surrounded them.

"Who would do such a thing?" Allen wondered aloud, his voice tinged with desperation.

"Patience, Emma," Sheriff Callahan advised, though his eyes betrayed his apprehension. "We'll uncover the truth soon enough."

It was then that they heard it – a sudden, chilling scream that echoed through the woods, freezing them all in their tracks.

"Jace!" Emma cried, her heart pounding as she raced towards the sound, the others close behind.

As she burst into another clearing, her breath caught in her throat. There, lying on the ground, was a figure – unmoving, silent. The moonlight revealed a pool of blood seeping into the earth.

"Who is it?" she whispered, her voice trembling with dread. "Is it…?"

"Stay back, Emma," Sheriff Callahan ordered, his own voice strained. "Let me check."

The group held their breaths as the sheriff approached the figure, his flashlight slowly revealing the truth. And as the beam of light fell upon the face of the motionless form, a collective gasp echoed through the night – for there, lying in a pool of blood, was someone they knew all too well.

But it wasn't Jace.

17

Kane

The sun was setting over the city of Malathar, casting long shadows on the ground as Jace and Raina stood atop a hill overlooking the ancient fortifications. The thick walls, built from the dark, impenetrable stone of Nelhelm, seemed to stretch forever into the horizon, a testament to the El's prowess in defense.

"Mitra's questioning made me feel like I'm on trial for something I didn't do," Jace said quietly, his eyes scanning the walls, assessing their strength.

Raina stood beside him, her blonde hair whipping around her face in the cool breeze. She shared his concern, her steel blue eyes reflecting the uncertain world they found themselves in. "I know," she replied. "It's like they don't trust us."

"Maybe it's not about trust," Jace mused, rubbing his chin thoughtfully. "Maybe it's about control. They need to know where we stand, how far he can push us."

As they mulled over their recent interrogations, a rustling sound caught their attention. Reynard emerged, his tall frame easily gliding through the underbrush, his red hair standing out against the fading daylight. He approached them with an urgency that sent a shiver down Jace's spine.

"Jace, Raina," he gasped, his breath coming in short spurts. "I've just heard something you need to know. Kane is going to try to remand you to your quarters again. I hear he thinks it's for the El's protection."

Jace and Raina exchanged a worried glance. They had been confined to their quarters before, with only occasional brief excursions allowed under the watchful eyes of Kane's guards. It was a suffocating feeling, being constantly monitored and restricted in their movements.

"Do you know why?" Raina asked, her voice tense.

"I overheard him talking to Mitra," Reynard replied, his expression grave. "He thinks that someone is targeting us and that it would be safer for you to stay in your rooms."

Everything around them seemed to freeze in time for a moment. Jace's heart was racing, and his face showed disbelief as he processed what was happening. Raina's mouth hung open, and her eyes widened in shock. It was difficult to believe that Mitra would allow this to happen once more.

"Are you certain?" Jace asked, his voice barely a whisper.

"Absolutely," Reynard replied solemnly. "I overheard Kane speaking with another El. He believes you're a risk to our people's safety."

Jace clenched his fists, anger flaring within him. But as the initial shock subsided, he forced himself to think rationally. The walls of Malathar stood strong in the distance, a symbol of the strength and unity they needed to face their common enemy. Turning to Raina, he saw a similar mix of defiance and determination in her eyes. They would not be imprisoned without a fight. Together, they would confront Kane and make their voices heard for the sake of both the El and the Gaians.

The air hung heavy with tension as Jace, Raina, and Reynard stood together, their eyes locked in a wordless exchange. Malathar's shadow loomed over them, its imposing walls a silent witness to the brewing conflict.

"Kane's suspicions could tear us apart," Jace said quietly, his steel-blue eyes darkening with concern. "If the El lose faith in us Gaians, we won't be able to stand against Belloch."

"Agreed," Reynard nodded solemnly, his red hair rustling in the breeze. "But we need to tread carefully. Confronting Kane might only fuel his paranoia."

Raina's knuckles whitened as she clenched her fists, defiance blazing in her steel-blue eyes. "We can't just sit back and let him imprison us. There must be a way to prove our loyalty without submitting to his whims."

As they spoke, Aydis and Ahat approached, anxiety etched on their faces. It was clear that word of Kane's plan had spread throughout Nelhelm, and the time for action was now.

"Jace, Raina, we must confront Kane," Ahat said, his voice trembling with urgency. "If we don't stand up to him, who knows what other measures he'll take to ensure the El's "safety"?"

"Let's go," Aydis agreed, determination shining in her eyes. "Together, we can make Kane see reason."

And so, the five of them marched towards Kane's quarters, each step echoing with the weight of their conviction. The sun dipped below Malathar's walls, casting long shadows as they entered the dimly lit chamber where Kane awaited them.

Kane sat in his chair, a stern expression on his face as he observed the group's approach. Jace noticed that there were several other Els in the room, their eyes flickering with curiosity and suspicion.

"What is the meaning of this?" Kane demanded as they came to a stop in front of him. "Why have you come uninvited?"

"Kane," Jace began, his voice steady and strong. "We've heard about your plans to lock us away again, and we've come to discuss this matter with you."

"Ah, so Reynard couldn't keep his mouth shut," Kane sneered, his black eyes narrowing as he glared at the scout. "You should know better than to question my decisions, Reynard."

Jace stood his ground, unfazed by Kane's hostility. "We are not questioning your decisions but rather seeking to understand them. Why do you feel the need to lock us away again? Have we not proven our loyalty time and again?"

Kane's expression softened slightly as he leaned back in his chair, studying each of them in turn. "It is not just about loyalty," he said slowly. "It is about protecting the El from potential threats."

"What threats?" Raina challenged, her voice sharp with anger. "We have worked alongside the El fighting against Belloch and his minions. We have risked our lives for the sake of Nelhelm."

"Or perhaps it was merely a ploy to gain our trust before betraying us," Kane retorted, his voice cold and unyielding.

"Enough!" Aydis shouted, her patience wearing thin. "We are here to protect Nelhelm, not destroy it. You cannot let fear and suspicion cloud your judgment!"

"Jace," Kane said, turning his gaze upon the young Gaian. "Do you truly believe all of you can be trusted? That your people won't turn on us when we least expect it?"

Jace hesitated, his heart pounding in his chest. He thought of Emma, of the life they'd left behind, and the sacrifices they'd made to protect the people of Nelhelm. In that moment, he knew with absolute certainty where his loyalties lay.

"Kane," Jace replied, his voice unwavering. "I would give my life for the El and their cause. I am willing to face whatever consequences you deem necessary, but know this: imprisoning us will only weaken our alliance when we need it most."

As the last words hung in the air, Jace could see the flicker of doubt in Kane's eyes. But whether it would be enough to sway him remained uncertain.

The air in the chamber seemed to grow heavy as if a storm was brewing. Voices grew quiet, and eyes darted between Kane and Jace, anticipating the next move in this dangerous game. Just as Kane opened his mouth to respond, a new voice cut through the tension like a blade.

"Kane, stand down." Mitra, the El's leader, strode into the room with an air of authority that demanded attention. Her golden hair shimmered in the dim light, and her piercing blue eyes locked onto Kane. "We will not imprison our allies."

Mitra's words hung heavy in the air, silencing any further arguments from Kane. She turned her attention to Jace and Raina, giving them a small nod of acknowledgment.

Jace and Raina exchanged a look of relief as they realized that Mitra was on their side. They had been worried that the El's mistrust would lead to their imprisonment, but now it seemed that they had an ally in Mitra.

"We have no intention of betraying you," Raina spoke up, her voice calm and resolute. "We are here to help in any way we can."

Mitra nodded, her gaze shifting to Kane. "Kane, I understand your concerns, but we cannot let fear dictate our actions. The Gaians have proven themselves to be valuable allies in our fight against Belloch."

Kane's expression remained stoic, but Jace could see a flicker of annoyance in his eyes. It was clear that he did not trust the Gaians, but he also knew better than to defy Mitra's orders.

"I will keep a close eye on them," Kane finally conceded, his tone begrudging.

Jace nodded solemnly, knowing that he and Raina would have to work extra hard to prove their loyalty to the El. He glanced at Raina, who returned his gaze with a determined look in her eyes. They were in this together.

As Mitra turned to leave the chamber, Kane stepped forward once more." It is not just about trust," he said. "We must also consider the safety of our people."

"I am well aware of that," Mitra replied firmly. "But we cannot let fear dictate our actions. We must find a way to coexist peacefully with our allies if we are to defeat Belloch and his army."

As Mitra's words echoed in the chamber, Jace could feel his heart racing, torn between relief and a growing sense of unease. He exchanged a glance with Raina, whose eyes were clouded with uncertainty. Could they trust the El? Even now, it felt as if there were secrets hidden just beneath the surface, threatening to unravel everything they'd built together.

"Jace, Raina," Mitra addressed them directly, her tone firm but compassionate. "I apologize for Kane's actions. He acted out of fear and misguided loyalty, but I assure you, your place among us is secure."

"Thank you, Mitra," Jace replied, his voice steady despite the tumultuous thoughts swirling within him. What did it mean to fight alongside beings who still harbored doubts about their loyalty? Would they ever truly belong?

"Very well," Kane grumbled, clearly displeased by the turn of events. He shot a dark look in Jace and Raina's direction before storming out of the chamber, his footsteps echoing loudly down the corridor.

"Please, don't let Kane's doubts shake your faith in us," Mitra said softly, her eyes filled with empathy. "We have a common enemy, and we must stand together if we are to have any hope of defeating Belloch."

With those final words, Mitra swept out of the chamber, leaving Jace and the others behind. For a moment, there was silence as they all processed what had just transpired.

Jace could sense that this was not over yet - there would still be doubts and suspicions lingering among some members of the El. But for now, they had been granted a chance to prove themselves and earn their place among their new allies.

As they left the chamber together, Jace felt a sense of relief wash over him. They had narrowly avoided imprisonment or worse - and now it was up to them to make sure it stayed that way.

"Raina," Jace whispered as they walked side by side through the dimly lit corridors. "Are you alright?"

She hesitated for a moment before answering, her voice barely audible. "I... I don't know, Jace. I want to believe that we can trust the El, but after all we've been through, I can't help but fear that our bond may unravel at any moment."

Jace never thought their fear could become a reality, slowly eroding the strength of their alliance. Giving in to despair would only benefit Belloch's agenda. Despite the looming doubts, they persevered in their fight for a future built on trust and unity.

Jace leaned against the cold stone wall, his breath forming small clouds in the chilly air. The vast expanse of the Malathar palace in front of him. The walls of the palace are cool and smooth to the touch, the polished stones giving off a faint sheen. The ground is made up of interlocking tiles cold against Jace's feet. He longed for the familiar woods of his home but knew that he was now irrevocably tied to this alien world.

"Kane's intentions, whatever they may be... are unsettling," Raina murmured, her steel blue eyes clouded with doubt as she stood beside him.

"Indeed," Jace agreed, rubbing his hands together for warmth. "But Mitra seems to have our best interests at heart."

Raina's brow furrowed, and she crossed her arms. "I don't know, Jace. I've seen firsthand what happens when you cross powerful people like Kane. It never ends well."

"Your past experiences weigh heavy on you," Jace observed gently, reaching out to touch her arm. "We must tread carefully, but also remember that Mitra holds sway here as well."

Raina nodded in agreement, her eyes lost in the memories of her own troubled past. "It's true," she admitted. "But having Kane constantly doubting us can create many challenges."

"We need to trust Mitra can handle Kane," Jace said, his mind torn between his desire to return home to Emma and the obligations he felt towards El and Nelhelm. "Yet, confronting Belloch alone is an insurmountable task. The assistance of the El is crucial, even if it requires sailing these perilous seas."

"Is it worth it?" Raina asked quietly, leaning into Jace's embrace. "Are all these sacrifices, all this uncertainty, worth the chance to defeat Belloch?"

Jace hesitated, his thoughts a whirlwind of emotions: loyalty to his people, love for Emma, and the weight of responsibility on his shoulders. "I don't know. But we've come this far – we can't turn back now."

"Perhaps," Raina sighed, her own heart heavy with doubt. "But do not forget, Jace, that in the end, we are all merely pawns in a larger game. We must choose our allegiances wisely."

Jace was confused by Raina's statement. He wasn't even sure of his own location, let alone any information about the three Gaians.

"We can't wait for someone else to save us," Raina declared. "We have to take control and find our own way."

"But how?" Jace questioned.

"By seeking out the truth at Mount Myra for ourselves," Raina answered confidently. "I'm sure Reynard would be willing to guide us there."

The heavy air of Nelhelm bore down on Jace and Raina like a suffocating blanket, the tension between them thick enough to cut with a knife. The city's ancient stone walls loomed over them, casting ominous shadows that seemed to reflect their mounting uncertainty. Jace ran a hand through his dark hair, his steel blue eyes clouded with indecision.

"I just don't know," Jace replied.

Raina's gaze flickered from the towering walls to Jace's troubled expression, her own blue eyes alight with determination. She squared her shoulders, steeling herself for the difficult decision she knew they must make together.

She addressed him with determination in her voice, "Jace, I am fully aware of the risks involved. But we must not let fear control our decisions. We did not come to Nelhelm by choice, and though Mitra has shown herself to be wise and just, trusting her puts us in Kane's crosshairs."

As the weight of their decision pressed upon them, Jace found himself torn between conflicting emotions – the desperate longing to return home to Gaia and the woman he loved and the El cause that had brought them to this strange new world. He clenched his fists, his heart racing with the force of his inner turmoil.

"Raina, my heart aches for home," he admitted, his eyes welling with unshed tears. "But I cannot abandon El when they need us the most. Perhaps trusting Mitra is the key to securing a future for us all."

"Jace," Raina murmured, reaching out to grasp his hand in a gesture of solidarity. "I, too, struggle with the ghosts of my past, but we must not let them cloud our judgment. We have come so far together, and I believe that Mitra will guide us on a treacherous path."

Raina suggested, "Let's just sneak away to Mount Myra instead of waiting for Kane's wrath here. We can find the information and figure out our journey home on our own."

At that moment, Jace felt a surge of determination and coldness course through him – a renewed sense of purpose that seemed to lift the oppressive weight from his chest. He met Raina's gaze.

"We must have faith in Mitra," he announced with conviction. "If you still wish to make the journey to Mount Myra, I understand completely."

After a moment of silence, Raina responded, "I have a strong sense that we should stay together, though I cannot explain why. And if I can't persuade you to leave, I will stand by your side."

As Jace and Raina stood before the ancient walls of Malathar, their decision echoing through the stillness of the night, they knew they had made a choice that irrevocably bound them together – a choice that would shape the very course of their destiny. The battle was far from over but united in their conviction, there was no force in this world or any other that could tear them apart.

With their decision made, Jace and Raina approached Kane with a steely determination in their eyes. The chamber they entered was dimly lit, the flickering torchlight casting eerie shadows across the stone walls. They found Kane standing at a massive, intricately carved table, his strong hands splayed out over a map of Nelhelm.

"Kane," Jace began, his voice echoing through the chamber, "we have something to say."

"Speak then, but choose your words carefully," Kane replied, not lifting his gaze from the map. His tone was cool and calculating as if he were already anticipating what they would say.

"Your plan to imprison us for the El's protection is misguided," Raina interjected, her voice unwavering. "We have proven ourselves, and we will stand by the El, no matter the cost."

Jace nodded, his heart pounding in his chest as he felt the weight of their defiance. "We trust Mitra's judgment," he added, "and we are committed to fighting together."

A moment of silence hung in the air before Kane finally looked up, his black eyes piercing into theirs. "You dare question my motives?" he asked, his voice heavy with menace.

Kane's words hung in the air, a tense silence falling over the chamber. Jace and Raina stood before him, their determination unshaken despite the looming threat of Kane's anger.

"We question any decision that divides us when unity is needed most," Jace retorted, feeling the familiar fire of resolve burning within him.

"Enough," Kane growled, slamming his fist down on the table. "I don't have time for this foolishness." He turned to leave, his cloak billowing behind him, when a messenger burst into the room, breathless with urgency.

"Lord Kane!" the messenger cried. "A large cambion army approaches Malathar! We must ready our defenses!"

The news struck like a thunderbolt, the words hanging heavily in the charged air. Instantly, the tension between them seemed insignificant compared to the impending threat. Jace and Raina exchanged a worried glance, their thoughts racing as they tried to process the gravity of the situation.

"Damnation," Kane muttered, his expression hardening. "This changes everything."

"Let us help," Jace offered, his eyes searching Kane's for a flicker of acceptance.

"Fine," Kane conceded, his voice strained. "But know this: if you prove to be a liability or betray the El in any way, I will show no mercy."

"Understood," Raina replied, her jaw set with determination. "We won't let you down."

With no time to waste, they hurried towards Mitra's chambers, the air thick with tension and anticipation. As they prepared to face the approaching Cambion horde, Jace and Raina knew that their loyalty to the El and their trust in Mitra would be tested like never before.

18

Preparations

The heavy oaken doors of Mitra's chamber groaned as they swung inward, a resounding echo announcing the arrival of Jace, Raina, and Kane. The room, vast and vaulted, was awash with the orange glow of torchlight that flickered against the walls, casting long, dancing shadows. A sense of ancient power lingered in the air, an invisible weight that seemed to press upon Jace's shoulders as he stepped into the sanctum.

Ahat, the tactician with eyes like polished obsidian, stood beside Aydis, whose presence was as serene as a still lake. They were deep in hushed conversation, their words lost beneath the ambient crackle of the nearby hearth.

Captain Forset, towering above them all, surveyed the newcomers with a gaze as piercing as the spears that adorned the chamber's corners.

"Silence," boomed Mitra's voice, arresting any whisper that dared persist. Her form was obscured behind a veil of incense smoke that curled around her like protective serpents.

Jace felt Raina's hand brush him, a fleeting touch that sent a current of unspoken understanding between them. He could sense her tension, a mirror of his own, as Kane moved past them, his footsteps deliberate and certain. The man's silhouette was rigid, the very embodiment of discipline.

"The Scouts have returned," Mitra continued, her tone cutting through the silence. "The Cambion army advances. Their numbers are like grains of sand in the desert—countless, unyielding."

Kane retorted, "The Cambions have never been this daring before."

Mitra responded, "Their numbers have never been this vast."

Jace's heart hammered against his ribs, a drumbeat of war that resonated in time with the pulsating fear that filled the chamber. He exchanged a glance with Raina, seeing his own dread reflected in the steel of her blue eyes.

"Darkness rides with them," Mitra declared, her face now emerging from the smoke, weathered lines etched into her skin like runes. "A devil leads their vanguard, cloaked in malice not seen for a thousand years."

Jace felt a chill run down his spine at these words, and he sensed that the others in the room were feeling it, too. A devil? It couldn't be true. Devils had been thought to be nothing but a myth, a bedtime story used to scare children into obedience. But if what Mitra said was true, then they were facing a formidable enemy indeed.

"Kane," whispered Aydis under her breath, her words barely reaching Jace's ear. "Do you believe this changes our strategy?"

"Every plan must adapt to the enemy's movements," Kane replied without turning, his eyes fixed on Mitra. "We knew Belloch would not hold back his foulest creations."

Mitra's words lingered in the air, weighing heavily on Jace's mind. But instead of succumbing to fear, he felt a surge of determination well up inside him. He was determined to protect his people and their homes, using every bit of strength he had.

"Let us not falter now," Forset intoned, his voice as steadfast as the mountains of old. "Their strength is formidable, but it is not unassailable."

"Indeed," agreed Ahat, his sharp gaze calculating, already dissecting battle lines and formations within the theater of his mind.

Aydis stepped forward, her voice a soothing balm amidst the brewing storm. "Fear can be a weapon, but so can hope. We stand united, each of us a bulwark against the coming tide."

Jace felt a swell of pride as he looked upon his fellow protectors. They were a diverse group, each with their own strengths and weaknesses, but united in purpose. He knew that together, they could face any challenge.

Mitra's gaze swept over them as if peering into the very depths of their souls. "Prepare yourselves," she commanded. "The walls of Malathar shall bear witness to our defiance. Let the battlements be lined with archers and siege machines ready to sing the song of resistance."

The chamber hummed with the energy of impending conflict, a symphony of clashing wills and fates intertwined. Jace felt the familiar pull of destiny tugging at his core, the weight of responsibility anchoring him firmly to the present.

"Let the Cambions come," he thought, the fire of determination igniting within him. "We are ready."

The air in Mitra's chamber hung heavy, saturated with the tang of heated steel and the undercurrent of magic that whispered through the ancient stones. Jace stood among the assembly, his steel blue eyes reflecting the flickering torchlight that danced across the walls like sparks from a forge. He felt the familiar weight of his father's hunting knife against his thigh, a grounding presence amongst the chaos.

"Let Belloch spread his corruption elsewhere," he proclaimed, his words slicing through the tension like an arrow. "We will not yield Nelhelm to his twisted desires."

Around him, faces turned; Ahat's calculating eyes narrowed, Forset's stoic expression softened, and Aydis nodded, her presence as reassuring as the gentle touch of a healer's hand. Kane's jaw set in solidarity, while Raina's unwavering gaze bolstered Jace's spirit.

"From the teachings of my youth to the untamed wilderness where I honed my skills," Jace continued, "every chapter of my life has been leading me to this moment." His heart thundered in his chest, a fervent drum rallying him to embrace his destiny.

"Jace Alexander," Mitra intoned, her voice carrying the wisdom of ages, "you are more than flesh and bone. Within you lies the essence of a true Gaian, one whose potential can turn the tides of war."

A shiver ran through Jace as if the very essence of Gaia had whispered secrets into his soul. His steely gaze lifted toward the vaulted ceiling, where shadows played among the etched runes of protection. He imagined them alive, coursing with energy, ready to stand sentinel over their fated battle.

"Then I shall stand tall as one of Gaia's chosen," Jace declared, the gravity of his role settling upon him like a mantle. His fingers brushed the hilt of his sword, the cool metal a promise of resistance, of battles to come.

"Your potential is vast," Aydis said, her voice a lyrical echo in the stone chamber. "And your spirit, unbreakable."

"Unbreakable," reluctantly echoed Kane, clapping a firm hand onto Jace's shoulder, a warrior acknowledging another.

"Unbreakable," Jace affirmed inwardly, his thoughts a fortress against doubt. He envisioned himself standing upon the battlements, bow in hand, an unyielding guardian between the darkness and the light.

"Indeed," Ahat chimed in, a smirk playing on his lips. "But remember, Jace, the potential is but the kindling. It is courage that sets it ablaze."

"Courage we have in abundance," Jace replied, allowing himself a small smile. His heart swelled with the camaraderie of these warriors, these protectors of realms unknown to his past self.

"Then let us sharpen our blades and ready ourselves," Mitra commanded. "For when the Cambions march, they will not find us weak or afraid. They will face our brave hearts and indomitable wills."

"Indomitable," Jace thought, savoring the word as he fixed the image of Emma, his anchor, in his mind. For her, for all of them, he would be the shield against the encroaching night. He was ready to write his story, not with ink, but with the steel of resolve and the fire of his newfound purpose.

The atmosphere in Mitra's chamber seemed to vibrate with the weight of the news they had just received. The faces around them were cast in shadow, their features flickering in the dim light of the torches. Every breath was a solemn pledge to fight against the encroaching darkness. Jace could feel it too - a heaviness not just on his shoulders but deep within his bones.

"Reynard's not yet returned from his scouting," Aydis said, her voice laced with concern. "He should have been back by now."

"His absence is... unsettling." The words slipped from Kane's lips before he could corral them, voicing the unease that gnawed at his insides. Reynard, the red-haired fox of a man, was never late, never careless.

"His delay speaks of risks taken for our sake," Mitra added, a grim undertone to his deep voice.

"Or dangers encountered," Ahat interjected, tilting his head. "The Cambions are no fools. They know the value of a good scout."

"Then let us hope Reynard's guile serves him better than their cruelty," Mitra stated flatly. There was steel in her gaze, a leader's resolve that brooked no argument.

Jace's thoughts raced. Reynard had saved his life more times than he cared to count, his keen eye and quicker wit finding paths through peril that would have ensnared lesser souls. He imagined the scout now, alone amidst the shadows, gathering secrets like so many scattered leaves, every moment stretching taut as a bowstring.

"Preparations must begin immediately," Mitra declared, breaking into Jace's reverie. "We cannot afford to be caught off guard."

"Agreed. We fortify the defenses, stockpile our resources, and train every ablebody to fight," Kane said, already listing tasks in his mind. "This will not be a simple siege to endure—it will be survival."

"Training..." Jace mused, rolling the idea around in his head. It was one thing to embrace his role as a Gaian, another entirely to step into the boots of a soldier. But his newfound strength thrummed within him, eager to be tested.

"Your skills with the bow will be vital on the battlements," Aydis said, meeting his gaze with a confidence that bolstered his own. "You've come far, Jace. Trust in your abilities."

"Every arrow will carry with it my vow to protect this land," Jace promised, the words resonating in his chest like the tolling of a great bell. He pictured the Cambion army in his mind's eye, a relentless, dark wave, and himself a steadfast breakwater against their fury.

"Each of us has a part to play," Mitra said, locking eyes with each person in turn. "We are the last line of defense for Gaia and Nelhelm. Our unity is our strength."

"Unity," Jace echoed silently, feeling the bond between them all. They were disparate threads woven into a single tapestry of defiance—a tapestry that would not unravel while he yet drew breath.

"Let this be the hour when we draw swords together." Kane's voice was a rallying cry, a call to arms that set Jace's blood aflame with purpose.

"Draw swords together," Jace repeated, the mantra solidifying his resolve. With Reynard absent, the urgency pressed upon them all the harder. But fear would not take root in his heart. Instead, determination blossomed, fierce and unrelenting.

"Ready yourselves," Mitra instructed. "For soon, the fate of all we hold dear will rest upon our courage."

And in that moment, Jace knew that whatever awaited them beyond the chamber's walls, they would face it as one. For Reynard, for Gaia, for Nelhelm—for the future that beckoned just beyond the horizon of war.

Jace watched as figures on the map shifted, tokens of wood and metal moving to form lines of defense. His mind raced with strategies and counter-strategies, playing out scenarios of battle like a grim game of chess. They spoke of positions and contingencies, but behind every word lay the unspoken truth: this fight would test their limits and, perhaps, be their last stand.

Jace addressed Raina, his companion, who had a determined expression on her face. "We have prepared for this," he reminded her. "Trust in your abilities and let your intuition lead the way."

Jace did not know what had come over him. He found himself taking charge with a cold calmness. It all felt so natural to him as if he had been born for this role.

"Always," she replied, her hand resting on the hilt of her sword—a silent vow that she was ready for whatever came.

"Good," Jace thought, feeling the cold touch of fear recede just enough to let hope shine through. "We will need every advantage."

As they dispersed to carry out their tasks, Jace's gaze lingered on the walls of Malathar, those venerable ramparts that had guarded generations. Their stones seemed to whisper with the voices of the past, urging him onward, steeling his spirit for the clash to come.

"Let the devils come," he murmured under his breath, squaring his shoulders. "We are the shield that guards the realms of men and El alike. We are the flame that burns against the dark."

And with that, Jace stepped forward to meet his destiny, the ember of defiance kindling within him into a blaze. He knew the hour was dark, and darker still it might become. But they would stand firm, for if they faltered, all the world might fall into shadow.

Jace's steely blue eyes swept over the ancient chamber, its walls etched with the intricate history of battles past as if each carving whispered secrets only the worthy could hear. The air hung heavy with foreboding, and the sense of an ending – or a beginning – clung to the cold stone like morning mist.

"Friends," Jace said, his voice echoing slightly in Mitra's chamber, "I came to Nelhelm seeking answers, but I have found more than just riddles in the dark." He stepped closer to the center of the room, where the light from the braziers threw dancing shadows across his determined face. "I have found a cause worth fighting for."

The others stood around him, their faces an array of stoic masks carved by the threat looming over their lands. Jace's gaze met Raina's, and he saw his own resolve mirrored in her. "I stand with you, and together, we will defend Gaia and Nelhelm against Belloch's corruption. We will not let darkness consume our homes."

"Your words are heartening, Jace Alexander," Aydis said, her voice as clear as the first light of dawn. "But the threat we face... it is not just about our homes. It is the very essence of life that hangs in the balance. If the Cambions breach our defenses, it will be the end of Malathar and will expose Mount Myra."

"Then we shall not let them pass," Kane interjected, his hands resting on the pommel of his sword, his eyes like flint, ready to strike fire.

"Indeed," Forset added, his broad frame casting a reassuring shadow. "Not just for ourselves, but for those who come after us. For the legacy we leave behind."

As they spoke, the door creaked open, and Reynard slipped in, his tall, thin silhouette unmistakable even in the dim light. His red hair was like a banner of defiance against the gathering gloom.

"Reynard!" Jace and Raina said in unison, with a sense of relief.

Jace persisted, "Where have you been?"

Reynard barely responded to Jace and Raina's presence before Mitra interrupted.

"Reynard, what news?" Mitra demanded, her voice cutting through the thick tension.

"None," he replied, shaking his head. His keen eyes scanned the chamber, noting every face. "The Cambions move in silence, and even the whispers of the wind hold no tales of their passing."

"Then we prepare blind," Jace thought, feeling the weight of uncertainty press upon his shoulders. "But not unready." Aloud, he said, "We know their strength, and we know our own. Let us make ready our defense. Reynard, you can join us once you've cleaned up."

"Already on my way," Reynard said with a nod, turning toward the door with the silence of a shadow.

Jace watched him leave and then turned back to the council. "We will fight with everything we have," he vowed, his voice ringing with a conviction that seemed to bolster the flickering hope in the chamber.

"Every arrow, every stone, every sword," Raina echoed, her hand gripping the hilt of her blade as if she could already feel the enemy before her.

The group dispersed, moving with purpose, their steps echoing off the stone floors. Jace's mind raced with battle plans, contingencies, and the haunting knowledge that, despite their preparations, the unknowns outnumbered certainties.

"Emma," he whispered to himself, the image of his fiancée a talisman against despair. "For you, for all of us, I will stand strong."

From the chamber that had become a war room, Jace looked out, his heart a drumbeat of war, his soul an anthem of resistance. The walls of Malathar awaited him, and there he would take his place among the defenders, a link in the chain that bound the present to the future, the living to the memory of the fallen.

"Let the devil come," he thought, the ember of defiance now a roaring inferno within him. "We are ready."

The twilight cast long shadows across the stone-hewn chamber, where the air hung heavy with the scent of burning incense and the quiet murmur of anxious voices. Jace's steel blue eyes scanned the faces around him, noting the grim set to every jaw, the determination in their postures as they gathered around Mitra. The ancient being, which seemed carved from the very rock of the chamber itself, raised a hand for silence.

As soon as Reynard returned, Mitra began to give out assignments.

"Here is what I have decided," Mitra's voice reverberated through the room like a solemn bell toll. "Jace and Raina, you will accompany Forset's battalion. Ahat and Aydis, you will join them."

"Reynard," Mitra continued, turning to the tall, red-haired scout who stood with an unreadable expression, "you are under Kane's command."

Kane, black-eyed and inscrutable, gave Reynard a nod so slight it could have been mistaken for a twitch. Jace caught Reynard's faint smirk before he turned away, leaving Jace to wonder at the strategy behind these pairings.

"Right," Ahat clapped Jace on the shoulder, his grin wolfish. "Let's see if those ancient texts you love taught you anything about slaying demons, eh?"

"Enough, Ahat," Aydis chided softly, her presence soothing. "We each have our strengths. Jace, Raina, we'll face this together."

Jace's heart thudded in his chest, a rhythm paced by the urgency of their plight. As they rallied, a sense of unity tightened around the group like the lacing of a warrior's boot. They were disparate threads woven into a single tapestry of purpose.

"Demons or not," Jace muttered, more to himself than anyone else, "we hold the line."

"Indeed," Raina agreed, the steely glint in her eye mirroring his own resolve.

"Remember," Kane's voice cut through the camaraderie, every syllable a command, "discipline is what will save us when the chaos descends."

"Discipline and a good sword arm," Reynard retorted, his humor a thin veneer over the tension in his voice.

"Both of which you possess," Aydis responded, placing a reassuring hand on Raina's arm, then on Jace's. He felt the warmth of her touch seep into him, bolstering his courage.

They moved toward the Armory, the sound of their boots on the stone floor a solemn march. Jace's mind raced with strategies, potential pitfalls, and the weight of lives in his hands. How many would stand after the battle? Would he?

"Protect Malathar, protect Nelhelm," Jace whispered under his breath, a mantra to focus his thoughts. His fingers traced the leather grip of his sword, a tactile promise of the fight to come.

"Will your sweetheart be watching over you?" Ahat teased, elbowing Jace playfully.

"Emma is always with me," Jace replied, his voice steady despite the ache in his heart. "Her spirit is my shield."

"Then we have nothing to fear," Raina said sarcastically.

As they strapped on their weapons and adjusted their armor, each movement was deliberate; each glance exchanged a silent vow. The eve of battle wrapped around them, a cloak woven of anticipation and dread.

"Let them come," Jace thought, his pulse a drumbeat echoing through the chamber and beyond, to where the walls of Malathar loomed, awaiting the storm on the horizon. "We are the storm that awaits them."

The golden hue of twilight seeped through the stained-glass windows of the armory, casting a kaleidoscope of colors onto armored figures who stood in silence. Jace felt the weight of his chainmail as if it were the collective hope of every soul that called this land their own. The air was thick with the scent of oiled leather and cold steel.

"Remember, we fight not just for the land beneath our feet but for the very essence of life," Forset's voice reverberated against the stone walls, steady as the ancient trees of Nelhelm. "For Gaia, for our future."

Jace caught Raina's determined gaze, her eyes like the steel blue of a winter sky, unyielding. He nodded, feeling an unspoken bond tighten between them. They were warriors of the same cloth, cut from the harsh fabric of necessity.

"May the valor of our hearts eclipse the shadow of Belloch," Aydis added solemnly, her voice a soft melody amidst the rising tension.

Reynard leaned against the cool stone, bowstring twanged tight between his fingers, a sly grin playing on his lips. "If they want a devil's welcome, let's indulge them with a taste of hellfire."

Jace's thoughts tumbled like river stones, smoothed over by years of contemplation and study. His father's words echoed in his mind, 'Always be true to your heart, son. It knows the way.' That truth now resonated with the clarity of a bell struck at midnight.

"Every arrow counts; every sword swing matters," Kane stated, his black eyes scanning the assembly, assessing, calculating. "We are the bulwark against the darkness."

"Tonight, we sleep with swords at hand," Mitra declared, her presence as formidable as the mountains themselves. "At dawn, we rise as one united force."

They dispersed, each to their quarters, the silence heavy with the gravity of what lay ahead. In the solitude of his own space, Jace sat upon the edge of his cot, tracing the runes carved into his weapon. The symbols spoke of protection, courage, and victory – he hoped they'd hold true in the clutches of war.

"Tomorrow, when I face that battlefield," Jace thought, "it will be with the heart of a protector, the resolve of a survivor." He envisioned Emma's face, the way her smile could cut through any gloom. "I fight for her, for all the silent prayers she whispers into the night."

Jace lay back, armor still adorning his body, and closed his eyes. There was no more planning or preparation to be done, only the wait for the first light of dawn. Sleep would be fitful if it came at all.

As slumber tugged at the edges of his consciousness, the voices of his companions mingled with the ghosts of his past, forging a chorus of fortitude within him. Ahat's jests, Aydis's comfort, Reynard's wry humor – they coalesced into the drumbeat of war.

"Let us meet destiny with blades drawn and spirits undaunted," he murmured into the gathering darkness.

The night passed in a blur of half-dreamt visions and restless anticipation. When Jace awoke, the chamber was filled with the gray prelude to sunrise. He rose, muscles taut, mind clear, and joined the others at the battlements. They lined up shoulder to shoulder, a mosaic of determination etched upon every face.

"Today, we write history with our courage," Jace proclaimed, his voice carrying over the embattled city. "For Gaia, for Nelhelm, for all that we cherish."

"Let the Cambions come," they whispered as one. "We stand ready."

And so, with hearts ablaze and eyes set upon the horizon, the alarm sounds, signaling the beginning of the end—or perhaps, the end of the beginning.

19

Battle For Malathar

Dawn was a grey smear on the horizon, a hesitant witness to the coming storm of war. Aydis strapped on her leather bracers, and each one embossed with runes of protection, her eyes fixed and resolute. The air was thick with the scent of oil as she ran a whetstone along the length of her sword, the blade singing a low, lethal note.

"Steel won't fail us this day," she murmured, not to her companions but to the very essence of battle itself.

Ahat, ever the giant among them, was clad in mail that glimmered faintly with an enchantment known only to his kin. He hoisted his sword, the pommel engraved with depictions of ancient victories, each a testament to fallen foes. His laughter rumbled like distant thunder.

"Let them come," he boomed. "We will write new legends upon their bones."

Jace Alexander felt the familiar weight of his longbow, a comforting presence in his callused hands. Emma's face flashed across his mind—sweet Emma, with her sunlit smile—and he pushed the image away. It was not the time for soft thoughts. He slung a quiver over his shoulder; arrows fletched with the feathers of the sacred roc, known to find their mark even in the hearts of shadows.

"Stay sharp," Jace said, steel blue eyes scanning the preparations. "The cambions won't fall to wishes and whispers."

"Nor to brute strength alone," added Raina, her voice steady as she tested the draw of her own bow. Her blonde hair, usually a bright flame, seemed muted in the

pre-dawn light. She caught Jace's gaze, and something unspoken passed between them, a shared resolve that needed no words.

"Here they come," Raina breathed out as they ascended the cold stone steps to the battlements.

The sight that greeted them was enough to squeeze the heart with dread. A vast, undulating sea of black smoke roiled across the plains, hiding the true number of their enemy. But it was the movement within the murk, the shifting, sinewy forms of the Cambion Army, that quickened Jace's pulse. Tendrils of darkness coiled around muscular silhouettes brandishing cruel weapons, eager for blood.

"Look at them," Jace muttered, more to himself than anyone else, "moving like wraiths in a nightmare." His fingers tightened on the smooth wood of his bow, finding some comfort in its familiar texture.

"Nightmares are but dreams, lad," Ahat grunted beside him. "And dreams hold no sway over the edge of my sword."

"Or the point of our arrows," added Aydis, her voice a low chant of readiness.

Raina shifted beside Jace, her eyes scanning the horizon. "They think to smother us in fear," she said, her tone laced with defiance. "But we stand as the breakwater against their tide."

"Let's give them a welcome they shan't forget," Jace replied, a steely edge cutting through the fog of his apprehension. He nocked an arrow, drawing back the string with practiced ease.

"Remember," Aydis called out, her silhouette a beacon of determination against the dimming light, "aim for the heart of the smoke—their generals hide there, commanding the throng."

"Then let us blind their eyes and silence their tongues," Jace responded, his focus narrowing to the shadowy figures emerging from the abyss.

The first rays of sunlight pierced the gloom, heralding the dawn of battle as the Cambion horde drew near, and the four warriors stood as one, united by a bond forged in the crucible of war and the unyielding spirit of survival.

The sky turned to a tapestry of chaos, the first volley of arrows from the El archers tearing through it like a hail of vengeance. Jace's arrow flew with them, its flight true and unwavering amidst the symphony of twanging bowstrings. As the arrows rained down upon the advancing Cambion Army, the ground seemed to quiver in response.

"Those blasted fiends," Ahat bellowed over the din, his eyes tracking the arc of the projectiles. "Like ants from the Pit, they come, but we shall crush them!"

"Stay focused," Aydis commanded, her voice cutting through the cacophony. "Hold the line, no matter what comes!"

Jace's gaze was drawn to the plains as he witnessed a terrifying spectacle: the Cambions retaliated with a barrage of their own—a maelstrom of smoldering projectiles that obscured the battlefield. The flaming orbs streaked across the sky, trailing dark smoke, a sight both mesmerizing and horrifying. With deafening roars, they exploded upon impact, shaking the very walls that sheltered them, the concussive blasts sending shockwaves that could be felt in Jace's bones.

"By the gods, why haven't we unleashed our siege engines?" Jace thought frantically, struggling to make sense of the one-sided onslaught. The answer came in a blaze of revelation as the El finally responded. From their positions, they launched glowing spheres of light, their beauty belying their deadly intent. These orbs detonated with thunderous force, bright as miniature suns, illuminating the nightmarish visage of the enemy: the siege weapons of the Cambions were now clearly visible within the infernal ranks.

"Finally," Jace muttered under his breath, a flicker of hope reigniting within him.

On the opposite end of the wall, Raina stood resolute, her silhouette outlined by an ethereal radiance. The newfound power within her surged, and as she released her next arrow, it transformed into a bolt of pure light, slicing through the darkness toward the heart of the enemy.

"See how they falter!" Raina cried out triumphantly.

"Keep at them!" Jace echoed, feeling the same energy coursing through his veins. His next arrow blazed forth, and each shot forged a path of destruction among the Cambions.

"Raina, aim for the—"

"Siege beasts," she completed his thought, her voice ringing clear even as the clamor of war threatened to drown all else.

The siege beasts towered over the battlefield, their massive frames clunking and clanging with every step as they trudged toward the walls. They were grotesque creatures with leathery skin and jagged fangs, their eyes glowing with a malice that made the skin crawl.

"Exactly," he confirmed, watching with satisfaction as their combined efforts began to sow discord among the enemy lines.

"Look at them," Aydis shouted her tone a mixture of awe and encouragement. "They fight like the legends of old!"

"Legends we'll be if we live through this," Ahat grunted, but his eyes shone with pride at the sight of Jace and Raina standing firm against the tide of darkness.

With every arrow imbued with light, with every Cambion felled by their hands, the momentum of the battle shifted. The El warriors took heart from the display of power, their cheers rising above the roar of combat, their swords and spears finding renewed purpose.

"Back, you devils! Back to the abyss that spawned you!" Ahat bellowed, firing his next arrow.

"Stand fast," Jace reminded himself, steadying his breathing. "For Emma, for home, we must prevail."

"Home," Raina whispered, almost inaudibly, yet Jace heard the word as if it were a shout. It was more than a place; it was a promise, a dream they dared to defend against nightmare-made flesh.

"Fight on," Jace said, not just to Raina or their comrades but to his own wavering spirit. "We are the dawn that banishes the night."

A shaft of dying sunlight pierced the murky sky, glinting off Jace's drawn bowstring as he perched atop the battlements. His eyes, reflecting the steel blue of a storm-ravaged sea, narrowed upon the advancing horde below. The Cambions loomed like nightmares given form—towering creatures with muscles like coiled serpents and horns ablaze as if they had dipped their crowns into the heart of a volcano.

"Raina!" Jace called out, his voice slicing through the tumult of battle. "Aim for the lieutenants—the ones with the twisted helms! They're rallying the grunts!"

"Understood," Raina shouted back from the distant wall, her silhouette framed by the fiery arrows she loosed into the darkening void. The light from her bow was a beacon, guiding her shots with unerring precision.

Jace exhaled, allowing instinct to guide his hand. He released a volley, each arrow singing through the air, trailing luminescence. One after another, they found their mark, severing the sinewy threads of command within the Cambion ranks. Monsters fell, their infernal light extinguishing upon the blood-soaked earth.

"See that, brothers and sisters?" an El warrior cried out, his voice brazen with newfound fervor. "The darkness falters beneath their light!"

"Let their courage ignite our own!" another rallied, and soon, the battlements echoed with the resolute cries of the El.

"By the skies, we hold!" Jace muttered under his breath, nocking another arrow. "For every soul still dreaming behind these walls."

"Push them back!" Raina's call resonated across the stone divide, bolstering the hearts of the defenders. Her presence, even at this distance, felt like a palpable force—a wellspring of hope amidst despair.

"Forward!" the El warriors roared in response, their voices a harmonic counterpoint to the cacophony of war. Their spears thrust forth like rays of dawn piercing the night, driving the enemy back step by relentless step.

Jace's mind teetered on the brink of a precipice, thoughts swirling between fear and focus. Each arrow he loosed was a prayer, a plea for survival—for Emma, for the simple life torn from his grasp.

"Is this what destiny feels like?" he thought, the question twining around his soul. There were no answers here, only the relentless rhythm of battle, the thrumming of bowstrings, and the thudding of hearts.

"Stay strong!" he called, his voice cutting through the din to reach every ear along the ramparts. "We are not alone in this fight!"

"Indeed," Raina replied, her affirmation clear even from afar. "United, we are a storm they cannot weather!"

"Storms end, but we endure!" an elder El added, his once-withered arms now steady as he launched a salvo of arrows into the abyss.

With each arc of glowing projectiles, the Cambions hesitated, their advance disrupted by the sudden ferocity of their prey. The tide of battle churned, and for a moment—just a fleeting heartbeat—the El sensed the possibility of triumph.

"Keep pressing!" Jace urged, his voice barely audible over the clamor. "Every fallen foe is a step closer to dawn!"

"Every breath a defiance!" Raina echoed her words blending with his own resolve.

"Until the sun rises again," Jace whispered to himself, drawing back his bowstring and aiming for the heart of the darkness below.

The Cambion horde, a seething mass of muscle and malice, surged forward with the relentlessness of a river bursting its banks. They swarmed at the base of Malathar's mighty walls, their inhuman strength turning them into living ladders as they clambered over one another, each warrior seeking to be the harbinger of doom.

"Looks like the devils fancy themselves climbers now," Ahat quipped, his sword gleaming with an oily sheen as he parried a descending blow from a Cambion that had managed to reach the top. He was always quick with a jest, even as his blade danced death among their foes.

"Then let's remind them of the fall," Jace shot back, stepping forward to meet the climbing menace. His sword, a length of sharpened resolve, cut through the air with a whoosh, severing the clutching hand of a Cambion that reached for the battlement's edge.

Aydis, her own weapon a blur of motion, stood shoulder to shoulder with Raina. "Remember, aim for the joints!" she shouted, punctuating her instruction with a thrust that found the gap in a Cambion's armor, sending it tumbling down into the abyss of its brethren.

"Joints got it," Raina responded her blade a silver flash as it followed Aydis's advice, slicing through sinew and bone. She moved with a grace that belied the ferocity of her strikes, a dance of destruction against the infernal invaders.

"Jace, left flank!" Aydis called out, and he turned just in time to catch a glimpse of a snarling Cambion face before his blade met it head-on, stopping the beast in its tracks. The creature fell back, its flaming horns extinguishing like candles in a storm.

"Nice save," Raina said, her eyes meeting his across the chaos. In that brief exchange, a current of shared purpose flowed between them, reinforcing the bond that the battle had forged.

"Always looking out for you," Jace replied, his chest tightening. Was it fear? Adrenaline? Or something more—a connection that transcended the carnage around them? He pushed the thought aside. There would be time for introspection if they survived this onslaught.

"Look at you two," Ahat teased, ducking a wild swing from a Cambion before delivering a counter that sent the monster plummeting. "If we weren't in the middle of a war, I'd say get a room."

"Focus, Ahat," Aydis snapped, though her lips twitched with amusement. "We've got more climbing vermin to deal with."

"Right you are, fearless leader," Ahat chuckled, moving to intercept another wave of Cambions.

Their camaraderie was a beacon in the darkness, a reminder that they were not mere defenders but a family forged in fire. With every deflected strike, every rallying cry, they stitched the fabric of defiance tighter, holding the line against a tide that sought to engulf them.

"Raina," Jace called, "take my six!"

"On it," she replied, moving with a fluidity that complemented his own style, her blade singing a duet with his. Together, they were a tempest that no infernal force could weather.

"Back to back!" Aydis commanded, and they formed a circle, their weapons extending outward like the spokes of a wheel designed to crush any who dared draw near.

"Circle of death, I like it," Ahat grinned, his blade carving arcs of silver through the air.

"Keep them off the wall!" Jace yelled, feeling the strain in his muscles, the burn in his lungs. Yet within him, a fierce joy bubbled up—an elation born of standing with allies against impossible odds. It was a sensation that filled the hollow spaces within him, lending strength to his weary limbs.

"Stay sharp," Raina warned, her voice steady despite the strain evident in her features. "They're relentless."

"Aren't we all?" Jace murmured, more to himself than anyone else. This was their crucible, the moment when they would either shatter or emerge tempered and unbreakable.

"Let's show this hellspawn what 'relentless' really means," Aydis declared, her gaze scanning the wall for any breaches.

"To the last," Jace agreed, his heart pounding a rhythm that matched the pulse of battle. "Until the end."

"Until the end," echoed Raina, and together, they held fast against the dark tide, united by a bond stronger than steel, a unity that even the Devil himself would struggle to break.

The onslaught had been relentless, a symphony of clashing steel and guttural roars that echoed off the ancient stones of Malathar's walls. But now, a subtle shift began to weave its way through the clamor. It started as a whisper—a murmur of surprise and disbelief among the El warriors—that grew into a roar rivaling the din of battle itself.

"Look there!" one shouted, pointing with a bloodied sword towards a crumbled section of the battlements. "They fall back!"

Indeed, the ranks of the Cambion Army, once locked in a monstrous ascent, were faltering under the weight of their own dead. Bodies tumbled from the high wall, crashing into the fiends still clambering upwards, sowing chaos in their previously unbreakable lines.

"Push them!" Jace bellowed, his voice tearing through the air. His eyes blazed with a light that mirrored the glow surrounding him—a manifestation of the power coursing through his veins. Raina, a mirror image at the other end of the wall, unleashed arrows that sang through the air, each finding its mark with lethal precision.

"By the gods," Ahat gasped, watching as one of Jace's bolts of light impaled a towering Cambion commander, its flaming horns extinguishing like snuffed candles. "He's become Death's own archer."

"Then let's not disappoint her efforts," Aydis replied, rallying the El around them. "We hold this fort or perish trying!"

Jace's mind raced, adrenaline and instinct merging in perfect harmony. He knew Emma was safe, far from this carnage, but here on these walls, he fought not just for survival but for the future they all yearned for—a future free of darkness and despair.

"Press on, my friends!" he cried out, his voice lifting the spirits of those who heard it. The El responded with renewed vigor, their blades flashing faster, their cries louder. They were the storm now, the hammer against which the anvil of the enemy would break.

Raina's laughter, wild and fierce, rang out over the fray. "See how they stumble? Like drunkards after a tavern brawl!"

"Let's sober them up with cold steel!" Ahat cheered, his teasing tone belying the deadly seriousness of his strikes.

And then, as if on cue, the tide turned. With each fallen foe, the invaders' morale seemed to wane, and the El found themselves pushing the Cambions back from the walls, reclaiming inch by precious inch of their besieged city.

"Forward! To victory!" Aydis commanded, her voice alight with the fires of triumph.

"Victory!" the El echoed, emboldened by the sight of the Cambions regrouping below. Panic set upon the enemy ranks, their formations breaking as the looming silhouette of Malathar became a beacon of defiance rather than a prize to be claimed.

"Keep up the barrage!" Jace ordered, pointing towards the siege engines. Bright orbs of pulsing energy were launched from the catapults, painting arcs of dazzling light in the sky before colliding with the enemy ranks, creating deafening blasts and chaos on the battlefield."

"May every shot be a prayer for peace," Raina whispered to herself, releasing another bolt into the abyss below, her aim guided by more than mere skill.

"Peace through annihilation," Ahat grunted, slamming his shoulder into a Cambion that had managed to gain a foothold on the wall.

"Annihilation it is, then," Jace replied

"Make them remember this day!" he roared, his determination infectious, his will indomitable. The El rallied to his call, their arrows blotting out the stars, their siege weapons thundering in righteous fury.

And as the Cambion hordes faltered, recoiling from the storm of wrath they had summoned, Jace allowed himself a moment of pride. They were few against many, the embattled guardians of Malathar, but they were unbroken. And in that unyielding spirit, they found their greatest weapon—the hope that even in the darkest of nights, dawn was ever on the horizon.

In the aftermath of their fierce counterassault, the El warriors breathed raggedly, leaning on battered shields and notched swords. The air above the battlements tingled with the electricity of hope as though the day itself had been pierced by the radiant siege weapons that continued to rain down upon the regrouping Cambion forces.

"Look at them, scurrying like rats," Aydis said, a note of triumph in her voice, eyes bright with the reflection of still-glowing embers.

"Rats can bite," Ahat cautioned, wiping his blade clean on the tunic of a fallen enemy. "Stay sharp."

Jace nodded, his gaze following the retreating shadows. He knew this was but an interlude in the symphony of war, and he let the silence between the percussions fill him with clarity. Raina caught his eye from across the wall, and he felt the silent communication pass between them; they were not done yet.

Suddenly, the ground trembled anew, and from the center of the Cambion host, a tumultuous roar erupted. The El soldiers stiffened, sensing an ominous shift. An enormous figure emerged at the head of a fresh onslaught, and Jace's instincts screamed a warning.

Aamon, the Devil himself, strode forth, towering and terrible. His skin was a tapestry of shadow, and his eyes burned with infernal light. Crowned with a set of twisted horns that blazed like molten gold, he wielded a scepter that seemed to draw the darkness of the abyss into its core. Wings unfurled from his back, vast and membranous, each beat sending ripples of dread through the ranks of the El.

"By all that is holy..." Jace muttered, recalling the depictions from the books he'd studied—the grand duke of hell who commanded forty legions, depicted now in flesh and fire before him.

"Is that...?" Raina's voice quivered across the distance, trailing off as the reality of Aamon's presence sunk in.

"Steady," Jace called back, trying to infuse his voice with more confidence than he felt. "Remember who we are. Remember why we fight." His words were meant for himself as much as for the others.

"Let's send him back to whatever pit spit him out!" Ahat bellowed with bravado, gripping his sword tighter.

But Aamon's entrance was not merely for show. With a guttural incantation, a vile miasma spilled from his lips—a poisonous breath that swept over the walls like a pestilential wind. Screams pierced the night as El warriors crumpled, clawing at their throats, their life force seeping away amidst spasms of agony.

"Fall back!" Forset yelled, his voice strained against the foul air. "Protect your faces!"

Jace, Raina, Aydis, and Ahat stumbled away from the ramparts, gasping for untainted air. They found shelter behind a bulwark, huddling together as the screams outside continued. Jace's chest tightened—not from the poison, but from the crushing weight of responsibility. Emma's face flashed in his mind, and he pushed the thought away. There was no room for fear here, only action.

Raina's frame shuddered as she coughed, struggling to catch her breath. "I can't...breathe," she managed to say. Forset quickly took charge, stepping in front and barking orders for Aydis and Ahat to get Jace and Raina to safety.

"Here," Aydis offered, handing her a cloth soaked in a sweet-smelling tonic.

"Thanks," Raina managed, pressing it to her mouth and nose. "We need a plan. We can't let that thing break us."

"Right," Jace agreed, his steel blue eyes meeting each of theirs in turn. "We have power too—powers we've barely tapped into. We need to find a way to use them against him."

"Any bright ideas, bookworm?" Ahat asked, half-mocking, half-desperate

"Books hold more than words, my friend," Jace said, his mind racing. "They hold knowledge, history... and if I recall correctly, they hold the ways to defeat such fiends."

"Then let's write our own damn chapter," Raina said fiercely.

"Let's," Jace echoed, feeling the unity among them solidify into resolve. Together, they began to weave a new strategy, one that might just turn the tide against the darkness that sought to claim Malathar.

20

Aamon

Beneath the crooked shadows of the crumbling parapets, Aydis, Ahat, Jace, and Raina huddled, gasping for breath that wasn't laced with poison. The air reeked of sulfur, a stench emanating from Aamon's relentless assault. Each breath they took was like drawing in a mouthful of invisible thorns, the toxic magic searing their lungs.

That's when they saw him. Forset's body lay slumped against the crumbling stone wall, his armor dented and singed from battle. His face, once noble and fierce, now lay contorted in a peaceful death. Blood seeped from wounds on his chest and arms, staining the grey stone beneath him. The sight of Forset's lifeless body shook Aydis to her core. She had known him for many years, and his death felt like a personal loss. But there was no time to mourn. They were still in danger.

"We need to keep moving," Ahat said firmly, breaking the heavy silence that had fallen over them.

With tears welling in her eyes, Raina nodded and gazed at Forset's lifeless form one last time before turning away. Jace led the way, cautiously maneuvering away from the walls. Suddenly, a brilliant light engulfed Forset's body, and it was gone.

"Here," Aydis rasped, passing around torn pieces of her cloak dampened with water. "Cover your mouths."

Jace pressed the wet fabric to his face, grateful for the scant respite it offered. His steel blue eyes darted through the chaos, watching as the world seemed to shatter piece by piece under Aamon's fury. Stone crumbled, screams echoed, and hope felt like a threadbare tapestry unraveling fast.

Raina leaned close, her voice barely audible over the cacophony. "We can't let this be the end."

He nodded, feeling the weight of his own resolve hardening like forged steel. "Aamon falls today," Jace declared, a silent promise etched within his thoughts.

His father's lessons and the countless hours spent training with the El —all culminated in this singular moment of destiny.

"By our hands," Raina agreed, her athletic frame poised like a coiled spring ready to unleash. Her blonde hair, once vibrant, now appeared muted, dusted in debris—a stark contrast against her fierce determination.

"Then let's make our stand." Jace reached out, taking Raina's hand in his, their fingers intertwining as if to weave their fates together.

"Together."

"Until the very end," she affirmed, squeezing back. The pact sealed between them was more than words—it was the confluence of shared experiences, the unspoken understanding that had grown between two hearts beating in sync against the tide of darkness.

As lethal miasma swirled beyond their meager sanctuary, Jace felt the pulse of newfound power coursing through him, a radiant surge that mirrored Raina's own burgeoning strength. It was as if the very essence of Nelhelm itself recognized their valor and whispered secrets of ancient might into their souls.

"Ready, Jace?" Raina asked, her gaze locked onto the battlements where Aamon, the embodiment of demonic legend, wrought havoc upon the living.

"For Forset," he replied, the timber of his voice carrying a certainty that belied the dire straits they faced.

With a final glance at Aydis and Ahat, who offered solemn nods of support, Jace and Raina prepared to step into the tempest. They knew that from this moment forward, there would be no shelter, no reprieve—only the clash of wills against an adversary born from the darkest annals of Christian demonology.

But within each other, they found an unyielding courage—the kind that turns the tide of battles and forges legends. And so, with the light of conviction burning bright in their eyes, they readied themselves to face the wrath of Aamon.

The battlements of Nelhelm, once a symbol of the kingdom's enduring strength, now quivered under the relentless assault of Aamon's poisonous fury. The stones themselves seemed to cry in agony as they crumbled and cracked, their ancient resilience tested by the onslaught of otherworldly malice. Great chunks of masonry lay scattered across the walkway, testament to the ferocity of the battle, while below, the clangor of steel rang out against the guttural cries of the Cambion army.

"By the Twelve," Reynard muttered, his lithe form slipping through the chaos to join the huddled group behind an upturned cart. His red hair, usually a bright flame against his pale skin, was darkened with the grime of war. "It's worse than any scouting report could have disclosed."

Aydis clutched her staff, her knuckles white, and Ahat stood grim-faced beside her. Their eyes were drawn upwards, where Aamon, a specter of smoldering wrath, directed his minions with cruel intent.

"Any longer out there, and we'd be lost," Aydis breathed, the words barely carrying over the din.

"Lost, but not broken," Jace replied, steel blue eyes flashing with determination as he looked at Raina. "We end this now."

"Agreed," Raina said, her voice steady despite the bedlam around them. "Reynard, we may need your eyes from above."

"Consider it done," Reynard answered, though his gaze lingered on the pair with a silent question.

Jace caught the scout's look and nodded. "We've got a score to settle with that demon."

"More than a score," Raina added, hefting her bow, its string humming with tension.

Jace's hand found hers, a brief touch that spoke volumes. "For Nelhelm. For all of us."

"Then let's not keep death waiting," she said, releasing his hand and stepping toward what remained of the battlement's edge.

"Death will wait for us today," Jace declared, following her lead, his own bow in hand. Each step they took was measured, a march toward the destiny that neither shied away from nor rushed into recklessly.

"Remember," Reynard called after them, his voice sharpened by the urgency of the moment, "aim true and let your arrows fly faster than his whispers of doom."

With the wind howling its mournful dirge around them, Jace and Raina strode out onto the ruined battlements. The sky above was a tumultuous canvas painted with roiling clouds and the sulfurous glow of Aamon's rage. Below, the battlefield stretched out like a tapestry of despair, the El and Cambion locked in a dance of death.

"Raina," Jace began his thoughts an echo of the storm within.

"Save it for after," she cut him off, her eyes never leaving the target of their vengeance. "Focus on the now, on every breath, every heartbeat. Let them guide your shot."

"Right," Jace agreed, feeling the power of Nelhelm thrumming in his veins, a symphony of ancient energies aligning with his purpose.

He nocked an arrow to his bow, the creak of the drawstring a familiar comfort amid the cacophony of battle. Beside him, Raina did the same, her movements precise and fluid, a warrior-poet in the language of survival.

"Whatever happens," he whispered, more to himself than to anyone else, "we fight as one."

"Always," Raina affirmed, her voice a beacon amidst the shadows.

And with that, two Gaians stood upon the precipice of fate, and their bows raised not just in defense but as instruments of hope, their arrows notched and ready to sing songs of light into the heart of darkness.

The air cracked with the ferocity of Aamon's onslaught, a relentless barrage of poison that scythed through the ranks of the El. Jace and Raina stood on the battlements, their silhouettes defiant against the chaos. The stone beneath their feet trembled with each impact, a reminder that death loomed as close as the shadow of the flame.

"Steady," Raina hissed through clenched teeth, her eyes darting from point to point, calculating trajectories and wind speeds with an intensity that could rival the storm above.

"Like we practiced," Jace replied, nodding to Reynard who hunkered down beside them, his own bow at the ready. "We hold nothing back."

Arrows were loosed, singing through the air like vengeful spirits. Each one was more than just wood and feather; they were extensions of Jace and Raina's will, coursing with the raw energy of Nelhelm itself.

"See it?" Jace whispered, not taking his eyes off Aamon, who stood in the midst of his havoc, a figure cloaked in dread—his horns curling skyward, wings unfurled like the banners of doom.

"Clear as day," Raina said, letting another arrow fly. Her voice was a subtle knife, cutting through Jace's anxiety, sharpening his focus.

A luminescent aura began to envelop them, the manifestation of their power and unity. It pulsed with each heartbeat, a beacon amidst the dark tide of war. Aydis and Ahat watched in awe from their cover, witnessing the emergence of something extraordinary.

"Feel that?" Raina breathed out, her gaze locked onto their foe. The light from their forms intensified, illuminating the dimmed battlefield.

"Power," Jace replied, a sense of clarity washing over him. His mind honed in on the moment, every lesson from his father, every scripture he had pored over, now distilled into this singular purpose.

"Let's show this bastard what Gaians can do!" Raina shouted, her voice carrying over the din, a rallying cry for all those who fought and bled below.

Their arrows transformed before their very eyes from mere projectiles to bolts of brilliance, searing across the distance to strike Aamon. The demon barely flinched at first, swatting the initial salvos away with a contemptuous sneer. But with each subsequent attack, the arrows struck truer, harder, brighter, until they detonated upon his hide, explosions of pure radiance that rocked the demon back on his heels.

"Again!" Jace roared, his voice threading through the maelstrom of fire and steel.

"Until there's nothing left!" Raina echoed, her dedication mirroring his fervor.

Aamon, the fiend born from the darkest pits of Hades, the grand marquis of hell, began to falter under their assault. With the last remnant of their combined strength, Jace and Raina fired once more. The arrows, now indistinguishable from celestial comets, found their mark, and the demon convulsed, his form unraveling.

"Impossible..." Aamon's voice was a guttural whisper, lost to the wind as the glow from Jace and Raina reached its zenith.

Aamon's body writhed and contorted, his skin blistering and peeling away as the light consumed him.

"Nothing is impossible!" Raina shouted back, defiance etched in every syllable.

With a final, thunderous roar, Aamon fell, his body igniting into a tempestuous tornado of fire that consumed him whole, leaving naught but ash and the echo of his defeat.

Jace and Raina stood panting, the luminescence around them fading but their victory shining all the brighter amidst the devastation. The immediate threat was neutralized, and for a brief moment, the din of battle seemed to quiet, allowing them to catch their breath and reflect on the impossibility they had just achieved.

"Raina," Jace said between gasps, his eyes reflecting the fires of war and triumph, "we did it."

"Jace," she replied, meeting his gaze, "Yes, yes, we did."

The battlefield lay in stunned silence as the ashes of Aamon, once a terror of the deep abyss, swirled and dissipated into the acrid air. Jace's chest heaved with exertion, and his hands trembled slightly from the release of adrenaline. Raina stood beside him, her own breathing labored, but her eyes alight with triumph. The cambion army that had surged forth like a relentless tide seemed to freeze, their monstrous forms slackening, the will to fight leached from them as though they were puppets with severed strings.

"Look at them," Raina whispered, an edge of disbelief in her voice. "They don't know what to do without him."

Jace followed her gaze, his pulse slowing as he took in the sight of the confused horde. "Like snakes with their head cut off," he mumbled, the comparison coming easily to his mind from his rural upbringing.

"Are we... Are we winning?" Aydis asked, peeking out from their makeshift cover, her question punctuated by the distant clangor of swords and cries of battle.

"Because of you two," Reynard said, gesturing toward Jace and Raina with a nod of respect.

"Let's hope it lasts," Jace replied, but there was a glimmer of hope in his steel blue eyes that hadn't been there before.

As if answering Aydis's question, the El warriors, emboldened by the sight of their vanquished foe, rallied with renewed vigor. Their armor gleamed under the blood-red sky, reflecting the light of dying fires as they moved in unison, a silver wave crashing against the faltering cambion ranks.

"Forward!" An El commander's voice cut through the haze, sharp and commanding. "For Nelhelm! For victory!"

Raina couldn't help but smile at the sight, feeling a kindred spirit among the El. She glanced at Jace, her grin infectious. "Our turn to inspire, it seems."

"Then let's not disappoint," Jace countered, his own smile matching hers.

Steel clashed upon steel as El warriors engaged the enemy, their movements precise and deadly. They fought not as individuals but as a single entity, each strike choreographed in harmony with the next. Through the chaos, Jace could see patterns emerging, the El exploiting weaknesses with the precision of master tacticians.

"Who would've thought," Jace murmured, "that we would be the ones to turn the tides of an otherworldly war."

"Look at us with our fancy glowing arrows," Raina joked as her gaze remained fixated on the chaos unfolding before us.

"Speaking of which, did you ever think we'd be capable of something like that?"

"Never in my wildest dreams, Jace," she admitted. "But then again, I never imagined half the things we've seen since this all began."

Jace nodded as he watched the El push the cambions back, step by laborious step. His father's words about perseverance echoed in his mind, how every small action could lead to significant change. He felt a swell of pride for what they had accomplished.

"Today, we made a difference," Jace said aloud, more to himself than to Raina.

"Today, we fight back the darkness," Raina agreed solemnly.

And fight they did. The El's advance was relentless, sweeping across the field like a storm. With every fallen cambion, the momentum shifted further into the realm of light. The once formidable army crumbled, scattering like leaves in the wind, their terror palpable even to the victors.

"Who knew that light could weigh so heavy on the damned?" Raina quipped, watching as the last of the cambions were routed.

"Guess we'll have plenty of stories to tell," Jace said, the corner of his mouth lifting in a tired but satisfied smirk.

"Only if we survive to tell them," Raina pointed out pragmatically, though her tone held an unmistakable note of optimism.

"Survive we will," Jace responded, clapping a hand on Reynard's shoulder as the El warrior joined them. "Together."

"Indeed," Reynard concurred, nodding solemnly. "Today, you've shown us all the power of unity. Together, we are unstoppable."

"Unstoppable," Jace echoed, the word resounding within him like a promise, a vow for the future. As he surveyed the clearing field, he allowed himself a moment to bask in the victory, in the knowledge that they had achieved the impossible. But deep down, he knew the journey was far from over. The road ahead would be fraught with peril, but for now, they stood triumphant, bathed in the light of their own making.

Jace stood atop the battlements, his gaze sweeping over the expanse of Nelhelm. The city, once shrouded in apprehension and despair, now thrummed with a palpable sense of hope. The El warriors, their swords still gleaming with the ichor of vanquished foes, raised their weapons skyward in salute to the courage that had turned the tide.

"Look at them," Aydis said, coming to stand beside Jace. Her voice held a note of awe. "You've given them back their spirit."

"Us," Jace corrected gently. "We did this together."

Ahat joined them, his eyes reflecting the fires of victory that burned throughout Nelhelm. "The people chant your names. Jace and Raina, the bearers of light."

"Let them chant for all of us," Jace insisted, feeling a surge of pride not for himself but for the collective strength they had all shown. "Today, every sword and bow was guided by the same hand of fate."

Below, the citizens emerged from their homes like blossoms after a harsh winter, and their faces lifted toward their defenders. Their cheers crescendoed into a mighty roar of gratitude and renewed vigor. In their eyes shone the fierce determination to stand against Belloch's darkness, whatever the cost.

"Jace," Raina said, her voice soft but firm as she placed a hand on his arm. "You've led us here to this moment. You've proven more than your worth—you've become our beacon."

He met her gaze, the steel blue of his eyes alight with the reflection of the setting sun. "It's one thing to hold a torch," he mused. "Another to know where to cast its light. We'll need that knowledge in the days to come."

"True," Reynard agreed, stepping closer. "But today, we follow your lead. Your instincts, your bravery—they are gifts, Jace. Gifts that have saved us all."

"Gifts that I didn't know I had until I was forced to use them." Jace's thoughts drifted inward for a moment to the boy who had left a small town with simple dreams. He could scarcely recognize that boy now, transformed as he was by the crucible of war.

"Your father would be proud," Ahat said softly, clapping him on the back.

"Emma always said my stubbornness would lead to something good," Jace replied, a bittersweet smile touching his lips.

"Let's hope it leads to the end of Belloch," Raina added, her expression hardening with resolve.

"Tonight, we celebrate," Aydis declared, her voice ringing out clear and strong. "For tomorrow, we plan. But know this: Belloch has met his match."

Cheers erupted anew from the walls to the streets, the sound carrying far into the evening sky. At that moment, Jace understood the true weight of leadership. It was more than just strategy and skill—it was inspiring others to believe that even in the darkest times, there would be a dawn.

"Let's make sure that dawn comes," he said, his words carried away on the wind, a promise to his allies, to Emma, and to himself.

The last vestiges of Aamon's army scattered like dark leaves in a gale; their will to fight crumbled to ash along with their fallen leader.

The battlements of Nelhelm stood victorious, silhouetted against the twilight sky that held the first promise of peace.

"Can you believe it?" Raina breathed out, her voice a mixture of exhaustion and elation as she leaned heavily against the stone wall, her bow dangling loosely from one hand.

Jace, his heart still thundering from the battle, looked out over the field littered with the remnants of conflict. "Believe it? I'm not sure I can even comprehend it," he admitted, raking a hand through his sweat-darkened hair.

"Neither can they," Aydis observed dryly, nodding toward the retreating figures of the enemy.

Raina chuckled wearily, dropping beside Jace. They sat shoulder to shoulder, their armor clinking softly, sharing the silence that spoke volumes of the camaraderie and relief that only those who have faced death together could understand.

"Look at us," Jace murmured after a moment, a ghost of a smile playing on his lips. "I never imagined... back in school, when the biggest worry was a history test..."

"Or getting caught sneaking out," Raina added, a twinkle of mischief in her eyes despite the fatigue lining her face.

"History tests seem so trivial now," Jace reflected. His thoughts drifted to Emma, to the future they had envisioned—one that didn't include battling demons and leading armies. But here they were, and here he was, a Gaian, changed forever by this war.

"Tomorrow begins the hard part," Aydis said, her tone sobering as she retrieved her bow from the ground. "Planning our next move. Belloch won't be taken down as easily as Aamon."

"True, but we've proven something tonight," Jace responded, the weight of his newfound leadership settling on him once again. "We've shown that we can stand together, that we're more than just survivors—we're fighters."

"More than that," Aydis interjected, stepping closer to them. "You've both shown that Gaians possess powers beyond what we understood. Powers that can change the tide of this war."

Jace met her gaze, feeling the enormity of their path unfold before him. "Then let's make sure we use them wisely," he said. "For everyone who's counting on us."

"Speaking of which," Raina interjected, "we need to ensure the defenses are set for the night. No telling if any stragglers might try to take advantage of the post-battle chaos."

"Agreed," Jace nodded, pushing himself up. "Let's see to it then."

"Enjoy this victory, my friends," Aydis called after them as they moved to rally the remaining troops. "But remember, the darkness is vast, and Belloch is but one star within it."

"Then we'll snuff out that star," Raina declared, determination steeling her voice. "One way or another."

As they walked among the defenders, coordinating efforts for the night, Jace felt the cold clarity that had washed over him during the battle return. It seemed to sharpen his senses, his purpose. He understood now more than ever that there was no going back to the life he had known. His destiny was entwined with the fate of Nelhelm, with Raina, and with the looming shadow of Belloch that still hung over them all.

"Tonight, we rest," Jace announced to those gathered. "Tomorrow, we begin anew. For Nelhelm, for the El, for our futures!"

A chorus of affirmation rose around them, a sound that carried with it the hope and resilience of a people ready to follow wherever he would lead. As the last light of day vanished, giving way to a blanket of stars, Jace felt a quiet assurance settle in his soul. This was just the beginning. The real battle—for their lives, their world, and their very souls—was still ahead.

The chill of the evening air bit at Jace's cheeks as he stood upon the battlements, his gaze drifting across the weary faces of those who had fought bravely. The stars twinkled above, indifferent to the turmoil that had unfolded beneath them. The smell of charred earth and the faint echo of distant sorrows lingered in the air.

"Feels like a dream, doesn't it?" Raina's voice was soft beside him, her azure eyes reflecting the night sky.

"More like waking up from one," Jace replied, turning to meet her gaze.

"Hard to believe Aamon's gone, that we did that." Her thumb brushed against his, a small gesture but grounding.

"Belief will come with the dawn," Jace murmured, watching as

Reynard approached them, a wry smile on his lips despite the fatigue etched into his face.

"Your arrows... they were like nothing I've ever seen. How did you learn such magic?" Reynard asked, curiosity lacing his tone.

"Sometimes, necessity forges new paths of power," Jace answered, his thoughts lingering on the cold clarity that had coursed through him during the battle.

"Indeed," Reynard nodded. "And it seems this newfound strength will be needed in the days to come."

Jace's gaze hardened. "We'll be ready. Whatever secrets Belloch harbors, whatever power he wields, we'll face it together."

"United," Raina affirmed, her voice carrying a decisive edge.

"Then rest well tonight, for tomorrow we plan, we prepare," Reynard said, clapping a hand on Jace's shoulder before turning toward the stairs leading down from the battlements.

"Rest," Jace echoed, the word tasting strange after-hours fueled by adrenaline. He watched Reynard's retreating figure, aware of how their fates intertwined, much like the constellations above.

As the quiet of the night enveloped them, Jace could feel the weight of what lay ahead. Doubts whispered like shadows at the edge of his mind, but he pushed them away, focusing instead on the solid presence of Raina beside him. Her determination was a beacon that pierced the uncertainty.

They descended the stone steps, their boots scuffing against the worn edges. The campfires below flickered like earthly stars, clusters of soldiers and mages gathered around them, the hum of conversation rising and falling like a healing balm.

"Tomorrow, we begin anew," Jace said again, this time more to himself than to anyone else. It was a promise, an acknowledgment that the path forward would not be easy, that darkness still loomed.

But as they reached the bottom of the battlements and melded into the crowd, Jace felt a sense of unity bind them all together. They were survivors, warriors, and protectors of Nelhelm. And though the future was shrouded in mystery, one thing was certain: they would face it as one.

"Let's get some food in you," Raina suggested, her practical words pulling him back from the precipice of his thoughts.

"Food sounds good," Jace agreed, allowing himself the simple pleasure of a shared meal. After all, even heroes needed sustenance.

As they sat by the fire, eating in companionable silence, Jace allowed the warmth to seep into his bones. The night stretched out before them, a canvas yet to be painted with the colors of their destiny. But for now, they had earned a moment of peace, a brief respite to gather strength for whatever lay ahead.

21

Seven Angels

Glenwood's night cloaked the town in an unsettling shroud, shadows coiling between the gnarled branches of ancient oaks like specters. A heavy mist crept along cobblestone streets, and the moon, a pallid wafer in the obsidian sky, cast a grim silver light upon the earth below. The air was thick with the kind of silence that weighs upon the soul, a harbinger of woe whispered by the rustling leaves.

The pallid moonlight threw a haunting glow over the scene as Allen and the Sheriff stood over the body. The corpse seemed almost to mock them from its resting place amongst the fallen leaves, clad in the same tactical gear that Emma's friends had worn—those who claimed to be searching for Jace.

The cause of death was clear: a gaping wound in his abdomen caused by some type of projectile. Evidence of burns surrounded the wound, indicating a violent and potentially explosive impact.

"Look at this," Allen murmured, his fingers brushing against the cold nylon of a hidden holster. "Two knives, a sidearm... and what's this? A garrote?" He picked up the wire weapon with a grimace, letting it dangle in the air, shimmering like a deadly serpent in the moonlit shroud of Glenwood.

"More than just prepared for a search party," the Sheriff commented dryly, his brows furrowed as he studied the body. "Seems like they were ready for a small war."

"Or an abduction," Allen countered, his voice low and tinged with concern. "Why would they need all this to find Jace?"

"Exactly what we're going to find out." The Sheriff's tone was decisive, a commander rallying his forces amidst the fog of uncertainty.

As the night deepened, Allen and the Sheriff continued their methodical search of the area. Every step seemed to add to the eerie ambiance, the silence broken only by their hushed voices and the crunch of leaves underfoot.

"Let's get him to the morgue," the Sheriff said, waving over the coroner's team. "I want a full report—every mark, every bruise. Anything that can tell us more."

"Right behind you," Allen agreed, the urgency in his chest mirrored in his swift footsteps. They followed the somber procession, the rhythmic cadence of their boots against the gravel path forming a dirge for the departed.

The morgue was a bleak, sterile place, its harsh fluorescent lights illuminating rows of metal gurneys. The sharp tang of disinfectant filled the air, mingling with the metallic scent of blood and the faint hint of decay.

The coroner's team quickly went to work, their gloved hands moving with practiced precision as they examined the body. Allen and the Sheriff stood by, watching intently as they awaited any new information.

"Keep me posted on everything," the Sheriff instructed the coroner. "No detail is too small."

"Understood," came the somber reply.

"The William's are hiding something," Allen whispered once they were alone, his gaze locked with the Sheriff's. "Why arm their friends like this? It doesn't add up."

"Maybe it does," the Sheriff muttered, turning to face the stainless steel table where the body now rested. "We just don't have all the pieces yet. But we will, Allen. We'll uncover the truth, even if it turns this town inside out."

Allen's heart thrummed in his chest, a relentless drumbeat urging him forward into the darkness of the unknown. There was no turning back; the path wound ever onward, deeper into the heart of the mystery that had ensnared them all.

"Let's find those missing pieces, Sheriff," Allen said, resolve hardening within him like forged steel. "Before whatever's lurking in the shadows finds us first."

The morgue's silence was profound, punctuated only by the hum of refrigeration units that lined the walls like crypts. Fluorescent lights flickered overhead, casting an unhealthy pallor on everything beneath their gaze. It was a place designed for the dead, and yet it made those still living yearn for the warmth of life.

"God, it's cold in here," Allen muttered, his breath visible in the frigid air as he moved closer to the table where the body lay draped with a stark white sheet.

"Death is always cold, Walker," the Sheriff replied his voice a low growl that seemed to merge with the somber ambiance of the morgue.

The coroners had finished with their initial investigation and left Allen and the Sheriff alone with the body.

Together, they peeled back the sheet, revealing the body. Moonlight streamed through a high window, bathing the scene in ethereal light. The dead man's eyes were closed as if in eternal slumber, but the lips were parted slightly, frozen in a silent gasp. Allen's hand hesitated over the chest, and then he drew in a sharp breath as his fingers brushed against the tattoo—a seven-sided star etched into the skin, stark and black against the pallor of death.

"Seven sides..." The Sheriff murmured, his mind racing. "That's not just some random ink. It means something."

Allen's head snapped up, meeting the Sheriff's gaze. "You think there's a connection to Jace's disappearance?"

"Maybe." The Sheriff's eyes narrowed. "Emma and her family... they're newcomers here, but they've never been open about their past."

"Her parents always struck me as odd," Allen confessed, the image of the seven-sided star burning behind his eyelids. "They have this arrogance to them like they're hiding something big."

"Look at this, too." The Sheriff pointed to the array of weapons now laid out on a table. "No person needs those for a search party."

"Or even for protection," Allen added, the implication clear. In Glenwood, a place where every shadow could harbor secrets, trust was as scarce as daylight during winter.

"The William's," the Sheriff mused, his thoughts a tangled web. "They are lying to us. But what are they protecting? Or who?"

"Could be Emma," Allen suggested his gut twisting. "But why would she want Jace out of the picture? Unless she wanted him gone for good."

"Unless Emma wanted him to escape," the Sheriff posited, his eyes narrowing. "Maybe she's playing both sides. Maybe she loves him enough to save him from her own flesh and blood."

Allen felt the weight of the revelation settle upon him like a shroud. The pieces were starting to form a picture, but it was incomplete, distorted by shadows and half-truths. Emma, the girl with the gentle smile and hidden depths. Jace, the survivalist with a penchant for ancient texts. And now, a secret society with a symbol marked in ink on a dead man's chest.

"Damn it," Allen whispered, a mix of anger and fear coursing through him. "We're missing something critical here. We need to confront them, get the truth before it's too late."

The Sheriff nodded, his jaw set in determination. "We'll get the truth, Allen. Even if it burns this town to the ground."

Together, Allen and the Sheriff returned to Emma's home, determined to confront her family about their lies and uncover the truth behind Jace's disappearance,

The night hung over Glenwood like a shroud, moonlight seeping through the dense forest and casting elongated shadows across the Williams' imposing estate. The house stood stark against the backdrop of wilderness, its modern lines and expansive windows a stark contrast to the rustic charm that typified the rest of the town.

Sheriff Callahan's cruiser crunched over the gravel driveway, its headlights cutting through the darkness as he parked beside Nicholas Williams's sedan. They both stepped out, their boots echoing on the stone walkway leading to the front door. Allen felt the unease in his gut tighten into a knot; confronting Emma and her well-heeled parents was not something he looked forward to.

"Remember," the Sheriff said, glancing at Allen, "cool heads prevail."

Allen nodded, though his heart beat like a drum in his chest. As they approached the entrance, the ornate door swung open, revealing Emma, flanked by her parents, Liz and Nicholas Williams. The interior light washed over them like a spotlight, and Allen noted how the trio seemed unfazed by the intrusion, an arrogance about them that was as palpable as the tension in the air.

"Good evening, Sheriff, Deputy Walker," Nicholas began, his voice dripping with condescension. "To what do we owe this unexpected visit?"

"May we come in?" the Sheriff asked, but it was more a formality than a question.

"Of course," Liz replied, stepping aside with a wave of her hand, but her eyes were sharp, observant.

The Williams' home was a study in ostentatious wealth, with marble floors, glittering chandeliers, and plush furnishings. Allen couldn't help but feel out of place as he followed the Sheriff into the living room, Emma trailing behind them. Nicholas and Liz took their seats on a luxurious sofa while Emma perched on an armchair opposite them.

"Please, have a seat," Nicholas said with a smooth smile, gesturing to the matching armchair beside Emma.

Allen obliged, his eyes never leaving the trio. The tension in the room was palpable like electricity humming through the air.

"Let's cut to the chase," the Sheriff said, standing firm. "The body we found tonight." He paused, allowing the weight of his words to sink in. "One of Rick Water's men. Armed to the teeth and sporting a tattoo of a seven-sided star."

Emma's gaze flickered for just a moment before she composed herself, a portrait of innocence. "I don't understand," she said, her voice steady. "What does that have to do with us?"

"Come now, Emma," Allen interjected, unable to contain his frustration. "You know as well as I do that ain't normal. Why would Rick's men need to be armed like that?"

"Assumptions can be dangerous, Deputy," Nicholas chided, crossing his arms. "Are you implying that we're involved in some sort of... conspiracy?"

"Nobody's accusing anyone yet," the Sheriff countered. "But you can't deny there's something strange about your friends walking around armed like soldiers."

"And this symbol," Allen added, watching their faces closely. "It doesn't strike you as odd?"

Liz let out a laugh that held no humor. "The world is full of oddities, Deputy. Perhaps you've been living in Glenwood too long."

The air in the living room grew thick with tension as the four of them stared at each other, all waiting for someone to break the silence. Allen's heart beat faster with every passing second, and he could feel his hands start to sweat.

"Or maybe you haven't been living here long enough," he shot back at Liz, his eyes locked on Emma's. He saw a flicker of fear in her eyes before it was quickly replaced with a stony expression.

"Enough," Nicholas interjected. "This conversation serves no purpose. You have no evidence linking us to any wrongdoing."

"Besides, Jace is still nowhere to be found, and we have to find him," Liz added with apparent sincerity. "We don't have time for baseless accusations."

Allen took a deep breath and tried to calm himself. He knew that they were right - without any solid proof, there was no point in continuing this line of questioning.

"Perhaps not," the Sheriff conceded, his tone even. "But we will find out the truth. Make no mistake about that."

"Is that all, gentlemen?" Liz asked, her voice cool as she ushered them towards the door.

"Thank you for your time," the Sheriff replied, tipping his hat mockingly.

As Allen followed the Sheriff out, he couldn't shake the feeling of being played. The Williams had deflected their questions with ease, revealing nothing. What secrets did they hold behind their cultured veneer? And Emma, sweet Emma, what role did she play in all of this?

"Something's not right," Allen muttered once in the grand foyer.

"Agreed," the Sheriff responded in a low voice, his eyes narrowing to thin slits beneath the brim of his hat.

As they made their way to the door, Allen's thoughts swirled with doubts and suspicions. The seven-sided star burned in his mind, a symbol of a mystery that threatened to unravel the very fabric of Glenwood. Emma's face haunted him – the girl he thought he knew now, a stranger wrapped in an enigma. What was she hiding? And at what cost?

The Williams' ornate front door closed with a resonant thud, leaving the Sheriff and Deputy Allen standing on the porch in a pool of yellow light that spilled from the windows. A chill autumn breeze whispered through Glenwood, carrying with it the musty scent of fallen leaves and the distant echo of an owl's call – harbingers of the dark secrets that seemed to fester beneath the town's surface.

"Damn, Allen," the Sheriff spat, his voice a low growl, "they're hiding something. I can feel it in my bones."

Allen nodded, fingers drumming restlessly against his thigh. "I know, but what? Emma's always been like an open book, and now..." His voice trailed off as he looked back at the house, its facade deceptively tranquil against the backdrop of brooding pines.

"Let's keep our eyes open and our heads clear," the Sheriff said, stepping off the porch. "We'll unravel the Williams' web one thread at a time."

Nicholas Williams leaned against the window; his arms crossed over his chest in a display of nonchalance that didn't quite reach his eyes. His normally charming smile was replaced by a hard scowl as he watched the Sheriff and Deputy Allen disappear into the night.

"Emma," he said, the word a blade wrapped in velvet, "what have you done?" as he closed the door.

Inside, Emma stood flanked by her parents in the opulent living room, the grandeur of the space dwarfed by the gravity of the situation. The air was thick with accusation, the luxurious rugs and antique furniture bearing silent witness to the tension that crackled between them.

"Father, I..." Emma began, her voice trembling, betraying the calm she tried to project.

"Silence," Liz commanded, her professorial authority undiminished by her retirement. "We know about Kiera's... misstep. And now Jace is gone."

"Kiera acted on her own!" Emma protested, but her gaze shifted, unable to meet her mother's piercing stare.

"Enough, Emma," Nicholas interjected, his posture rigid. "You may fool the Sheriff with your innocent act, but not us. We know you influenced Kiera to take Jace before the wedding. Why?"

"Because I love him!" Emma exclaimed, the words bursting forth like dammed waters. "I didn't want—"

The confession hung in the air like a lead weight, the silence stretching on as the Williams' stared at Emma in disbelief.

"Love?" Liz sneered, her lip curling. "Your dalliance has endangered everything. The Order of the Seven Angels has informed us Jace has reached Emmon. He was never supposed to get there."

Emma's heart pounded, a caged bird seeking escape. The Order's symbol, the seven-sided star, seared her conscience. She had never wanted to be part of their clandestine machinations.

"Emmon..." she whispered, clutching at the locket around her neck, a trinket that felt like a shackle. "But he's alive."

"His survival is inconsequential if he exposes us," Nicholas said coldly. "The Order's plans are paramount."

"Plans that involve sacrificing the man I was supposed to marry?" Emma's voice broke, and she could feel the foundations of her world crumbling.

"Your feelings are irrelevant," her father replied, his tone dismissive. "Prepare yourself; we must act swiftly to correct this."

"Correct this? How?" Emma's mind reeled, fear and defiance waging war within her. Her parents stood united, a formidable front of aristocratic steel and scholarly ice.

"Leave that to us," Liz said, her brown eyes dark pools of resolve. "For now, keep up appearances. The town must not suspect."

"Remember, Emma," Nicholas added, "you are a Williams. Duty before desire."

With those words hanging heavy in the air, the three of them remained locked in a tableau of strained allegiance, each contemplating the next move in a game where the stakes were life and death.

The silence in the Williams' living room was suffocating, broken only by the soft ticking of the grandfather clock—a metronome to Emma's racing heart. She stood motionless, her gaze lost in the intricate patterns of the Persian rug beneath her feet. The air was thick with the scent of old books and the faintest trace of her mother's jasmine perfume.

"Emma," her father's voice cut into her thoughts like a blade, "what will you do?"

She raised her eyes slowly, her parents' silhouettes framed against the dim glow of the hearth. Though she could not see them clearly, she knew their expressions well—the expectant arch of her mother's brow, the rigid set of her father's jaw.

"Enough!" Liz stepped forward, her presence commanding. "We've given you everything, Emma. Your life of comfort, your education—"

"An education in deceit?" Emma retorted, her voice rising. "All my life, I've been nothing but a pawn in your games!"

"Lower your voice," Nicholas warned, his tone frigid. "Remember who you are speaking to."

"Who am I speaking to?" Emma breathed out, her mind a whirlwind of fragmented thoughts and unspoken pleas. "My parents or my puppeteers?"

"Emma." Liz's hand reached out, hovering uncertainly before retreating. "We do what we must for the greater good. You know this."

"Jace is innocent," Emma whispered, the locket's metallic chill seeping into her skin. "I can't—I won't be party to this madness."

"Then you choose him over The Order? Over your own family?" Nicholas's query was more accusation than question.

"Over murder? Yes."

"Even if that decision destroys us all?" Liz's voice was softer now, almost pleading.

"Perhaps it's already destroyed enough," Emma shot back, her resolve hardening.

"Think carefully, Emma," Nicholas said, pacing now, the heel of his shoe clicking ominously against the wood floor. "Your next actions will determine much."

"Actions that could save a life or end it," she murmured, her mind racing to find another way, any way, to shield Jace from the fate the Order had decreed.

"Time is a luxury we do not have," Liz reminded her, checking the ornate watch clasped around her wrist.

"Then give me time to think," Emma pleaded, her eyes darting between them, seeking a flicker of compassion.

"Very well," Nicholas conceded after a tense pause, "but remember, time is the enemy of secrets."

As her parents retreated, leaving her alone with her turmoil, Emma sank into an armchair, the leather cold and unwelcoming. Outside, the wind howled as if mourning for the innocence Glenwood had lost. She clutched the locket tighter, knowing within it lay the key to Jace's survival—or his doom. Emma sat in the armchair for what felt like hours, her mind racing and her heart heavy with the weight of her decision.

She reached into her pocket and pulled out the locket, its cool metal a reassuring presence in her hand. She opened it, staring at the image of Jace that lay inside. His eyes, bright and full of life, seemed to plead with her as if he could sense the danger that loomed over him. "Jace..." The name escaped her lips, a prayer, a curse, a beacon in the darkness of her soul. He was alive, for now. But for how long?

"Emmon," she whispered again; the word burned in Emma's mind, its letters formed from fiery red tongues, dancing and twisting like serpents in the shadows.

And then, from the depths of her despair, a spark ignited. A plan began to form, wild and dangerous—and perhaps, just perhaps, it could work.

"Jace," she said once more, her voice steadier, "hold on."

The grandfather clock chimed, marking the hour. Midnight in Glenwood, where secrets bred in the shadows and loyalty faced its ultimate test. Emma rose from her seat, her decision made, yet the truth of Jace's disappearance—a truth she had crafted with lies—remained unsaid, hanging in the balance.

With this chapter closed, leaving the question hanging in the air unanswered. What would she do? What could she do?

22

Rebuilding

The city of Malathar lay in tatters, like a grand tapestry torn and trampled upon by a host of shadowy marauders. The once-majestic spires and domes, symbols of the El's ancient glory, were now but fractured skeletons reaching for a sky that seemed to mourn with a palette of grays. The ground was littered with the remnants of what had been - shards of crystal, splintered wood, and the dimming light of arcane energies dissipating into the ether.

Jace Alexander stood amidst the rubble, his steel blue eyes reflecting the devastation around him. His hands, toughened by survival and battle, bore the stains of soot and blood - a testament to the sacrifices demanded by this foreign land. Raina, ever his echo in determination, moved beside him, her blonde hair now a tangled veil that whispered tales of the fray.

"Look at this place," Jace muttered, his voice barely above the wind's sorrowful tune, "It's like the bones of the earth are laid bare."

Raina nodded silently, her eyes scanning the horizon where smoke curled into the air like wounded serpents seeking refuge in the clouds. They had come to Nelhelm as outsiders, strangers to its magic and customs, yet through fire and fear, they had become part of the very fabric of the El.

"Remember our first day here?" Raina asked, breaking the silence that hung between them like a delicate shroud. "We were so out of our depth."

A wry smile touched Jace's lips as he turned to face her. "I'd never have imagined it. Us, becoming warriors... leaders, even." His gaze fell upon his hands again, the scars etched upon his skin a record of their trials. "My dad always said life was the best teacher. Guess he was right."

"Your instincts," she said, touching his arm lightly, "they've saved us more times than I can count. And your knowledge... it's like it was preparing you for this all along."

Jace shook his head, a laugh escaping him despite the desolation. "And you, with your secrets," he teased gently. "Turns out they were the keys we needed at times. We've grown, Raina. We're not who we were when we stumbled into Nelhelm."

"True," Raina agreed, her steel blue eyes locking with his. "But I'm glad we haven't done it alone."

They exchanged a look of shared understanding, their bond forged and tempered through adversity. Their reflections were cut short by the sound of movement as the people of Malathar emerged from hiding places, faces set in grim determination. Together, they began the slow process of healing and rebuilding, lifting stones and clearing debris, their actions a silent vow to restore the heart of their world.

"Help me with this," Raina said, bending to lift a heavy beam that lay across the path of an elderly El whose steps wavered with exhaustion.

"Of course," Jace replied, moving to assist her. They heaved the timber aside, muscles straining in unison, and the old one passed with a nod of gratitude that spoke volumes.

As they worked, shoulder to shoulder with the El, Jace felt a surge of pride. This was more than a duty; it was a kinship that transcended worlds. He knew that no matter where their journey took them next, the lessons learned and the ties formed in Nelhelm would forever be part of their story.

"Ready to keep moving?" Raina asked after a moment, brushing dust from her hands.

"Always," Jace affirmed, offering her a grin that held both the weight of the past and the promise of the future. "Let's see what else we can do."

Together, they stepped forward, weaving through the canvas of destruction and rebirth, their footfalls echoing the heartbeat of Malathar rising anew.

The air was thick with the scent of charred wood and fallen embers as Jace and Raina stood amidst the ruins of Malathar. The once-proud spires that reached for the heavens now lay broken, their jagged remnants poking through the smoky haze like skeletal fingers. In the distance, a lone figure approached, her silhouette ghost-like against the backdrop of destruction.

Mitra, the stoic commander of the El, her indomitable spirit evident in the determined set of her jaw, came forward clutching a missive—an unlikely beacon of hope amidst the desolation. The people around them paused in their toil, a hush falling over the crowd as Mitra unfurled the parchment. Her voice, when she spoke, was laced with an emotion they had not heard before anticipation.

"Word has come from Mount Myra," Mitra announced, her eyes finding Jace and Raina across the clearing.

As the news began to spread throughout Malathar, the El within earshot quickly passed the word of the announcement. Soon, word would reach all corners of the city.

Jace felt a jolt of excitement, a spark that ignited the longing he'd harbored in the recesses of his heart. Beside him, Raina's expression mirrored his own—a mix of elation and an unspoken fear of the unknown that awaited them back in Gaia.

"Seems like destiny isn't done with us yet," Jace said, turning to Raina, their hands brushing as they moved debris aside, continuing their work even as their minds raced.

"Destiny or not," Raina replied, her voice almost lost in the sound of stone scraping against stone, "I can't help but wonder if we belong here, with the El, more than we do back on Gaia."

"Gaia is our home," Jace reminded her, though his tone held a question he couldn't quite articulate. He lifted a timber, muscles straining, as he cast a glance at the faces around them—the El who had become family.

"Home is more than a place, Jace," Raina said, her gaze lingering on the children of Malathar, who were forming a human chain, passing stones hand to hand. "It's where you're needed, where you've shed blood, sweat, and tears. It's where you've forged bonds in the face of adversity."

"Is that here...or Gaia?" he asked, wiping the soot from his brow. His steel-blue eyes searched hers for an answer neither of them had.

"Maybe it's both," she offered, her blonde hair catching the light of the setting sun as it broke through the cloud of ash and sorrow. "We've changed, Jace. The people we love back home have stayed the same."

"Or maybe they've changed too, in ways we can't fathom," Jace countered, dropping his voice so only she could hear. "Emma..." His sentence trailed off, choked by the thought of his fiancée waiting in a world free from magical wars and ancient prophecies.

"Your love for her, it's a compass pointing you back," Raina said, understanding etching her features. "But your duty to Nelhelm, to what we've fought for, that's a tie that won't easily be severed."

"Both are pulling me in different directions." Jace exhaled sharply, his thoughts a tangle of loyalty and love, duty and desire. "Leaving might be harder than staying, but I can't shake the feeling that we're meant to walk this path."

Raina nodded. "Then let's walk it together," she affirmed, her hand finding his among the detritus of the fallen city. "As long as we remember what we're fighting for, I think we can find our way."

"Remember and honor," Jace agreed solemnly, looking out over the laboring forms of the El and the people of Malathar. They were a testament to resilience, each one a story of survival and strength. And soon, he and Raina would carry those stories with them across worlds and, through the mists of time, back to Gaia.

The ruins of Malathar whispered of desolation as if the very stones mourned their fallen guardians. Amidst this somber dirge, Jace and Raina stood before Mitra, the wise El matron whose ageless eyes held a glimmer of nascent hope.

"Listen well," Mitra began, her voice carrying the weight of ancient secrets. "With our successful defeat of Ammon, Mount Myra sees no other imminent threats for us to fear. The remnants of Ammon's army are in chaos and retreating from Malathar."

A tired cheer resounded from the crowd of El gathered before her on the ruins of their once-glorious city. Jace and Raina stood among them, their faces etched with exhaustion and loss.

Mitra's eyes swept over them, taking in each tired but determined face. "But let us not forget those who have fallen," she continued, her voice softening as she spoke of their comrades-in-arms who had made the ultimate sacrifice in the battle against Ammon.

The El nodded solemnly, understanding the weight of their words.

"Our focus now must turn to rebuilding," Mitra said, her gaze sweeping over the crumbling buildings and charred remains of Malathar. "We must rebuild our city and restore it to its former glory."

Mitra turned towards Jace and Raina, her voice filled with hope. "In this time of chaos, Mount Myra has become a refuge for other Gaians. Its sacred aura offers protection to those who seek shelter there."

Jace and Raina's eyes lit up at the mention of other Gaian's seeking refuge at Mount Myra. Jace couldn't help but wonder how many more of them were out there.

"Other Gaians?" Jace asked, his curiosity piqued. He had heard the stories of the Triumvirate and their powerful magic. He wondered how many more there were at Mount Myra.

Mitra nodded, her gaze turning towards the distant horizon. "Yes, there are others like you out there," she confirmed.

Jace and Raina stood before Mitra, their minds reeling at the revelation that there were others like them out there in the world. The thought of these other Gaians seeking refuge at Mount Myra filled them with a sense of hope and excitement.

"You are to go to Mount Myra as well," Mitra continued.

Jace's gaze met Raina's, both sets of steel blue eyes reflecting a shared determination. They had been tested by fire and emerged as leaders; now, they were to embark on a new journey.

"Your time in Nelhelm has honed your senses, heightened your awareness," Mitra explained. "You are no longer mere visitors in our realm; you are part of its legacy."

Raina felt a surge of pride swelling within her chest, a testament to the arduous path they had traversed. She turned to Jace, and their hands found each other once more, an unspoken pact formed in that simple touch.

"We're ready," Jace stated, his voice steady despite the whirlwind of emotions. "For Gaia, for Nelhelm."

"Crossing into the unknown with nothing but faith and each other," Raina added, her voice a soft murmur that carried the fierceness of her spirit. "To meet the others, to share our stories, and to fight for our home."

Mitra nodded at their resolve, a smile touching her lips that seemed both proud and melancholic. "Go with the blessings of the El. May the fog guide you safely to your destination."

"Are we able to travel using the fog again?" Jace questioned Mitra.

"Yes," Mitra answered with a knowing smile. "With the Cambion army defeated and none left in our realm, they will not be able to track you through the fog."

"Prepare yourself for the journey when the time comes," Mitra instructed. "For now, I must supervise the reconstruction in Malathar."

Jace and Raina exchanged a nod and departed to ready themselves for the journey ahead, while Mitra went to guide her people.

Jace stood amidst the ruins of Malathar, his gaze sweeping over the once grand city now reduced to rubble and ash. The golden light of dawn spilled over the broken stones, casting long shadows that seemed to reach for the survivors like the hands of the past, urging them to rebuild, to restore what had been lost.

"Looks like we've hammered out a little hope from all this destruction, haven't we?" Raina's voice cut through the crisp morning air, tinged with a weary optimism as she joined him, her eyes reflecting the same steel blue determination he saw in the mirror every day.

"More than a little," Jace replied, watching a group of El working alongside the people of Malathar, hoisting beams and clearing debris. "We've forged something stronger than before. Bonds that won't be easily broken."

Raina nodded, her blonde hair catching the light as if to echo her agreement. "The El... they've shown us the meaning of resilience. And friendship." She paused, looking up at the silhouette of workers against the sky. "I never thought I'd find a family in another world."

The sounds of hammers and chisels rang out like a relentless heartbeat, and Jace felt it sync with his own—a rhythmic testament to the enduring spirit of those around him. The reconstruction of Malathar unfolded like a scene from an ancient tapestry, each stone laid with precision, each carved column a promise of rebirth.

"Like Malathar is rising from the dust," Jace mused aloud, his interior monologue spilling over into words. "An old civilization lending us its strength."

"Through the fog of war, we've glimpsed what can be," Raina added, her hand finding his, gripping it tight as if to transfer her resolve into his veins.

"Yet we owe it to our loved ones back home," Raina's voice wavered, betraying her conflict. "Emma... your Mother... they're part of this too. We carry them with us."

"Gaia is our home, but Nelhelm has changed us. Made us warriors. Healers. Friends." Jace's voice was firm, his words a vow etched into the very fabric of his being.

"Let's make sure we leave a piece of ourselves here, in the heart of Malathar," Raina suggested, her gaze locking with his. "So that no matter where we are, we'll always be connected to this place, to these people."

"Agreed." Jace squeezed her hand back, a silent acknowledgment of their shared journey. Together, they turned to watch as a massive cornerstone was set in place, the beginning of a new edifice that mirrored their own internal transformations—the foundations of their courage, the structure of their newfound wisdom, and the sheltering roof of their love for two worlds.

The air in Malathar was thick with the scent of fresh timber and mortar. Workers, both El and human alike, moved about with a sense of purpose that belied the recent chaos. Somewhere amidst the clatter of stone on stone and the distant ring of metal, Jace found himself standing before the three who had become more than just allies—Aydis, Ahat, and Reynard.

"Never thought I'd be saying goodbye to another world," Raina said softly, her eyes glistening as she clasped hands with Aydis. The

El woman's strong grip was a testament to the battles they had faced together.

"Nor did I think I'd find such kinship with those from beyond the Veil," Aydis responded, her voice carrying the warmth of embers.

Jace turned to Ahat, the towering figure who had taught him the way of the blade. "Your guidance... it's been invaluable."

"Keep your guard up, Jace. In every sense," Ahat replied, a glimmer of humor in his eyes. He leaned in closer, lowering his voice to a conspiratorial whisper. "And try not to get too lost, eh? There's a whole world out there."

"Speaking of worlds, we've decided—you're not getting rid of us that easily," Reynard chimed in, his thin frame leaning casually against a half-rebuilt wall. "We're coming with you to Mount Myra."

"Really?" Jace couldn't hide his surprise. "But why?"

"Because, my friend," Reynard grinned, his red hair catching the sunlight like a flame, "our fates are intertwined now. Plus, I can't let you have all the fun teasing Ahat about his newfound soft spot for humans."

Ahat rolled his eyes but didn't deny it, and Jace laughed, feeling the tension ease from his shoulders. Raina smiled at their exchange, her gaze meeting Jace's with a silent message of excitement—and maybe, just maybe, a touch of relief.

"Then it's settled. We journey together," Jace declared, shaking hands with each of them in turn.

"Let's get our supplies. We leave at dawn," Raina said with resolve, already scanning the area for what they would need.

They moved through the bustling city, gathering rations, medical herbs, and the few personal items they could carry. Jace paused to strap a newly forged dagger to his belt, its weight a comforting presence against his thigh.

"Emma's waiting," Jace thought, his heart aching with the anticipation of the reunion. But alongside that yearning ran a current of reluctance, a shadow of doubt that he could ever truly leave Nelhelm behind.

"Hey," Raina nudged him gently, drawing him back to the present. "You ready for this?"

"More than ever," Jace replied, though his mind wrestled with the duality of his longing—for home and for the adventure that beckoned just beyond the horizon.

As they secured their packs, Jace looked around at the reborn Malathar, its resilience a mirror of their own. The city was rising like a phoenix from the ashes, grander than before, its people united by a shared vision of hope.

"Mount Myra awaits," he said, his voice steady even as his spirit wavered between two worlds. "Let's not keep destiny waiting any longer."

"Agreed," Raina nodded, her steel-blue eyes reflecting the first light of dawn. "To new beginnings, Jace. To new beginnings."

The sun had begun to dip below the horizon, painting the sky in hues of crimson and gold as Mitra approached Jace and Raina. The air of Malathar was heavy with the scent of woodsmoke and the distant echo of hammers against the stone. Amidst the rebuilding, there stood these two figures, now familiar yet forever transformed by their journey in Nelhelm.

"Your paths have been wrought with trials that would break lesser spirits," Mitra said, her voice carrying the timbre of a gentle wind. Her eyes, ancient and knowing, held Jace's gaze with an unwavering intensity.

Jace nodded, feeling the weight of her words like a mantle upon his shoulders. "We've come so far, seen so much," he murmured, more to himself than to anyone else. His hand unconsciously found the pommel of his new dagger, gripping it for assurance.

"Indeed," Raina agreed. She stood beside him, a mirror of strength and resolve. Her hands were steady, but her mind raced with thoughts of what lay ahead. Mount Myra, she thought, will it be the end or another beginning?

Mitra stepped forward, placing a hand on each of their shoulders. "In you, I see the fire of courage and the resilience of the earth. Your hearts have grown vast enough to embrace the challenges before you."

"Sometimes, I still feel like that person who stumbled into this world unprepared," Jace confessed, his steel-blue eyes reflecting the fading light.

"Yet, you are not," Mitra countered warmly. "You have become more than you once were, Jace Alexander of Gaia. You and Raina both have woven your essence into the tapestry of Nelhelm. And no matter where you tread, that strength will remain with you."

Raina felt a surge of gratitude for Mitra's words. They were a balm to the uncertainty that gnawed at her. She believes in us, Raina realized, her heart swelling with newfound confidence.

"Look at this city," Mitra gestured to the rising spires and the people working in harmony. "Like Malathar, you have been rebuilt from the ashes of hardship, stronger and more majestic."

"Thank you, Mitra," Jace replied, his voice firm despite the emotions swirling within him. "Your guidance has been a light in the darkness."

"Remember," she continued, her gaze sweeping over them both, "no matter how vast the distance, you are never alone. The bonds you've formed are eternal."

"Your words mean the world to us," Raina responded, her throat tight with emotion. "We'll carry them with us, always."

"Go now, with the blessings of Nelhelm upon you," Mitra intoned, stepping back to allow them space to embark on their path. "And should fate decree, may our roads lead us back together." Their hearts filled with Mitra's final words of encouragement and the promise of tomorrow.

23

Another Chapter

The morning sun pierced the misty dawn, casting a pale glow over Malathar's central courtyard, where Jace and his companions stood amid the hum of early risers. The city's ancient stones whispered tales of bygone eras as the group—Jace, Raina, Aydis, Ahat, and Reynard—bustled about, their movements infused with an electric current of anticipation.

"Check your packs one last time," Jace advised, his steel blue eyes surveying the courtyard, taking in the rooted ivy that clung to the walls like desperate hands reaching for the sky. He hoisted his own pack, feeling its weight as a tangible reminder of the journey ahead.

Raina, standing tall and composed, nodded at his words, her athletic frame bending to adjust the straps on her rucksack. "Every extra ounce counts," she said, her voice carrying the edge of experience. She caught Jace's gaze for a moment, both understanding the gravity of silence.

"Ah, but do not forget a morsel for joy, my friends!" Reynard chimed in, producing a small pouch from within his cloak. His red hair seemed to catch fire in the sunlight. "A little sweet can turn the bleakest path into a parade!"

Aydis, ever the pragmatist, rolled her eyes. "Sugar won't save us from what lies beyond these walls," she retorted, checking the fletching on her arrows with meticulous care.

"True," Ahat interjected, his voice steady as the earth itself. "But Reynard speaks a truth of the soul. It is the little joys that fortify our hearts against despair."

Jace couldn't help but smile at the banter, feeling it lighten the coil of nerves in his gut. Yet, underneath the camaraderie, an undercurrent of solemnity ran deep. These were more than mere preparations; they were rites of passage, each strap fastened a step closer to destiny.

The energy of Malathar pulsed around them, the city awakening to another day while their small fellowship prepared to leave it behind. The echoes of merchants setting up stalls and the clank of armor from patrolling guards all faded into a backdrop for their focused intent.

"Enough delays," Reynard announced, slinging his own pack over a shoulder. "Adventure, like a shy maiden, waits not for the hesitant."

Jace took a deep breath, letting the crisp air fill his lungs. Then, with a nod to his companions, he stepped forward. Each footfall resonated against the cobblestone, a drumbeat to their collective pulse.

"Let's move out," he said, a silent prayer escaping his lips. Would Emma understand the necessity of his leaving? Would the love they shared endure the trials to come?

"Stay sharp. Stay alive," Raina added, her stride confident as they crossed the threshold of the courtyard, leaving the embrace of Malathar's watchful spires.

Their departure was not grandiose nor laden with fanfare. It was a quiet assertion, a determined crossing into the unknown. And as they ventured forth, the Emmon Fields stretched before them, a vast canvas awaiting the story they would paint with their courage.

Under the arching gate of Malathar, Jace Alexander adjusted the straps of his leather backpack, feeling its weight settle against his broad shoulders. His steel blue eyes scanned the courtyard, taking in the cluster of buildings that had been his home for these past weeks. His gaze caught Raina's, and for a moment, time seemed to hold its breath. In her eyes, an ocean of unspoken thoughts churned—a mirror to his own trepidation and resolve.

"Remember why we're doing this," her voice was a whisper meant only for him, yet it cut through the hum of the city like a blade.

"Always," he replied, his words more than a promise, more than an oath—they were the very beat of his heart.

A shiver coursed through him as he took in her athletic form, the way her blonde hair caught the light of the morning sun, creating a halo around her determined face. She was so much like him, yet so different—her secrets locked away behind those steel blue eyes of hers.

From the shadowed alcove of an ancient watchtower, Mitra watched the pair with a steady gaze. Her features were inscrutable as she turned to Kane, whose large frame loomed beside her like a silent sentinel. The black of his eyes reflected the scene below, but the furrow of his brow betrayed his inner turmoil.

"Jace has the fire of destiny in him," Mitra murmured. "It burns bright."

"Fire is dangerous," Kane replied, his voice low and measured. "It can guide or consume. And destiny is no shield against folly."

"Indeed," she conceded, letting out a sigh that held both hope and the weight of centuries. She clutched a woven shawl tighter around her shoulders as if warding off a chill that came from within.

Jace felt Raina's hand brush against his, a fleeting touch that sent a current of warmth through him. He met her glance once more, a silent vow passing between them. They would see this through together.

"Let's not keep fate waiting," Reynard quipped, breaking the moment as he passed by Jace with a knowing smile.

"Nor our enemies," Aydis added, her grip tightening on the hilt of her sword, eyes scanning the horizon beyond the city walls.

"Both are equally impatient," Ahat chimed in, his voice a deep rumble, as he hefted a sealed satchel over his shoulder.

Jace took a step forward, and the others fell into step beside him. Their path lay open, their wills aligned. As they moved, echoes of their footsteps rang out, each one a declaration, each one a defiance of the darkness that threatened their world.

Raina's words wove through his thoughts, lending him strength. "Stay sharp. Stay alive." Those words were a beacon, a reminder of all they stood to lose—and gain. Emma's face flashed in his mind, her smile a bittersweet ache in his chest. Would she still be smiling when he returned?

"Watch over us," he whispered under his breath, a prayer or perhaps just a hopeful thought tossed into the winds of fate.

"Always," Raina echoed, though whether she'd heard him or simply shared the sentiment was unclear.

"May the earth guide your steps and the stars light your way," Mitra called out from the shadows, her voice carrying the depth of ages.

Kane said nothing, but his nod was grave, full of unspoken understanding. He knew the perils that lay ahead better than anyone.

The group crossed the threshold of Malathar's embrace, their silhouettes blurring into the golden haze of dawn. Adventure beckoned, and they answered its call, leaving behind the grandeur of the city for the vastness of the Emmon Fields. Ahead, Mount Myra awaited, shrouded in mystery and promise.

"Look at them," Mitra mused aloud, the timbre of her voice resonating with the wisdom of centuries. "The Gaians return, walking upon soil that has yearned for their touch since time out of mind."

Kane stood beside her, his towering frame casting a long shadow in the morning light. His gaze was not upon the preparations but fixed on the horizon, where the sky kissed the earth in a delicate caress. "Yes, they walk our lands once more," he said, his voice a low rumble, "but the scrolls speak of three, Mitra. Three Gaians to turn the tide. Yet there are four."

In the hush that followed, the rustle of parchment seemed to whisper through the air. Mitra's eyes darkened like storm clouds gathering strength. "The scrolls are old, Kane," she countered softly. "Older than any of us. Perhaps they speak in riddles, or perhaps the world has changed its own weave. We must trust that Gaia knows the hearts of her children."

"Or," Kane interjected with a glance as sharp as the sword at his side, "there may be forces at play we do not yet comprehend. I cannot shake the sense that there is more to this tale—threads unseen that could unravel all our plans."

Mitra considered this, her eyes narrowing as she traced the lines of magic that pulsed through Malathar's ancient architecture. "Then it falls to us to watch and guide, to see the pattern emerge," she replied. "We must have faith in those who embark on this quest. They carry our hope as surely as they carry their blades."

Kane grunted, the sound echoing like a stone dropped into a still pond. He turned to Mitra, the weight of strategy pressing down upon him. "Hope is a fragile thing in war," he said. "I will remain vigilant, ready to act should the need arise."

"Vigilance is wise," Mitra acknowledged, "but do not let it blind you to the promise of dawn. Even the darkest night yields to the light."

Kane nodded, though his black eyes remained impenetrable pools of thought.

As Jace and the others entered the open gates, Mitra's lips moved in silent incantation, a blessing invisible to all but the wind. Kane watched them go, his mind turning over and over like a key in a lock without a door. He knew battles, strategies, the ebb and flow of conflicts across the ages—but this uncertainty was a different kind of foe, one that gnawed at the edges of his certainty.

"May Gaia's hand guide them," Mitra whispered, almost to herself, her eyes following the figures until they became part of the landscape beyond—the Fields of Emmon stretching out like a canvas awaiting the first stroke of destiny's brush.

"May the winds favor your journey," an elder of the El intoned, his voice a deep well of sorrow and hope.

"Thank you," Jace replied, clasping the elder's hand firmly, feeling the parchment-thin skin and the history etched within it. Raina, Aydis,

Ahat, and Reynard echoed his gratitude, their voices braiding together in a tapestry of unity.

"Keep the light of Gaia burning in your hearts," another chimed, her voice lilting like a song lost to time.

"We will," Raina vowed, her steel blue eyes reflecting the same determination that mirrored Jace's own.

Reynard, ever the jester even at times of departure, offered a rakish grin. "I'll keep my eyes sharp, the path clear, and my quips ready."

Laughter rippled through the group, easing the tightness of impending separation. Aydis, the quiet force among them, nodded solemnly, her expression a mask of resolve. And Ahat, with the wisdom of ages in his gaze, simply placed a reassuring hand on each shoulder in turn.

"Remember," Ahat said, his voice carrying the weight of prophecy, "the scrolls speak of trials but also of triumphs. Trust in yourselves, as we trust in you."

Jace felt the mantle of responsibility settle upon him, heavier than his pack, more vital than his sword. He glanced at his companions, seeing the echo of his own thoughts mirrored there—a fierce yearning to rise to the destiny that awaited them.

"Let us walk the path laid out before us," he declared, his voice steady despite the tremor of anticipation that quivered through his limbs.

The group crossed the threshold of Malathar's embrace, their silhouettes blurring into the golden haze of dawn. Adventure beckoned, and they answered its call, leaving behind the grandeur of the city for the vastness of the Emmon Fields.

"Look not back, for the future is the direction of heroes," Raina said softly, her words not meant for the ears of others but for those who stood beside her.

And so, with one last sweeping gaze at the towering spires and the faces of the El, Jace led the way forward. Each step was a promise, a defiance of the darkness that loomed on the horizon. In his mind's eye, he carried the image of Malathar—a bastion of strength and beauty, a reminder of what they were fighting to protect.

The fields of Emmon opened before them, a vast expanse of untamed wilderness stretching towards the fabled slopes of Mount Myra. They walked on, five silhouettes against the canvas of a waking world, their shadows long and their spirits undaunted. The chapter of Malathar closed behind them, and ahead, the pages of an unwritten saga fluttered eagerly in the breath of dawn.

Jace halted a stone's throw from the gates, the heavy ironwork an intricate dance of dragons and wyverns. With the city's majestic skyline receding behind him, he felt the stark contrast between the secure grandeur of Malathar and the looming uncertainties that lay beyond its protective embrace. A cold breeze tugged at his cloak, a spectral hand urging him away from contemplation and into action.

"Jace?" Raina's voice cut through the crisp air, her tone laced with the strength of tempered steel. "We mustn't linger in the shadow of what was."

He turned to find her standing steadfast, her blonde hair a banner in the wind. Her steel blue eyes locked onto his, and for a moment, they shared an unspoken language as ancient as time itself—fear, resolve, and camaraderie melded into one.

"Every step we take is a step towards our destiny," she continued, her words punctuated by the sound of snapping leather as she tightened the straps on her pack. "Remember the prophecies, Jace. We are the chosen of Gaia, the harbingers of change."

A breath escaped him, visible in the morning chill—a ghost of doubt exorcised by her conviction. "It's just... Forset," he murmured, the name of his betrothed a talisman against the darkness. "Leaving his memory in Malathar—"

"Is not leaving him at all," Raina interjected firmly, yet not unkindly. "He travels within your heart, Jace. And our bond—ours— is the kind forged in the very fires that reshape worlds. Together, we'll face whatever trials await."

Jace nodded, feeling the weight of his sword against his thigh, a comforting presence. He reached out, clasping Raina's shoulder in a gesture that spoke volumes. She returned the grip, their alliance sealed in the silent oath of warriors.

"Then let's go forth and write our legend across the skies," he said, a renewed vigor infusing his words. "For Emma, for Gaia, and for the future that beckons."

With a determined step, Jace resumed their march, Raina falling into stride beside him. The rhythm of their boots upon the earth was a testament to their purpose, each thud a chorus of defiance against the brewing storm. In the deep recesses of his mind, Jace knew that the path would be fraught with peril, but he also knew that the shared strength between them was mightier than any foe they could encounter.

They did not look back again.

The silhouette of Malathar dwindled behind them as Jace and his companions marched towards the embrace of the fields of Emmon. The city, with its spires that clawed at the heavens and gargoyles that whispered secrets of ancient times, had been a sanctuary of stone and sorcery. Now, it was but a memory set against the canvas of the sky, its edges softening like ink in water.

"Look at it," Aydis murmured, her voice tinged with wonder, "the plains stretch on forever, don't they?"

"Like the promise of tomorrow," Ahat added, his gaze fixed on the horizon where the earth kissed the sky. The vast expanse before them was a tapestry of rolling hills and fields awaiting the tread of their boots. Wildflowers nodded in the breeze as if to salute their passage, and the air carried the scent of freedom and wild thyme.

Jace took a deep breath, filling his lungs with the untamed zephyr. His heart matched the rhythm of the land—unfettered, boundless. This was no longer the structured geometry of cobbled streets and towering edifices; this was nature's design, chaotic and perfect.

"United by hope," Jace added under his breath. His thoughts turned inward to the countless lives hanging in the balance, to the love he bore for Emma, now a ghostly presence in his heart—a beacon guiding him forward.

"Hope," Raina echoed softly, pulling her cloak tighter against the breeze. "It's as vast as these plains and as resilient. Belloch thrives on despair, but we... we are harbingers of dawn."

"Then let the dawn be ours," Jace responded with a quiet intensity. He reached out, brushing his fingers against the tall grasses that flanked their path. Each blade seemed to whisper encouragement, bolstering his resolve.

"To Mount Myra and whatever awaits," Jace continued, his words weaving through the company like a binding spell. "We march not only for ourselves but for all those who cannot stand with us."

"May our footsteps echo as a testament to our courage," Aydis said, her eyes reflecting the vastness of the sky above.

And so, step by step, they started into the plains, their silhouettes cutting a stark contrast against the sprawling vista. With each stride, the hope within them grew, fertilized by the rich soil of determination and camaraderie. Their journey was more than a mere crossing of land; it was a pilgrimage—a testament to the belief that even against the darkest of powers, light would find a way to prevail.

The horizon was a smear of twilight, the last fingers of day caressing the contours of the distant Mountains of the Stars. As the five companions stepped forward, a mist rose from the earth like an exhalation of the land itself, cloaking their departure in a shroud of opalescent gray.

"Feels like we're stepping into a storybook," Reynard mused, his voice tinged with a reverence befitting the sacred quest they were on. His long shadow flickered and danced within the fog as he moved.

"Or leaving one behind," Aydis added softly, her eyes locked on the path ahead, where the veil of mist thickened with every step. Her hand rested on the hilt of her sword, a silent promise to any who dared threaten their passage.

Jace took in a deep breath, the cool droplets of fog clinging to his lashes. He could feel the weight of Emma's absence, a hollow space inside him, but he also felt the presence of his companions, the shared courage that bound them together.

"May the tales spun of this journey be worthy of the telling," he said, his words nearly a whisper, blending seamlessly with the ghostly tendrils swirling around them.

Raina glanced back at Jace, her steel blue eyes catching the last glint of daylight. "We'll make sure of it," she replied, her tone steady as ever. A small smile played on her lips, a silent message of solidarity to the man with whom she had forged an unbreakable bond.

"Look there," Ahat pointed toward the barely visible outline of the mountain, now just a darker shape within the fog. "Mount Myra awaits. And so does our destiny."

"Destiny," Jace mused internally, the word resonating within him. It was a heavy burden, destiny, filled with unknowns, yet it was theirs to meet head-on. His father's lessons rang clear in his mind—fate was crafted by action and will, not by waiting for signs and portents.

"Let's keep moving," Reynard urged, breaking through Jace's reverie. "The night grows bold, and the fog with it."

Their boots sunk softly into the earth, leaving transient marks soon to be swallowed by the mist. The rhythmic sound of their steps became a mantra, propelling them forward, away from the safety of Malathar and into the arms of uncertainty.

"Remember why we fight," Raina whispered, so low that Jace wasn't sure if the words were meant for him or for the wind.

"For Gaia. For those, we've lost. For those we refuse to lose." Jace's heart swelled with resolve. They were more than wanderers in the fog—they were warriors of light against the encroaching darkness.

"Gaia guide us," Aydis intoned, her gaze fixed on the hidden peaks beyond.

"Gaia guide us," the others echoed in a chorus that seemed to stir the very air.

The mist enveloped them fully now, each figure becoming little more than a wisp, a phantom blended with the ethereal landscape.

"Let the fog claim our forms," Jace thought, "but never our spirit."

As they disappeared into the dense fog, the last remnants of daylight surrendered to the night. The chapter closed with the finality of a sealed tome, their silhouettes dissolving as though ink absorbed into the parchment of the fields of Emmon. Mount Myra awaited, stoic and unknowable, the next page of their story ready to be written upon arrival.